"I didn't know what I was getting into," Jillian said,

the dark despair of those days coloring her voice even now. The night they had made love, she had never intended to let things go so far.

"You sure as hell acted like you did."

"*Acted.* I think that's the operative word."

"Are you telling me you were *acting* that night?"

She couldn't truthfully tell him that. She hadn't been. She had simply been swept away by what had been happening between them.

"No," she said, willing to leave it at that.

"Then what the hell *are* you saying?"

"That...I wasn't ready for what happened, I guess. I wasn't prepared."

"And you regret it," he said. Statement and not question.

But of course he was unaware of all the tangled issues in regretting what had happened between them that night. She could never regret having Drew. He was her life. She opened her mouth, knowing it was past time to tell Mark the truth. Long past time.

Dear Reader,

I hope very much that you'll enjoy *The Cowboy's Secret Son*. This is a story close to my heart for many reasons, primarily because it concerns the reuniting of a family, a favorite theme in many of my books, both historical and contemporary.

Also, just like the hero of this novel, my husband is a former army helicopter pilot. He has over 5000 flight hours, many acquired during two tours of duty in Vietnam flying a gunship. While there, he was awarded the Distinguished Flying Cross, as well as an impressive variety of other medals. He is truly my hero, not only for his courage and dedication to country, but for his many acts of love, support and sacrifice for our family through the years of our marriage.

And finally, I loved writing this book because I love Texas. Although we never lived in the Panhandle, my family and I were fortunate to live along the Texas/Mexican border for several years. We fell in love with the beauty and grandeur of the desert Southwest and with the warmth of its people. It was very exciting for me to revisit another part of the state with which I feel such a connection. I hope you're enjoying all the rich Texas diversity the Trueblood series showcases.

Best wishes for good reading!

Gayle

TRUEBLOOD, TEXAS

Gayle Wilson

The Cowboy's Secret Son

HARLEQUIN®

TORONTO • NEW YORK • LONDON
AMSTERDAM • PARIS • SYDNEY • HAMBURG
STOCKHOLM • ATHENS • TOKYO • MILAN • MADRID
PRAGUE • WARSAW • BUDAPEST • AUCKLAND

Gayle Wilson is acknowledged
as the author of this work.

To Marsha Zinberg
For her endless patience and kindness

And to Texas, my "other" home

HARLEQUIN BOOKS
225 Duncan Mill Road, Don Mills,
Ontario, Canada M3B 3K9

ISBN-13: 978-0-373-65082-8
ISBN-10:   0-373-65082-5

THE COWBOY'S SECRET SON

Visit us at www.eHarlequin.com

Printed in U.S.A.

TRUEBLOOD, TEXAS

THE TRUEBLOOD LEGACY

THE YEAR WAS 1918, and the Great War in Europe still raged, but Esau Porter was heading home to Texas.

The young sergeant arrived at his parents' ranch northwest of San Antonio on a Sunday night, only the celebration didn't go off as planned. Most of the townsfolk of Carmelita had come out to welcome Esau home, but when they saw the sorry condition of the boy, they gave their respects quickly and left.

The fever got so bad so fast that Mrs. Porter hardly knew what to do. By Monday night, before the doctor from San Antonio made it into town, Esau was dead.

The Porter family grieved. How could their son have survived the German peril, only to burn up and die in his own bed? It wasn't much of a surprise when Mrs. Porter took to her bed on Wednesday. But it was a hell of a shock when half the residents of Carmelita came down with the horrible illness. House after house was hit by death, and all the townspeople could do was pray for salvation.

None came. By the end of the year, over one hundred souls had perished. The influenza virus took those in the prime of life, leaving behind an unprecedented number of orphans. And the virus knew no boundaries. By the time the threat had passed, more than thirty-seven million people had succumbed worldwide.

But in one house, there was still hope.

Isabella Trueblood had come to Carmelita in the late 1800s with her father, blacksmith Saul Trueblood, and her mother, Teresa Collier Trueblood. The family had traveled from Indiana, leaving their Quaker roots behind.

Young Isabella grew up to be an intelligent woman who had a gift for healing and storytelling. Her dreams centered on the boy next door, Foster Carter, the son of Chester and Grace.

Just before the bad times came in 1918, Foster asked Isabella to be his wife, and the future of the Carter spread was secured. It was a happy union, and the future looked bright for the young couple.

Two years later, not one of their relatives was alive. How the young couple had survived was a miracle. And during the epidemic, Isabella and Foster had taken in more than twenty-two orphaned children from all over the county. They fed them, clothed them, taught them as if they were blood kin.

Then Isabella became pregnant, but there were complications. Love for her handsome son, Josiah, born in 1920, wasn't enough to stop her from growing weaker by the day. Knowing she couldn't leave her husband to tend to all the children if she died, she set out to find families for each one of her orphaned charges.

And so the Trueblood Foundation was born. Named in memory of Isabella's parents, it would become famous all over Texas. Some of the orphaned children went to strangers, but many were reunited with their families. After reading notices in newspapers and church bulletins, aunts, uncles, cousins and grandparents rushed to Carmelita to find the young ones they'd given up for dead.

Toward the end of Isabella's life, she'd brought together more than thirty families, and not just her orphans. Many others, old and young, made their way to her doorstep, and Isabella turned no one away.

At her death, the town's name was changed to Trueblood, in her honor. For years to come, her simple grave was adorned with flowers on the anniversary of her death, grateful tokens of appreciation from the families she had brought together.

Isabella's son, Josiah, grew into a fine rancher and married Rebecca Montgomery in 1938. They had a daughter, Elizabeth Trueblood Carter, in 1940. Elizabeth married her neighbor William Garrett in 1965, and gave birth to twins Lily and Dylan in 1971, and daughter Ashley a few years later. Home was the Double G ranch, about ten miles from Trueblood proper, and the Garrett children grew up listening to stories of their famous great-grandmother, Isabella. Because they were Truebloods, they knew that they, too, had a sacred duty to carry on the tradition passed down to them: finding lost souls and reuniting loved ones.

PROLOGUE

"I'LL BE DAMNED," Dylan Garrett said under his breath.

Lily Garrett Bishop looked up from the work spread across her own desk, loving amusement lifting her lips as she watched her twin brother. His eyes were on one of two letters that had been hand-delivered to the offices of Finders Keepers.

"Something interesting?" she asked after a moment.

She stacked the report she had just finished and inserted it into its folder, which would eventually be filed with the others in the agency's growing list of successfully completed cases. At her question, Dylan's blue eyes lifted from the paper he held.

"A voice from the past," he said.

"Are you deliberately *trying* to be mysterious, or is this 'voice from the past' strictly personal?"

"Personal? In a way, I guess it is. Part of it, anyway."

"And the part that isn't?" Lily asked patiently.

"Involves an assignment for the agency."

The agency was the investigative venture the Garrett twins had recently formed, using skills developed in their previous occupations in law enforcement. The goal of Finders Keepers was to find people, especially those who had, for one reason or another, been torn apart from their families.

"Something you're obviously interested in accepting."

Lily believed she knew every nuance of her brother's voice. This one contained a tinge of nostalgia. Perhaps even regret.

"Someone," he corrected softly.

Lily's smile widened. She knew him too well to be able to resist the opportunity that offered for teasing. "Oh, let me guess. Someone young and beautiful. And female, of course."

"Young at heart, in any case. Or…at least she was."

The past tense and the subtle shift in tone warned her, and Lily's smile faded. "Someone I know?" she asked gently.

"Someone Sebastian and I met years ago."

Dylan's eyes fell again to the letter, and his sister waited through the silence, anticipating that eventually he would go on with the story he had begun. By now she understood it was one that had engaged her brother's emotions as well as his intellect.

"Young at heart doesn't sound much like one of your usual romantic encounters," she ventured finally. "Or Sebastian's."

When Dylan laughed, Lily felt a surge of relief. Whatever this was, apparently it didn't involve the disappearance of Julie Cooper, which had occupied her brother's time and energy since his friend Sebastian had come pleading for help to find his missing wife.

Actually, Lily hadn't heard this much interest in Dylan's voice in weeks. Not for anything other than Julie's disappearance. Whatever was in that letter, she could only be grateful for the distraction it was providing her brother.

"We had car trouble," Dylan said, that subtle hint of nostalgia back. "Down in Pinto."

"*Pinto?*" Lily repeated disbelievingly.

"Pinto, Texas, home of Violet Mitchum and not much else."

"Violet Mitchum is your mystery woman?"

"There was no mystery about Violet. Except this, I guess."

"This?"

"It seems I've been named as one of her heirs."

"Should I congratulate you on your inheritance?" Lily teased, assuming that whatever her brother had inherited from a chance acquaintance in Pinto, Texas, wouldn't be substantial.

Dylan inclined his head slightly, as if in polite acceptance of those congratulations. With the movement, the strong Texas sun shining through the wide second-story windows behind him shot gold through the light-brown strands of his hair.

"You may congratulate me along with the seven other recipients of Violet's largesse," he said.

"Too bad you have to share your inheritance with so many," Lily mocked. "And is Sebastian another of Miss Mitchum's heirs?"

"*Mrs.* Mitchum. And no, he's not. Violet didn't take to Sebastian," Dylan said, the amusement suddenly missing from his narrative. "She said he had…an impure heart."

That assessment of the handsome and charismatic Sebastian Cooper, especially by a woman, was surprising. Usually it was Sebastian who made an indelible impression on females, Lily thought with a trace of bitterness. Just as he had with Julie.

She had hoped for years that Julie would realize Dylan was the one who really loved her. The one who was so obviously right for her. She hadn't, however, and when she and Sebastian had eloped, Dylan had continued to be a friend to both of them, despite what Lily suspected was a badly broken heart.

"But she took to you?" The mockery had been deliberately injected back into her question, hiding that swell of bitterness.

"Of course. After all, I took her riding," Dylan said. "And part of my inheritance is the horse we rode on."

"The horse *we* rode on?"

"She said she hadn't been riding in years. I held her before me in the saddle so she could have one last ride on one of her beloved horses. It just seemed…the right thing to do."

"Just exactly how *old* was Violet when you met her."

"According to this, Violet was eighty-one when she died.

The fishing trip was before Sebastian and Julie married...."
The sentence trailed, and Lily felt unease stir. After a few
seconds, however, her brother continued, his voice un-
changed. "So, maybe...four years ago. Maybe a little more."

The tough-as-nails Dylan cradling a fragile old lady before
him in the saddle was not hard to imagine. Not if one knew
her brother as she did. "And in gratitude, she left you the
horse."

"Considering its bloodlines, that would be no small be-
quest in itself. But it isn't all Violet left me."

Dylan walked across the room and laid both letters on the
desk in front of her. Lily scanned the first one quickly, finding the initial paragraphs to be confirmation of what he had
just told her. And in the third paragraph...

"Mitchum Oil? Your Violet was *that* Mitchum?" she
asked.

"She and her husband Charles. They had no children.
Only Violet's horses and...that."

That was a fortune, one of the largest in Texas, where
millionaires were not rare. The size of the old Mitchum strike
was justly famous even in this oil-rich state.

"And the other heirs?" Lily asked, after she had skimmed
the rest of the first letter.

"People who meant something in Violet's life. They're all
listed in the other letter. That one's from her lawyer. There's
an old friend, Mary Barrett, who stayed in touch by letter,
despite their changing circumstances. There are several who
had done Violet favors, like Stella Richards, who sent meals
out to the Mitchum house every day until Violet died. And
Stuart Randolph, who loaned Charlie the equipment to dig
his first well. John Carpenter, who tended her horses," Dylan
enumerated. "And then there are those, like me, who had a
chance encounter with her that...changed their own lives."

"Is that what Violet did? Changed your life?" Lily asked,
hearing again the thread of emotion in his deep voice.

"She granted me absolution."

"Absolution?" Lily asked, surprised at the word, which

had such strong religious connotations. "Absolution for what?"

"For not being here when Mother died," he said quietly.

"Dylan," Lily said, pity intermingled in her equally soft protest. "I never knew you felt that way. You have to know she understood. She always understood. And she loved you so much."

"That's what Violet said. I guess she just said it at the time when I most needed to hear it. She reminded me that a mother's love has no conditions," he added. "Mom's certainly didn't. Somehow, stupidly, I had managed to forget that."

Lily nodded, blinking back the sharp sting of tears those memories evoked. "You said there was an assignment for us in this," she reminded him, not sure that reliving the pain of her mother's death was what either of them needed right now. Not with Dylan so worried about Julie, and her own pregnancy—

"The other heirs," Dylan said, interrupting the remembrance of that very private joy. "We've been asked to find them and to let them know about Violet's bequests."

"And those all involve sums like this?" Lily asked, her eyes again considering the amount that had been left to her brother.

"Some of them are much larger. And each is accompanied by a memento from their association with Violet. Does that sound like an assignment we'd be interested in taking on?"

"Changing lives," Lily said thoughtfully.

"What?"

"That's what this amounts to. Changing lives. Changing circumstances. Can you imagine what a gift like this could mean to some of these people? Do you know anything about them?"

"At this point, nothing but their names," Dylan said, reaching over her shoulder to turn the page, revealing the names of the three still-missing heirs.

"Jillian Salvini, Sara Pierce and Matt Radcliffe." Lily read the names aloud. "And if we agree to the lawyer's proposal, we're supposed to find these people?"

"*And* tell them what Violet has left them."

"Do you suppose she meant as much to any of them as she did to you?" Lily asked, looking up from the letter into his eyes.

"If she did…then, despite the money, I would bet they'd rather not be found. I know I'd like to think about Violet still alive and vital, living in that Victorian monstrosity her husband built for her. Still watching her beloved horses and writing her endless letters. Frankly, I'd much rather be allowed to believe that than to have the money."

"But you can't speak for everyone. And this much money—" she began to remind him again.

"Can change lives," Dylan finished for her. "Not exactly the purpose for which we started Finders Keepers, but still… I think I'd like to do this, Lily, providing you're agreeable. And who knows, we might even manage to reunite a few families in the process."

"Whether we do or not," Lily said, "I think this is something you need to do. For Violet. To repay the debt you owe her, if for no other reason."

"I think you're right. For Violet," Dylan agreed. And his voice was again reminiscent. *For Violet.*

CHAPTER ONE

LIKE A WHIPPED DOG with his tail between his legs, Mark Peterson thought, fighting the bitterness that always boiled up to the surface when he approached the ranch from this direction.

He dropped the chopper low enough that its powerful rotor kicked up dust from the arid ground below. There were no power lines or trees to worry about in this desolate terrain, and it had become his habit to low-level over the Salvini ranch whenever he was coming in from the west.

After a few pointless trips across the deserted ranch, which stirred up memories as well as dust, Mark had given up trying to figure out his motives for doing this. Maybe it was simply a form of masochism. Or maybe it was the fact that this was the last place on earth where he still felt a connection to Jillian. And that in itself was a totally different kind of masochism.

He had never forgotten her, of course, but since he'd come back to Texas, back to his family's land, all those memories had become stronger. And much harder to deal with.

The For Sale signs were still up, he realized, which meant that the price on the property hadn't yet dropped enough to make the co-op snap it up as they had most of the land around here. It would soon, of course, because the people who currently owned the ranch would be increasingly eager to get out of it whatever they could and move on with their lives.

The house had been unoccupied for a couple of months

and was beginning to show the effects. Despite the fact that the last owners couldn't afford to hold on to the ranch, they had at least kept it in good shape. Now...

Mark eased the cyclic back, bringing the nose of the helicopter up, and increased the pitch. As the chopper rose and then leveled out, he forced his eyes away from the familiar buildings spread out across the flat High Plains countryside below. He didn't need to look at them. He knew every square mile of that ranch almost as well as he knew the one next door. The one where he had grown up.

It already belonged to the cooperation, as did most of those in the area that had come on the market in the last few years. Few individuals could afford the investment it took to make ranching up here a financial success. The cooperation had the backing of a couple of major banks and the monetary wherewithal to ride out the volatile ups and downs of the cattle market.

Families didn't. They couldn't afford to hold on through the hard times. That's why more and more land was being sold to groups such as the one he now worked for. And as much as Mark hated to see that happen, he couldn't blame anyone for choosing a less heartbreaking road than the one that had broken his father.

The thromping blades of the rotor startled an antelope into flight. It raced along under the shadow of the copter for a few hundred feet before it veered off to the right and disappeared beneath him.

Mark's lips slanted with the pleasure of watching that brief display of grace and power. The country below was too dry and forbidding for much of the wildlife that flourished farther south. Of course, the High Plains were different enough from the rest of Texas that they were almost a separate entity—one Mark loved with a passion that rivaled his father's.

Although the doctors had put his dad's death down to a stroke, Mark knew that bitterness and failure had played as big a role as his physical condition. A longtime widower, deeply estranged from Mark, who was his only child, Bo Peterson had died a lonely and sour old man. And if he wasn't careful, Mark told himself, coming in now over the ranch that had killed his father, that could be his own epitaph as well.

In contrast to the old Salvini place, the buildings below showed the effects of having enough money. There were only a few hands, including himself, living on the ranch now that the fall roundup was over, but it still had the well cared for air that all of the co-op's properties possessed.

He wondered how his father would have felt about that. He sometimes wondered how he himself felt about it.

He set the chopper down with the ease of long practice. Even after he had completed the shutdown procedures, he remained in the comfortable warmth of the enclosed cockpit, delaying a moment because he dreaded the bite of the November wind, despite the protection of the leather jacket he wore.

There was nowhere in Texas as prone to bitter cold as the top of the Panhandle. The frigid gusts from the north swept ruthlessly across the flat landscape, chilling to the bone.

And his bones were a lot more susceptible than they had been before he'd left here ten years ago, Mark acknowledged. He remembered the pleasure he had once taken in a long day of hard physical labor or in the equally demanding leisure pastimes.

It had been a long time since he'd wrestled a steer or done any saddle bronc riding. And, he admitted ruefully, his lips quirking slightly, it would be a hell of a long time before he did either again.

He climbed out, feeling the jolt of the short step to the ground in every one of the damaged vertebrae of his spine. He gritted his teeth against the pain, trying to stretch out his back unobtrusively as he walked away from the chopper.

Too many hours in the cockpit without a break. He

wasn't making any complaints, though. Flying was the only activity he had ever found that he loved with the same passion he had once felt for rodeoing. He had been strictly an amateur, not nearly on a level to go pro, but he had been good enough to win some of the local prizes.

And good enough to win a few admiring glances from the women and slaps on the back from the men of the close-knit ranching communities of the Panhandle. Those had meant more to him than the money or trophies he'd won.

Especially at the last, when some of those glances had come from the doe-brown eyes of the once skinny little girl who had tagged along at his heels, hero-worshiping him the whole time they'd been growing up. Tagged along until in the space of one year, while he'd been away at college, Jillian Salvini had become a woman. A woman he'd seen with newly awakened eyes and fallen head over heels in love with.

"Back mighty late, boy," Stumpy Winters yelled from the door of the bunkhouse. "Boss been calling you. He said for you to be sure and give him a ring when you get up to the house."

Mark waved an acknowledgment to the old man, hunching his shoulders against a blast of wind that carried with it a stinging assault of dirt. Most nights he stopped at the bunkhouse to talk, delaying the lonely hours he would spend in his father's house until it was time for bed. Tonight he needed to take a hot shower and stretch out his aching back more than he needed company.

Stumpy wouldn't be offended. The old man had known him from the time he had ridden his first horse. Actually, he wasn't sure Winters hadn't been the one who'd put him up on that swayback.

Out of sight of the bunkhouse now, Mark slowed his pace, stretching his spine again. He climbed the three steps that led to the ranch house's back stoop as if he were as old as Stumpy.

Once inside, he shut the door, blocking out the howl of

the wind. Closing his eyes, he leaned back in relief against the solid wood behind him.

After a moment he straightened and walked across the kitchen, boot heels echoing on the vinyl-covered floor. He filled the glass standing beside the old-fashioned enamel sink and drank down the same clear, sweet well water of his childhood in a couple of long thirsty drafts. As he stood there drinking his water, he noticed that the shadows were beginning to lengthen over the yard, revealed through the windows above the sink.

He wondered idly what Tom Shipley wanted. Probably instructions about another errand to be run tomorrow. That was mostly what the chopper was used for during periods when cattle weren't being moved. Bringing in supplies and shuttling guests from the airports in Amarillo and Lubbock out to the spread the co-op ran as a dude ranch. Or taking its owners, like Shipley, into market or meetings. Occasionally doing medevac duties for the few injuries that required more than the first aid available on the ranches themselves.

He put down the glass and turned to face the phone on the opposite wall. Make the call, get squared away with Shipley, and then grab a hot shower, he promised himself, imagining the heat relaxing muscles tensed by a long day in the air.

Maybe tensed even further by that little side trip into the past he took every time he flew over the Salvini place. Tensed every time he thought about Jillian. Which had been too often lately for his peace of mind. Especially since he'd come home.

Home, he thought, glancing around his mother's kitchen. Not all that much had changed about it since she'd died. Just over twenty years ago, he realized with a small sense of disbelief.

There was a different color of paint on the walls. New curtains on the windows he'd been looking out. But the scarred wooden table and four chairs were exactly the same. He could still remember the night he'd brought Jillian here so they could tell his dad—

He stopped the playback of that image, closing his eyes against the painful strength of it. Too damn many memories. Too many ghosts. And none of them, except maybe his mother's, would rest easy with him living here. He pushed away from the counter and walked over to the phone.

After he'd dialed Shipley's number, he stood listening to the distant ringing, his eyes once more considering the chair where Jillian had sat that night. When he realized what he was doing, he turned around, facing the wall instead. And he knew that action was a physical enactment of what he needed to do mentally. To turn his back on the past.

He had been here long enough to know that coming home had been a mistake. It was time to start looking for another job. Time to move on. Time to forget about what had happened here and to get on with the rest of his life.

After all, he thought, the bitterness surging relentlessly to the surface again, that's exactly what *she* had done. Jillian Salvini had turned her back on him and everything that had been between them. In doing that, she had been wiser than he. Apparently Jillian had known, even then, that no matter how badly you might want to, you could never really go home again.

"VIOLET," Jillian Sullivan said. "Oh, God, not Violet."

She touched the edge of her desk and, using it for support, eased down into her chair like someone who had suffered a hard blow to the midsection. Which was exactly what this felt like.

"I'm really sorry to be the bearer of such bad news," the man who had introduced himself as Dylan Garrett said.

Jillian forced herself to look up, taking a calming breath as she nodded. "I didn't know. I didn't have any idea. I should have, I suppose. I had written her a couple of times and gotten no reply, which for Violet was so far from the norm…''

She shook her head, moving it slowly from side to side as she tried to assimilate the unwanted information that Violet Mitchum was dead. More unwanted than it would have been had they not had that silly argument the last time they'd met.

That was what those two letters had been about—an attempt to reassure Violet that she really did know what she was doing as far as marrying Jake Tyler was concerned. And as far as Drew was concerned as well, Jillian conceded.

That was what had eroded her confidence in her decision the most—Violet's doubts about whether or not Jillian was doing the right thing for her son. The question of whether she was cheating him out of something that he was entitled to. And yet, one of the reasons she had agreed to marry Jake—

"Mrs. Sullivan?"

Dylan Garrett's voice brought her back to the present, a present she was still having a hard time facing.

"I'm sorry," she said blankly. "What did you say?"

"I was wondering if you had known Violet Mitchum long."

Long enough to feel for her the kind of love usually reserved for family, Jillian thought. She didn't say it aloud, but there was no doubt the old woman had assumed a parental role in her life. And therefore the loss was almost as devastating as if she had been one of Jillian's parents.

Maybe even more so, she realized in regret. After she had left her family and ended up in Pinto, Jillian had desperately needed someone as supportive as Violet in her life. And through the years, she couldn't have asked for a better friend.

"More than nine years. She was both a friend and a mentor."

"A mentor?"

"She taught me a lot of what I know about this business," Jillian said, glancing around the interior design studio. "When I came to Pinto, the only job I could get was in the local antique store. I learned a lot from the owner, who was a friend of Violet's, but even more from Violet herself. Despite the rather...unusual appearance of her house, she had collected some really lovely things when she and Charlie traveled. Violet might not have had any formal education, but she had the eye, and the instinct, to discern quality and value."

"And she shared those with you?"

Jillian smiled at him, thinking about all Violet had shared through the years. "That and far more. She paid for my classes in design and baby-sat my son so I could attend them. When I finished school, she helped secure this job for me by contacting a friend of hers who lived here in Fort Worth. I owe her more than I could possibly say, and now I discover that she's gone, that she's been dead for over a month. And I didn't even know."

Despite the depth of her grief, Jillian hated the catch in her voice when she spoke. Through the years she had learned the hard lesson of hiding her emotions. At first she had done it out of pride, and a determination that no matter what her father said to her, he would never see her cry. Then she had done it for Drew's sake, keeping up a brave front for her son, despite the struggle those first years had been.

By now, guarding her feelings was a deeply ingrained habit. One that even a grief this profound apparently couldn't break.

"I'm so sorry," Dylan said again.

"Thank you. It's just...such a shock."

"And I have what will probably be another for you."

"I beg your pardon?"

"Another shock. Not more bad news," he clarified quickly. "Violet's death was enough, I know."

"What kind of shock?" Jillian asked carefully.

"Mrs. Mitchum remembered you in her will."

Remembered you in her will. Which could mean almost anything. Violet had a lot of money, of course. Jillian had always known that. Not that it was evident in her person or in her treatment of others. It was simply that Violet loved to tell the story of her beloved Charlie's strike. And considering how well-known Mitchum Oil was in Texas...

"She left me something?" Jillian asked.

"A couple of things, actually."

Mementos then, Jillian thought, relieved. For the first time in years her financial situation was stable and promising, and much of that was due to Violet's past generosity. She didn't really want her to do more.

"What are they?"

"One I couldn't bring with me," Dylan Garrett said, smiling at her for the first time.

Again Jillian shook her head. "I'm not sure—"

"Violet left you her piano."

Memories she had been fighting flooded Jillian's brain. How many afternoons had she taken refuge in Violet's huge Victorian house rather than go back to that dreary apartment over the antique store. It was all she could afford, and she was grateful for the owner's generosity in making it available to her, but her loneliness for adult companionship had been almost unbearable.

At Violet's, there had always been a welcome. Jillian remembered the long, happy evenings she'd spent there, her heart filling again with the warmth of the unconditional love she had felt emanating from the old woman for both her and her son. She would play the piano and Violet would hold Drew until he fell asleep. It had been idyllic. And a balm for the rejection Jillian had felt in every other aspect of her life.

"I can have it delivered whenever and wherever you want it."

He meant the piano, Jillian realized. "I—I don't know what to say," she said softly.

"I'll leave you my card, and you can think about it. Just give me a call when you've decided."

"I used to play that piano for her."

Even as she said it, Jillian realized this man couldn't possibly care about that. Dylan Garrett was simply acting at the request of Violet's lawyers. He had told her that at the beginning.

"She left *me* a horse," he said.

Surprised, she looked up into his blue eyes, which were almost amused—maybe at Violet's choice of mementos. And yet, at the same time, they exuded a sympathy that made Jillian feel as if perhaps he did understand what she was feeling.

"And she also left me one of these," he added.

He laid something down on the desk in front of her. It took her a few seconds to break the strange connection that had grown between them to look down at whatever it was.

"My God," she whispered when she did. And then she added truthfully, "I don't want this."

She didn't. She would have given every penny this check represented to have had the opportunity to clear up the disagreement that had marred her last visit with Violet, the one where she had taken Jake Tyler with her.

That had been her mistake. It wasn't that Violet hadn't liked Jake. She had said as much herself. But she had also warned Jillian that there was too much "unfinished business" in her past. Too many things she had never put behind her. Violet had warned her that she must clear those up before she could hope to start a new life for her and Drew. A life with someone else.

"I'm afraid giving it back isn't an option," Dylan said, his voice amused. "The money's yours to do whatever you want."

"What I *want* is to see Violet again," Jillian protested, knowing how childish that probably sounded.

"I know," Dylan replied, and the way he said it somehow made Jillian feel that he didn't think her plea was childish at all. "I felt the same way when I found out she was gone. I'd lost touch with Violet, and I'll always regret that. She told me something very meaningful, something that made an incredible difference in my life, and...I never got the chance to tell her that. Or a chance to thank her."

Something very meaningful... The words seemed to echo in Jillian's heart. She had tried to ignore what Violet had told her. She had tried to dismiss the old woman's wisdom as something that wasn't feasible or realistic. But none of the advice Violet had given her through the years had been wrong. Jillian had known that, even as she had stubbornly denied the sagacity of what Violet had said to her the last time they'd met.

"She told me something, too," she said in a low voice.

Dylan tilted his head a little, as if he were trying to read her tone. "And...?"

"And...I didn't listen because I didn't want to hear what she was saying. I didn't want to believe it."

"I certainly wouldn't presume to try to tell you—"

"Violet would," Jillian assured him.

Dylan laughed.

"I don't know if she was right about what she said," Jillian went on. Despite her grief over the way she had left things the last time she'd visited Pinto, she managed to smile at him. "But...she was right about most of the things she told me through the years. Maybe I owe it to her to try to find out if she was right about this one, too."

Again her eyes fell to the check lying in the center of her desk. She wondered if Violet had intended her to use this money to do what she had suggested. Of course, it had come with no strings attached. No demands made. And what Violet had said had only been a suggestion. Still...

"I'll let you know where to send the piano," she said.

It was intended as a dismissal. Now that she had made the decision, Jillian found she was eager to get started. Maybe it was an eagerness to do exactly what Violet had said, and then put it all behind her. Or maybe... Maybe

Violet had been right about the unfinished business of her life, she acknowledged.

There were too many things that Drew would have questions about as he grew older. Too many things, Jillian realized with a sense of surprise, that she herself still had questions about. And there was only one way to answer them. And really, only one place to start.

"YOU'VE LOST your mind," Jake Tyler said.

"I know it must sound like that," Jillian admitted.

His gaze held hers a long moment before he turned and paced to the other end of his enormous penthouse office, his fury apparent in every step. When he reached the wall of glass that looked down into the heart of Dallas's financial district, he turned, meeting her eyes again.

His lips were compressed, and Jillian understood, because she knew him so well, that he was trying to gather control before he said anything else. His hands had been thrust into the pockets of the charcoal-gray suit he wore so that she wouldn't see that they were clenched angrily into fists.

"I thought everything was set," he said finally, the fury tamped down enough to allow him to speak almost naturally.

"I'm sorry, Jake, but this is something I have to do."

"Because that crazy old woman told you to do it."

Jillian suppressed her own anger at his characterization of Violet. Her grief was too new to shrug off Jake's disparagement, although she recognized it was his disappointment speaking. And she couldn't blame him for being annoyed. Any man would be.

They had all but set the date before she had taken him to Pinto that weekend. And since they'd returned, even before she had known about Violet's death, she had been putting Jake off about finalizing plans for the wedding. The news Dylan Garrett had brought her, along with Violet's legacy, seemed almost a sign that she had been right in postponing things a bit.

"And because of Drew," she said, wondering as she spoke if she was using her son as an excuse for something *she* wanted to do. And that, too, created its own sense of guilt.

"A good private school and a father's discipline," Jake said. "Those are the only things he needs. You know that."

"I'm not sure another school would be any better."

"He needs to be with children who are bright enough to judge on something other than physical attributes."

"Like how much money their fathers have?" she asked pointedly.

"Not all children bully those who are…different. That doesn't have to be a part of growing up. It shouldn't be."

"He'll be in a new school when we move."

"And you think it's going to be any different in the back of beyond? You think those kids are not going to bully him?"

There was no guarantee of that, and she knew it.

"There's more to this than just Drew," Jillian said.

"Then tell me. Explain to me why you're giving up a client base you've worked so damn hard to build. Your career is just now starting to show the kind of success you said you'd always dreamed of. Why the hell are you throwing that all away?"

Unfinished business, Violet had said. And that about summed it up, Jillian thought. "It's just something I have to do, Jake," she said aloud. "If I don't…"

"If you don't, then…what?" Jake asked after the silence had stretched too thin between them.

"If I don't, then I won't be able to be your wife," she said, looking down at the emerald-cut four-carat diamond she wore on her left hand. "If you still want that."

"If *I* still want it? You know I do, Jillian. Is that what this is about? Is there someone else—"

He broke off when her eyes came up too quickly from

the ring he'd given her. Again the silence expanded, filling the space between them. Finally, almost reluctantly, she twisted the engagement ring off her finger.

Holding it in her right hand, she walked across to the huge mahogany desk that was the focal point of the office she had designed for him a little less than two years ago. She laid the ring on the edge, allowing her fingers to rest on it a moment before she removed them, then clasped both hands together in front of her waist because they were trembling.

"I have to know," she said softly. "We both have to know."

"Don't do this," he said, his voice as low as hers.

"If we're right—if this is right," she amended, nodding toward the ring, "then I'll be back. I'm not asking you to wait. But…whatever you decide to do, I have to go."

"Are you telling me I won't even be allowed to see you?"

"Are you sure you still want to?" she asked, smiling at him.

"Of course, I want to. I'm in love with you, Jillian. I thought you were in love with me."

"So did I," she said. "But that's something we both need to be right about, and I promise you, what I'm doing is the only way I know to be sure."

"And if you aren't in love with me?" he asked, every trace of anger wiped from his tone. It held a note of uncertainty she had never heard in Jake Tyler's voice before.

"Then…I guess that's something we both need to know."

CHAPTER TWO

"SOLD?" Mark repeated in surprise.

"Somebody bought it right out from under their noses," Stumpy Winters said, grinning. "I guess they waited a little too long this time, trying to drive the price down to nothing."

"An individual?"

"With enough money to get the paperwork done overnight. Seems like they even took Dwight Perkins by surprise."

That wasn't the way things normally worked around here. Most of the Realtors, like Perkins, were in the co-op's hip pocket, which was pretty deep, giving them inside information on the market that allowed them to get the best deals.

Mark even understood why Stumpy was grinning with such unabashed delight as he told him about the sale. It did feel like a victory for the little man to have the Salvini place sold out from under the co-op's nose. And to a family, apparently.

"Poor bastards," Stumpy said, spitting tobacco juice into the five-pound coffee can that had been provided in the bunkhouse for that purpose. "They don't know it yet, a' course, but there ain't nothing except bad luck and heartbreak waiting for 'em."

Stumpy would know. Although Mark hadn't thought about it since he'd been back, that ranch had once belonged to Winters's family, long before Tony Salvini bought it.

"Maybe it'll be different this time," Mark said.

Stumpy snorted, his disdain for the prediction clear. "And

maybe pigs'll fly, too, but I ain't hanging around expecting it.''

"Speaking of which…" Mark said.

He threw the dregs of his coffee out the open bunkhouse door. Considering the strength of the brew the old man boiled up on the woodstove every morning, he half expected it to sizzle in the dirt when it hit the ground. Despite the taste, though, there was nothing guaranteed to clear the head and get the heart pumping faster than Stumpy's coffee.

"You take care," Stumpy said. "We're gonna have us some weather 'fore the day's out.''

Weather. In the vernacular of the High Plains that meant a storm, which this time of year could include sleet or snow. Like most old cowpunchers, Stumpy's battered bones were a better indicator of the local conditions than the six o'clock news.

"See you tonight," Mark said, taking the bunkhouse steps two at a time.

Whatever Stumpy's bones were telling him, Mark's back felt better than it had for a couple of days. Of course, that might be due to the fact that he hadn't had any marathon sessions in the cockpit lately. And today wouldn't change that pattern. A run over to Albuquerque to take one of the co-op's owners to a meeting was the only thing on his agenda.

That could always change, but it looked as if he might have the afternoon free to take the résumés he'd been work- ing on to the post office in town. He didn't want to mail them from the ranch. That was something that his dad had drummed into him from childhood. The fewer people who knew your business, the better.

Not a bad philosophy, Mark admitted. Not in this case, anyway. Until he had another position lined up, he couldn't afford to alienate the owners of the co-op. He'd keep his mouth shut about his plans to move on. After all, that deci- sion was nobody's business but his.

JUST A GLUTTON for punishment, he thought as he found himself easing the stick to the right.

Flying over the Salvini place hadn't been a conscious decision, but on the return leg of his trip, Mark had ended up again on the northern boundary of the property. Although the distance this route added to his flight time would be no more than a few minutes, they could be critical on a day like this.

The old man had been right about the storm. The sky was low, the clouds were dark and threatening, and the temperature had dropped at least fifteen degrees since this morning. He needed to get the chopper down before the storm hit, but the temptation to see what the new owners were doing was too strong to ignore. At least that was what he told himself as he headed south.

Out of the corner of his eye he caught a glimpse of movement on the tabletop flatness below. Hoping for something like the antelope he had startled into motion a few days ago, Mark looked down, carefully scanning the area. And when he found what had attracted his attention, it took a second or two for him to comprehend what he was seeing, because it was so unexpected.

Beneath him was a kid. On foot. And alone.

The impressions bombarded his brain, but it took another minute to adjust his course so that he was flying back over the spot where he'd seen the child. As he did, he realized that he hadn't been mistaken about any of those things.

The kid looked up, watching the helicopter's approach. As Mark drew nearer, details became apparent. Boy, he decided, although with today's unisex clothing and hairstyles, gender could be hard to distinguish.

As soon as the child realized the chopper was coming back, he turned, too, heading off in the opposite direction. Although he was hurrying, he wasn't really moving very fast. He was limping, Mark realized as he watched the uneven gait. And his limp was slowing down what was obviously supposed to be an escape attempt.

Despite the threat of the predicted storm, Mark's lips tilted into a smile. He'd be willing to bet the kid was wearing new boots of a kind not designed for hiking in this terrain. He could visualize them in his mind's eye. The pointy-toed tourist-variety cowboy boot, gaudy with decoration. And if the boy thought he could outrun him in those things...

Mark brought the helicopter alongside and just above the child, jabbing his finger toward the ominous cloud bank that lay above the horizon. He was near enough to see brown eyes widen in a pale face as the child looked up. Near enough that he could tell that the flapping windbreaker would not offer nearly enough protection from the cold that would come sweeping in across the plain.

He increased pitch, pulling up a little and moving in front of the kid, who was still trying to run with that loping awkwardness. Then, very carefully, he set the chopper down maybe thirty feet in front of the boy. As soon as he realized what Mark was doing, the child changed directions again, heading north this time. Right into the heart of the approaching storm.

"Damn it, kid," Mark said under his breath.

He could lift off and land in front of the boy again. He could keep doing that until he'd worn him into exhaustion. Or he could get out and try to talk some sense into him. Maybe try to figure out what the hell he was doing way out here alone, a good five or six miles from the nearest habitation, which was...

New owners. New boots. The kid must belong to the family who had bought the Salvini place. He had probably set out to explore and gotten turned around. That wasn't hard to do, given the unchanging sameness of the landscape. There weren't any landmarks up here, and unless you had a compass...

Mark lifted the chopper off the ground again, closing the distance between them, and landed directly in the boy's path. The kid's lips were parted now, as if he were panting from the exertion of trying to outrun his pursuer.

Mark throttled down to flight idle and locked down the controls before he unfastened his seat harness and opened the door of the cockpit. By the time he'd stepped down, ducking under the blades, the kid had twirled again and was heading in the opposite direction.

It took Mark only a few strides to catch up. The boy must have heard him, although he never looked back. When Mark put his hand on his shoulder, the child twisted, pulling out of his grip.

He darted away to the left, and as Mark turned to follow, he felt a twinge of pain ripple through his back. He ignored it and ran after the boy, using the advantage of his longer stride to quickly lessen the distance between them.

When he was close enough, he reached out again, grabbing the boy's upper arm. His hand closed around it hard enough to withstand the attempts the child made to pull away. The kid must be more panicked than he'd realized, Mark thought, holding on despite the frantic struggle the boy was making to escape.

"Calm down," Mark said, his tone the same he had once used to gentle spooked horses. "I'm not going to hurt you. There's a storm coming, and believe me, you aren't equipped for the kind we get up here. I'm going to take you home."

The boy's efforts to free his arm ceased, but Mark didn't release him. And for the first time, he got a good look at the kid's face. There was a dusting of freckles across a slender nose. Dark eyes were fringed by equally dark lashes. And compared with the thick brown hair and those eyes, the skin that surrounded them seemed awfully pale.

City kid, Mark guessed. Any boy this age who had spent the summer out in the rural Texas sun would still have a pretty good residual tan. This kid didn't.

Of course, part of that noticeable paleness might be put down to fright. Odds were the kid had never been chased by a stranger in a helicopter before. That would be enough to scare almost anyone, especially a kid who had gotten lost in unfamiliar territory. Mark was about to offer more reassurances, when the boy spoke for the first time.

"I don't *want* to go home," he said, jerking his arm free.

So much for the scared spitless theory, Mark thought, realizing only now that what he was seeing in those eyes wasn't fear, but defiance.

"I told you, kid. There's a storm brewing, and up here, that's nothing to fool around with. Not in November."

The eyes changed a little, holding Mark's a moment before they cut back to consider the line of clouds. When the boy looked back, he seemed less certain—and less antagonistic—than he had only seconds before. "My mom send you?"

"I don't know your mom. And nobody sent me. I didn't have any idea you were out here. Not until I saw you."

The boy stared hard at Mark, obviously trying to decide whether to believe him or not.

"You running away?" Mark asked into the silence.

After a few more seconds of scrutiny, the kid nodded. Apparently Mark had passed the test for trustworthiness that had just been administered.

"I've done that a couple of times myself," he said easily, smiling in memory. "And I can tell you from experience, it never solved anything I wanted it to."

"I didn't want to come here," the boy said. "I told her that. There's nothing out here."

His tone was almost plaintive, and Mark laughed, provoking a flash of resentment in the dark eyes.

"Well, you aren't wrong about that," he admitted, attempting to regain the ground that unthinking laughter had lost. "Nothing at all, unless you're partial to sky and dirt. We've got plenty of that. And cows, of course. Horses."

"She said I could have a horse."

Those words were less defiant, but there was something beneath the surface Mark couldn't quite read.

"That's good," he ventured.

"I don't *like* horses."

"You ever been around any?"

"No," the boy admitted after a brief hesitation.

His gaze skated again to the line of clouds, a little anxiously this time. Mark realized that the wind had picked up as they'd been talking. It was whipping the boy's hair into his eyes and billowing inside the back of the light cotton jacket he wore.

"Your mom's probably worried sick about you," Mark said, bringing the boy's eyes back to his face.

"You like horses?" the kid asked.

"Always have. Since long before I was your age."

As he said the word, he tried to estimate how old the child was. He hadn't really been around enough kids to make it an accurate evaluation, but...six or seven, he guessed. He wondered why the boy wasn't in school. Maybe with the move and all—

"I don't," the boy said. "They smell."

Mark laughed again, unable to argue with that assessment.

"You get used to it. After a while, that smell will seem like perfume. Cookies baking. Something good, anyway."

He resisted the urge to reach out and ruffle the dark hair that was blowing around the pale, freckled face.

"She likes them."

"Your mom?"

"Yeah. I told her I didn't want a horse. Then I told her I didn't want to be here, and she got all upset."

"So you left."

"She worries about me," the kid said.

I'll bet she does, Mark thought. He put his hand on the back of the narrow shoulders, directing the child toward the waiting chopper. There was no resistance this time, and as they walked, Mark noticed the uneven stride again. He glanced down at the boy's feet, which were shod in ordinary sneakers.

"Blister?" he asked, still using his hand to direct the kid around to the other side of the helicopter.

He opened the door on the passenger side of the cockpit and put his hand under the boy's elbow, preparing to help him inside. The kid squirmed away, the move almost like the one he'd made to throw Mark's hand off his shoulder. And it was as effective.

"I can do it," he said, that hint of defiance back.

Again Mark refrained from arguing. After all, there was nothing wrong with wanting to stand on your own two feet, even if they were blistered. It took the kid a few seconds to assess the unfamiliar situation. When he had, he put one foot on the skid and grasped the leather loop above the door. He scrambled into the seat, shooting a triumphant glance downward at Mark.

Resisting the urge to smile at that rather obvious, if silent, "I told you so," Mark closed the door and walked around the nose of the chopper. He climbed inside, automatically fastening his harness as soon as he was settled in the seat.

The boy watched and then began fastening his own, making quick work of the procedure. Since Mark occasionally had to help adults figure out how to work the device, his opinion of the kid's intelligence edged upward a notch or two.

He reached behind the adjacent seat and pulled out a flight helmet. Very few of his passengers wanted to wear one, and given the fact that most of them were his employers, he didn't insist.

"Put it on," he ordered this time, handing the helmet to the boy. If he had expected resistance, he was disappointed.

"Cool," the kid said with a touch of awe in his voice.

Mark hid his grin by putting the helicopter into the air. The wind had picked up quite a lot in the short time he'd been on the ground, but he'd be flying south, away from the storm. At least he would until he got to the Salvini ranch, which was, of course, no longer the Salvini ranch, he reminded himself.

He wasn't sure he'd ever known the name of the last owner. If he had, he couldn't remember it. And he didn't think Stumpy had mentioned the new owner's. "What's your name?" he asked.

He had to raise his voice to be heard over the engine. The kid had been watching the ground whip beneath him, which was an awesome sight the first time you experienced it. He turned his head, the helmet sliding around despite the chin strap. He raised both hands to straighten it as his eyes met Mark's.

"Andrew Sullivan."

"Nice to meet you, Andy."

"Drew," the child corrected.

"Drew," Mark repeated obediently. "Mark Peterson."

"You live around here."

"Next door."

"Cool," the kid said again.

Mark allowed the smile he had resisted before. He glanced over at the boy, receiving an answering one. Wide and unabashed, it lit up the narrow features and lightened the dark eyes.

After a second or two, the kid turned back to watch the scenery below. Mark found himself hoping their passage would stir up some wildlife. He thought the kid would like to see that. It, too, would probably be deemed *cool*.

He was a little surprised at how gratified he was to have won that appellation. It had been a while since anyone had approved of him with quite that much undisguised enthusiasm. And that was definitely *cool*, he thought, again fighting a grin.

"I WISH YOU'D called me earlier," the sheriff said.

"If I'd known he was missing earlier, believe me I would have," Jillian said, not even bothering to hide her sarcasm. She hadn't liked Ronnie Cameron when they had gone to school together. Nothing that had happened today had changed her opinion. All she wanted him to do was to organize some kind of search, and instead, he seemed determined to let her know what a bad mother she was. Right now she didn't need anyone else telling her that. Her guilt over letting Drew out of her sight while he was still so angry was quite sufficient without Ronnie's comments.

"When's the last time you saw him?" the sheriff asked, flipping the pages in the small spiral-bound notebook he had taken out of the pocket of his suede jacket. He licked the point of his pencil in preparation and glanced up at her expectantly.

Jillian wondered, her irritation growing, how long it had been since she had seen anybody do that and what it was supposed to accomplish. What was any of this supposed to accomplish?

Apparently Ronnie intended to write down everything she had already told him before he did anything. Jillian gritted her teeth over the delay, working to keep her temper in check. Not that she had much choice.

When she'd discovered Drew was gone, she couldn't think of anything else to do except appeal to the sheriff for help. She had given the dispatcher all the information. And then she had repeated it for the sheriff as soon as he'd shown up, almost thirty minutes after she'd called the emergency number.

And she had searched the ranch herself before she'd called. Once she had, she had realized there was just too much very empty territory surrounding it for her to investigate alone. Besides, she couldn't be sure how long Drew had been gone.

"A little after ten," she said, trying to hold on to her patience. "He was playing a computer game."

"And you didn't see him after that?" Ronnie asked, carefully writing something in his notebook.

"That's right," Jillian said, taking a deep, calming breath.

"And you think he might have gone out exploring?"

"I said it's possible. We just moved in a couple of days ago. I thought maybe… I don't know. Maybe he just decided to take a look around and got lost."

"Uh-huh," the sheriff said, still writing.

"But…"

She hesitated, hating to confess the strained relationship with her son this move had caused. Ronnie's blue eyes had lifted from his notebook at the pause. They held hers, waiting.

"He might have run away," she said softly.

"Run away from home?"

She resisted the urge to state the obvious, nodding instead.

"Got his dander up about something?" Ronnie asked.

"He wasn't too thrilled about the move."

The sheriff's eyes drifted over the buildings clustered around the house before they came back to hers.

"Could be hiding," he said. "Lots of hiding places around here for a boy."

"I called him. I went inside every one of the outbuildings and called."

"That don't mean he's gonna answer," Ronnie said, smiling at her. He flipped the top of the notebook over whatever he'd written and stuck it back in his jacket pocket.

"And why would he do that?" Jillian asked. "Why would he not answer? Exactly what are you implying?"

"That maybe the kid don't want to be found. He's got himself a mad on, and he's trying to rattle your chain. Seems to be working, too."

The smile widened, and Jillian, the most nonconfrontational person in the world, wanted to slap it off his face.

"There's a storm coming," she said. "I don't want my son out in it. I called you to help me find him."

"I expect he's curled up somewhere watching us right now. He probably liked the idea of you calling the county out to look for him. Liked seeing the cruiser coming."

"You can't know that."

"Best guess," Ronnie said, seemingly unaware of her anger. "Based on eight years' experience in this business."

"And you aren't going to do anything to find him," Jillian said flatly, finally realizing that he wasn't.

"I'll take a look around. Drive out a ways."

"I've already done both of those things."

"But you're his mama. *I'm* the sheriff. Kids react differently to a uniform. To somebody in authority."

"I thought you'd decided Drew was enjoying watching this."

"One or the other. Let's start with the barn," Ronnie said.

He began to walk in that direction without waiting to see if she was coming. As a child, the barn had always been her refuge, Jillian remembered. Its horse-scented darkness had given her a sense of safety unmatched anywhere else on the ranch. Reluctantly, knowing this was nothing but a wild-goose chase and a waste of what might be valuable time, she turned to follow him.

As she did, she realized that the sheriff had stopped, seeming to study the clouds to the north. As she glanced in the same direction, she became aware of a sound disturbing the prestorm quiet.

Helicopter, she identified automatically. She put her hand up, shading her eyes from the swirling, wind-driven dust more than from the sun, which had been dimmed by the clouds.

The chopper grew larger as she and the sheriff watched. After a minute or two, it became apparent that it was preparing to set down in the yard. Now that it was this close, Jillian could see it wasn't any kind of official aircraft. There were no markings that would indicate it belonged to law enforcement or to the military.

It was small and sleek, its body white with bright-red numbers. There was a logo of some kind on the door, but Jillian couldn't quite make it out from here.

She shielded her eyes again, this time from the dust the rotor was stirring up. Whoever was flying the chopper set it down with hardly a bump and shut off the engine. The sudden silence made her realize how noisy the thing had been.

"Co-op," the sheriff said.

"Co-op?"

"Outfit that owns most of the land around here. They wanted this place, but I guess you beat 'em to it."

She had been told someone else was interested in the property, which had helped her make up her mind very quickly that this was what she wanted to do with Violet's money. Once she'd made that decision, writing the check for the full purchase price was all that had been required to close the deal. That and signing her name on the bottom line.

Foolishly, she had done that before she had approached Drew. Because her childhood here had been so idyllic, she had never expected that he'd react the way he had. After all—

The door of the chopper slid open and the pilot climbed down. Head lowered a little, he walked around to the other side and opened the passenger door. By now, Jillian had begun to suspect what this was all about. Still, her heart leaped into her throat when Drew came running around the nose of the chopper.

She fought the maternal instinct to shout a warning to him to be careful of the still-rotating blades. Biting the inside of her lip, she simply watched as he approached, so relieved to see him that her knees felt weak.

His steps slowed the closer he came, especially when he noticed the sheriff. *You know you're in trouble,* Jillian thought, *when you find out your mom's called out the law.*

"Hi, Mom," Drew said, his tone wavering somewhere between apprehension and excitement.

The latter she could credit to his recent ride in the helicopter, something he'd never done before. And the former was self-explanatory. Drew knew from experience that she wasn't going to put up with this kind of nonsense.

He knew that, and yet he had done it anyway, which proved exactly how upset he was about the move. And she felt like a fool and a failure for not having any idea about how he'd react.

"Where have you been?" she asked, giving him a chance to tell his side of the story. Besides, listening to his explanation would give her a few seconds to decide what she was going to do about his disappearing.

"I was leaving, but...I got turned around."

"You were running away?"

"I was going back to Fort Worth," Drew said.

He sounded almost as determined as he had when he told her how much he hated the ranch. She wished she'd listened.

"And you got lost instead," she guessed.

He nodded, his eyes cutting back to the pilot, who was rounding the nose of the chopper.

"You're a little old for that kind of thing, aren't you?" Jillian asked, bringing his attention back to her. "You must have some idea of how worried I've been."

As she talked, she was aware of the pilot's approach. She wanted to thank him for bringing Drew home, but she also wanted to make the point to her son that something like this wasn't going to happen again. This kind of escapade was not allowed.

"He says there's a storm coming, so he brought me back."

He glanced away again, focusing on the man who was walking toward them. Jillian raised her own gaze this time, noticing the man's sun-streaked hair first, since he was in the act of pushing it away from his face by running long tanned fingers through it.

And when he looked up, hazel eyes meeting hers, her heart stopped. Skipped a beat. Did something different, at least. Whatever she called it, something strange and terrifying happened in the center of her chest as recognition washed over her in a scalding wave of emotion.

The same weakness that had invaded her knees when she'd seen Drew run around the chopper moved up to her stomach. And then lower. Its effect was so unexpected that for a second or two she didn't realize what was happening. After all, it hadn't happened to her in more than ten years. Not since the last time she had seen this man, whose eyes locked on hers and then widened with what looked like the same sense of shock she had just experienced.

He recovered first. Although she didn't believe she could manage to utter a coherent sound, Mark Peterson's voice seemed perfectly normal. A little deeper than she remembered it, but other than that, exactly the same as it had always been.

Exactly the same as the night he'd made love to her. The night Drew had been conceived.

"Hello, Jillian," he said. "It's been a long time."

CHAPTER THREE

JILLIAN TRIED to think of an appropriate response. What Mark had said was nothing less than the truth. It *had* been a long time. A damn long time, better measured in events than in years.

"It has been, hasn't it," she said, thankful to find that her voice still worked, although to her own ears it was thready, a little breathless. "How are you, Mark?"

It's been a long time.

It has been, hasn't it? How are you?

The merest commonplaces. Phrases either of them might have said to a chance acquaintance. But beneath lay all the memories she suspected neither of them had forgotten.

Or maybe she was wrong about that, she thought, watching him turn to Ronnie. Maybe that was just her fantasy—that what she and Mark had shared that summer had meant more to him than a quick roll in the hay.

"Ronnie," Mark said, nodding at the sheriff.

"Looks like you did my job for me," Ronnie replied. "Much obliged. I wasn't looking forward to searching for the kid all afternoon in a storm. Probably would have been calling on you to help, so I guess you saved us both some trouble."

Mark nodded again, his mouth flattening as if he had wanted to say something and then thought better of it. "Glad I could help," he said finally, his eyes coming back to Drew.

"You know what's good for you, young man," Ronnie said to the boy, "you won't ever pull a stunt like this again. Worrying your mama and wasting the taxpayers' money. I got gas and time tied up in coming way out here. Ought to make you work those expenses out. And I will the next time you get the notion to send everybody off on a wild-goose chase.''

As much as she knew Drew was in the wrong, Jillian found herself resenting the sheriff's lecture. *Overprotective.* Jake had accused her of that, and she had resented his lecture, too.

He needs a man's discipline in his life, Jake had said. *He needs a father.* Maybe he did. After all, Violet had told her the same thing. Of course with Violet...

Involuntarily, her gaze found Mark's face. Now that her shock had faded, she was able to evaluate it dispassionately. He was still looking down at Drew, so she allowed herself to examine his features more freely than she might have otherwise.

His skin was as darkly tanned as it had been since she'd known him. Although his hair was much lighter than hers, Mark never burned, not even when working all day in the grueling heat.

In the years since she'd last seen him, that exposure to the relentless Texas sun had etched its marks on his face. Faint lines fanned from the corners of his eyes. His lashes were as long and thick as she remembered them, and still tipped with the same gold the summer sun always brushed through his chestnut hair. A crease had begun to form in the center of his cheeks, which were no longer boyishly rounded.

A man's face, she acknowledged. Hard, lean and tempered by the years. Whenever she had thought of him, she had pictured him exactly as he had been that summer. Young, strong and so beautifully male. He was different now. Certainly not less attractive. If anything—

"I'm sure Drew won't head out without permission again," Mark said. He smiled at Drew, whose eyes had shifted gratefully from the sheriff's accusing ones to his. "We all make mistakes."

As he added the last, Mark glanced up at Jillian. She wasn't sure what he was implying, but then no one could argue with the sentiment. *We all make mistakes.*

Of course, maybe that phrase didn't mean anything, she

cautioned her volatile emotions. Maybe he was just making conversation. Just because he said something didn't mean it was related to their shared past. Or to her.

"Well, you best not make this one again, young fellow," Ronnie said pompously. "Nobody's got time to be chasing down kids who don't have sense enough to get in out of the rain."

The word seemed a signal. The first drops began to splatter down around them, large enough to be audible as they struck the dry earth.

"Gotta go," the sheriff said. "You mind your mama, boy. If you don't, I'll know about it, and then you and me's gonna have to have us a talk. You hear me?"

"Yes, sir," Drew said.

The bravado with which he had told Jillian in no uncertain terms this morning that he hated this place seemed to have disappeared. Even his excitement over the chopper ride had evaporated, and as angry as she was with him for running away, Jillian found herself regretting that loss.

The three of them watched as Ronnie trotted to his car. As soon as he had gotten settled into the seat, he picked up the radio and spoke to someone. The exchange was inaudible and brief, maybe just a location report or the assurance that he was headed back into town. Then he put the car into gear, backing it into the yard before he headed out the dirt road. He lifted his hand in farewell as he drove past them.

"I have to get back, too," Mark said. "I'll see you later."

She glanced up, an incredibly powerful surge of hope flaring inside her, to find he was addressing Drew.

"Promise?" her son said, brown eyes meeting hazel. And the same hope she had just felt was expressed in that single word.

"You can count on it," Mark said.

He reached out and put his hand on top of the boy's head, but he didn't ruffle the darkly shining hair. That was something Jake did, and Jillian had never been sure Drew appreciated the gesture. Mark's was more of a touch. A goodbye. Maybe even a benediction of sorts. As was his smile.

Without looking at her, he turned and began to retrace his steps. She realized then why it had taken her so long to recognize him. Just as his face had changed, so had his body. The shoulders were as broad, maybe broader than the last time she'd seen him. His hips and waist had narrowed, leading down to long, muscular legs, now eating up the distance to the chopper.

A man and no longer a boy, she thought again.

Before she had time to think anything else, Drew's hand slipped into hers. That was unusual enough these days that she glanced down in surprise.

"I'm in big trouble, huh?" he said, his eyes still on Mark.

"What do you think?"

"I think…it was worth it," her son said.

"Worth being in big trouble?"

"If I hadn't been out there, I'd never had gotten to ride in the chopper. He let me wear a flight helmet," he added.

Jillian shielded her eyes from the dust as the rotor began to turn. She didn't particularly want to be standing out here, watching Mark Peterson leave, but she didn't seem to be able to do anything about the fact that she was.

"You think he meant what he said about seeing me again?"

At least Drew hadn't asked how she knew Mark, she thought with gratitude. But she understood how her son's mind worked well enough to know that he would put two and two together soon enough. After all, Mark had called her by name.

"Who knows?" she said softly, forcing the words between lips that felt stiff. And not just with the cold.

Once she had been foolish enough to think she could predict what Mark would do in any situation. And she had been wrong. This time she wasn't going to make any predictions. Not even for Drew's sake. Especially not for Drew's sake.

JILLIAN, he thought, going mindlessly through the motions of flying without any conscious awareness of what he was doing. He didn't seem capable of thinking about anything

other than the woman he had left behind him, standing out
in the rain. *Jillian Salvini.*

Sullivan, he reminded himself. The kid had said his name
was Sullivan. He wondered briefly about Jillian's husband,
feeling nausea stir in the pit of his stomach at the thought.

And then, deliberately, he blocked out images he didn't
want to deal with. Couldn't deal with. Images from their
past followed by images of Jillian married to someone else.
Sleeping with someone else. Conceiving another man's
child. His head moved slowly from side to side in denial.
A pointless denial.

What the hell did you think she'd been doing for the last
decade? he asked himself angrily. So she was married and
had a kid. Big deal.

In the back of his mind he had always known that was
a possibility. A probability, he amended. After all, Jillian
was almost thirty now. Twenty-eight, he calculated.

And she still didn't look much older than she had that
summer when she was seventeen. Not with her hair pulled
back like that. Her skin was still pale and smooth, but without the ever present tan of her childhood. The freckles that
had always decorated the bridge of her nose, unless it was
the dead of winter, were no longer visible.

Except they were, he realized. Those same freckles were
splayed across her son's equally delicate nose. He wondered how he had missed noticing the resemblance.

He shouldn't have. Drew Sullivan was a masculine rep-
lication of the skinny little tomboy, that other sometimes
lonely only child who had followed at Mark's heels
throughout his childhood.

Jillian's son. Who might also have been his son. That
thought was as sickening as the images of Jillian lying in
the arms of another man, sated and fulfilled. Just as she
had once lain in his. Once. A long time ago.

If there was one thing Mark had learned in the last ten
years, it was that there was nothing more damaging than
thinking about the ''what might have beens'' of your life.
That's what his father had done. And after the crash, he

himself had indulged in more than his share of those kinds of thoughts.

It certainly wouldn't do him any good to think about what might have been as far as Jillian Salvini was concerned. And he realized he'd been doing that on some level since he'd been back.

Now he knew with unwanted clarity what she had been doing since the last time he'd seen her. A reality that included a husband, a son and a life that had nothing to do with the girl who had given herself to him with the same sweet innocence with which she had lived her entire childhood. A girl who had then disappeared as completely as if she and her mother and father had been wiped off the face of the earth.

His father had muttered bitterly about Tony Salvini's Mafia ties and had cursed Jillian's father until the day he'd died. A man broken by life, who had owned nothing at the last but the shirt on his back and an unquenchable hatred for Salvini.

It was an animosity that had been born the morning he'd discovered the Salvinis and their daughter had fled in the middle of the night, leaving everything behind them, including the unpaid loans Bo and Jillian's father had signed jointly.

And Mark had never seen Jillian again. Until today. Until he had stepped around the nose of the chopper and come face-to-face with the woman who had haunted his dreams for the last ten years. Especially since he'd come back here. And now, so had she. Perhaps if things had been different...

Except they weren't different, he reminded himself as he started the familiar descent to the land that had belonged to his family for three generations. Your birthright, his dad used to say. A birthright his father believed Tony Salvini had stolen.

Whatever the truth of what had happened between their fathers ten years ago, Jillian was married, and Mark was leaving. And those were the only two things he ought to be thinking about. Not about all those what might have beens.

Unbidden, the thin face of Drew Sullivan appeared in his mind's eye, looking up at him as he begged for that promise Mark had foolishly given before he'd left. An eerie reflection of a little girl who had once pleaded with Mark not to leave her behind.

I didn't, Jilly, he thought bitterly. *I never did. You're the one who left me. And it's too late to even ask you why.*

WHY THE HELL *can't I sleep?* Jillian thought.

She turned on her side, pushing the old-fashioned feather pillow into a more comfortable shape. It wasn't really that she didn't know why, of course. It had more to do with an unwillingness to admit how disturbed she had been by seeing Mark again. She just hadn't been prepared, she'd told herself. It had been the shock combined with her worry over Andy that had thrown her. Drew, she corrected herself, remembering the sound of that single syllable spoken in Mark's deep voice.

Andrew had been her maternal grandfather's name, and Jillian had loved the strong Scots sound of it. It had seemed too grown-up, though, too serious for the minute scrap of an infant—a preemie with so many problems, including that tiny twisted and misshapen foot—that they had placed in her arms. Although she had written Andrew on the birth certificate, from the beginning she had called her son Andy.

Then last year, he had declared that Andy was a baby's name and that the kids at school made fun of him because of it. And he had been right, she admitted. The diminutive did make him sound like a baby, and he was growing up. Despite the maternal urge to keep him small so she could hold him close and make him safe, she knew this was the way things were supposed to happen.

She sighed, the sound an outward expression of all the frustrations she had felt since her encounter with Mark this afternoon. She turned over again, trying to find a cool spot on the pillowcase to rest her cheek. There wasn't one. The pillow had been turned and poked and restlessly prodded into shape until it was as worn-out with the long hours of this night as she was.

And it was nowhere near dawn, she thought, judging by the lack of light seeping in through the east-facing window. She sighed again, wondering if she should just give up and go unpack another box, when she heard a noise that sounded like something falling.

Or someone, she thought, that same mother instinct she had just acknowledged kicking into overdrive. Had Drew gotten up to go to the bathroom and stumbled over something in the unfamiliar darkness?

She threw the covers off and slid her feet into her slippers. As she hurried across the room, she pulled on the robe that she had tossed on the foot of the bed. Normally she wouldn't have taken time for that, but the house seemed strangely cold, a damp, pervasive chill left from the afternoon storm.

She hurried down the hall to Drew's room, the same one that had been hers when she was growing up. She had given him his choice, and that's the one he'd chosen, which for some reason had pleased her. Of course, the window seat her father had built to her specifications, and which doubled as a toy chest, had undeniable appeal.

The door to his bedroom was open to allow the old-fashioned heating system to circulate the air better. She stopped in the doorway, looking inside. The small mound of her son, sleeping in a near fetal position as he had since he was an infant, was clearly visible. Nothing in the room seemed disturbed. Nothing had fallen. Obviously, whatever she'd heard hadn't originated here.

Turning, she looked back down the dark hallway, and was again conscious of the cold. Maybe she should check to see if the pilot light on the furnace had gone out. After all, she was up, and it didn't seem likely that she would go back to sleep now. Especially since she hadn't been sleeping before.

She walked past the door of her own bedroom, which

had been her mother and father's room. Shivering, she wrapped her arms around her body, rubbing her hands up and down the sleeves of her robe. Maybe it was just jumping out of a warm bed so quickly—

As she stepped out of the hall and into the main room of the house, which her mom had always called the den, she realized that the front door was standing wide-open. Her first inclination was to rush across and close it, but the trickle of ice that was now in her veins had nothing to do with the cold air rushing in from outside.

She had locked that door before going to bed. She was sure of it.

During the last ten years, Jillian had become accustomed to living in apartments. To having neighbors. To law enforcement that responded in much less than half an hour. The kind of isolation inherent in living on a ranch was no longer familiar. It had made her nervous enough to be cautious and to double-check that lock and all the others. The fact that the door was now standing open...

Her gaze examined the shadows, moving slowly along the perimeter of the room. Although she couldn't see behind each piece of furniture, nothing seemed out of place.

She glanced back at the door. Had the wind been strong enough during the night to blow it open? Except she'd been lying awake for at least an hour, and she hadn't heard any wind. She hadn't heard anything at all, but that one noise.

The door hitting the wall? Or someone hitting the door?

Again she was conscious of the cold. She ought to at least close the door, she thought, turning toward the kitchen now. Given the angle of the wall, she couldn't see into that room, and she directed her gaze back to the front door.

For the first time in her life she wished that she had a gun. Although she had grown up around them, she had never thought she was the kind of person who would ever want or need a firearm. Faced with the realities of where she was living now...

She forced herself to move across the den, tiptoeing so that her slippers made only a slight shuffling noise on the hardwood floor. When she was near enough, she could stand behind the protection of the open door and look through it into the yard. Maybe there would be enough moonlight to allow her to take a look around without leaving the house.

Taking a deep breath, she took the final step to the door and grasped the knob in her right hand. The metal was cold under her palm, and for some reason, now that she was here, she couldn't seem to make herself move any closer to the opening. If there was someone waiting outside—

Idiot, she chided herself. Why kick in the door to a house and then wait around outside? If someone was that eager to get inside, they'd already be here. A thought that was hardly more comforting.

So why hadn't she turned on the lights? Why didn't she now? The switch that controlled them was just on the other side of the doorway. All she had to do was step across, closing the door in the process, and flick it on. All she had to do, and yet she seemed paralyzed, unable to act.

She drew in another deep breath, gathering her courage, and in the silence she heard movement out on the porch. As if released from a spell, she pushed the door hard, and as it swung closed, she reached across the narrowing opening, intending to flip up the switch.

A dark shape loomed before her, seeming to spring up from the floor of the porch. The terrifying image lasted only a split second—too short a time for identification—before the door slammed closed. Quickly she turned the lock, putting a barrier, however fragile, between her and whatever—whoever—was out there.

CHAPTER FOUR

"PE-EW," Ronnie Cameron said, wrinkling his nose in disgust and drawing the sound out. He hurriedly closed the black garbage bag, pulling the plastic strings tight.

A little late for that, Jillian thought.

"What in the world is in there?" the sheriff asked, carefully laying the bag back on the floor of the front porch.

"It seems to be roadkill," Jillian said. "*Aged* roadkill from the smell. Armadillos and a few less recognizable victims."

Her voice was very quiet. Anyone who knew her well could have told the sheriff that she was exerting enormous self-control. Which she was. Now that it was daylight, her fear had been replaced by anger, and much of it was self-directed because she had let herself be so terrified.

"You're saying somebody dumped this on the porch and then kicked in your door?"

"The door was open when I got up to investigate," she clarified. "I'm not sure it was kicked in. I would think there would be some damage if it had been. But it *was* open."

"You see who it was?"

"I saw a shape. Nothing else. Certainly not enough to make an identification."

She didn't confess that she had been too frightened last night to realize that if she'd turned on the outside lights and opened the door, she might have been able to do exactly that—make an identification. Instead, she had turned the lock and sagged against the door, trembling all over. It wasn't until the running footsteps outside faded into the distance that she'd even thought about opening it again and looking out.

"I plain don't know what to tell you," the sheriff said, shaking his head and looking down again on the foul-smelling bag in disbelief. "I haven't seen anything like this since I've been in office. Never heard of anything like it since grammar school."

"So who was responsible for this kind of thing back then?" Jillian asked, the edge still in her voice.

"I didn't mean that literally. It's just that this business seems so…juvenile."

That was the perfect word, Jillian thought. *Juvenile.*

"Any idea why somebody would do this?" Ronnie asked.

"That's why I called you," she said. "Because I don't have any idea. I thought maybe you did. I was also hoping you could get fingerprints off the bag or something."

"That's not likely. I can guarantee you that whoever put this together was wearing gloves. And not just because everybody who's going to commit a crime nowadays knows enough from television to do that, but for sanitary reasons. Trust me, nobody would handle the stuff that's in there with their bare hands."

He was probably right, Jillian acknowledged bitterly. She had known that finding usable fingerprints would be a long shot.

"Not much of a welcome home, I guess," Ronnie said.

"You think that was the message this was supposed to convey? That I'm *not* welcome?"

"A lot of folks don't remember your family any too kindly."

"What exactly does that mean?"

"When your daddy ran off, he left a lot of people holding the bag." He glanced down at the sack at his feet.

Involuntarily Jillian's gaze followed his. She wondered if he had meant to suggest there was some connection between that metaphoric "bag" and this.

"I don't understand," she said.

"He left here owing a lot of people money."

Reluctantly, Jillian dredged up the memories of that time.

She had thought her life was ruined because she had been forced to leave Mark. And her father had forbidden her to even speak his name. Just as he had forbidden her to write or call him.

She had, of course. None of the things her father had threatened her with could have kept her from doing that, especially not after she had discovered she was pregnant.

"My dad left here owing people money?"

The sheriff studied her closely a moment before shifting his attention to the vista that spread in front of them.

"Your old man and Bo Peterson had taken out loans with just about everybody within a hundred miles. By the end, they didn't own a cow or a teacup that wasn't hocked or mortgaged."

"Are you saying my dad took out a mortgage on his ranch?"

That didn't sound like her father.

"A couple of them, or so I heard. Course, you could hear just about anything around here after your family run off in the middle of the night. Believe me, there were a lot of explanations offered for that."

"He had lost the ranch," she said softly.

It was only now that she realized that this loss, and not her relationship with Mark, was the reason her entire life had changed in the course of one night.

"They both did. Lost everything. Bo held on a little while longer, but even when your place was sold at auction, it didn't bring in enough to pay off both mortgages and the rest of the loans. That's when they foreclosed on the Peterson ranch."

"The Petersons lost their land, as well?"

"Bo never got over it. It killed him in the end."

"I thought Mark was still living there."

"Not in years. He was in the service for a while. Just came back here a couple of months ago. He's working for the people who own his daddy's ranch now."

That must have been a bitter pill to swallow for someone

with as much pride as Mark had always had. Jillian wondered why he had come home at all. But of course, so had she.

"Bo and my dad signed loans together?" she repeated, trying to make sure she understood what Ronnie was saying. "For what?"

This wasn't something she had heard before. And frankly, it didn't make a whole lot of sense. Why would her dad and Mark's father have taken out joint loans?

Ronnie shook his head. "Nobody knew. Maybe they were going in together on some kind of hybrid. Bo was always talking about finding the perfect breed for raising beef cattle up here."

"So they borrowed this money, and then my father leaves. He ran out on the loans he'd signed. Is that what you're saying?"

"Peterson was pretty steamed. Musta come as a shock."

It had come as a shock to her, too. There had been no warning. Her father had simply awakened her in the middle of the night and demanded she get dressed. Her mother was already in Jillian's bedroom, folding her clothes and putting them into a suitcase.

She had always believed that her dad had discovered what was going on between her and Mark. Although he hadn't said that the night they'd left, he had had plenty to say when he'd found out she was carrying Mark's baby. Now the sheriff was implying there might have been another explanation for that midnight exodus.

"You think whoever put this here," she asked, touching the bag with her shoe, "is angry because my father owed him money?"

"It's a possibility. You think of any other reason somebody would want to harass you?"

"Is that what you call this? Harassing me?"

"I figured that's what *you'd* call it," Ronnie said with a grin. "What *I'd* call it is a sack full of dead varmints. You want me to get rid of 'em for you?"

Jillian hesitated, not wanting to be in Ronnie Cameron's

debt. And that sounded like something her father might have said, she realized. He never wanted to be beholden to anyone. Which made the story the sheriff had just told her even more bizarre.

"I'd really appreciate that, Ronnie. If you don't mind," she said. The tone of her agreement sounded grudging and ungracious, despite its surface politeness. "What about my door? You think it's possible someone has a key to the house?"

"Anything's possible, I suppose. You just bought the place. You have the locks changed?"

"I never even thought about it. Not out here."

She would have in the city, of course. She had foolishly thought that because her family had never had to worry about crime while she was growing up, she wouldn't have to, either.

"You can do that," Ronnie said. "Or you can just get yourself a dead bolt. A big one."

The sheriff picked up the garbage bag, holding it gingerly. He walked down the steps and over to the patrol car he'd parked in the yard. When he reached it, he opened the trunk and dropped the sack inside, closing it quickly. Then, still standing behind the car, he looked back at her.

"Maybe this has nothing to do with that money. But it looks to me like somebody isn't too happy you've come back. You know how folks are around here. Memories are long, and grudges are held even longer. But one thing's for sure, whoever did this was trying to get your goat. If I were you, I wouldn't make too much of it. At least not in public. Don't give them the satisfaction of knowing they've succeeded in making you nervous. Or they might try it again."

She nodded, realizing he was probably right. But it made her furious not to have any recourse. Ronnie touched the brim of his hat and walked around to open the door of the cruiser. He settled into the seat, again making that brief radio report before he turned the car around and drove down her road.

Despite yesterday's rain, she could track his progress for quite a way by the plume of dust that followed the cruiser. She stood on the porch and watched it for a long time, maybe because she wasn't sure what she should do next.

One thing she was sure of was that this stunt wasn't going to make her do what her father had done. If they expected her to leave in the middle of the night, they had better think again.

As she stood there, she realized that the aroma from the sack still permeated the air. She'd put some disinfectant in a bucket of water and mop the porch, even though the contents of the bag hadn't touched the wooden boards.

With that thought, she acknowledged that this all could have been much worse. Those poor, long-dead creatures could have been dumped on the porch itself. Or even inside the house, which would have been a real pain in the neck.

That hadn't happened. Apparently, somebody wasn't thrilled there was a Salvini living here again, but as pranks went, this one was relatively minor. She could only hope that whoever had done it had gotten whatever animosity that had precipitated it out of his system.

"MOM," Drew whispered, tugging on her elbow.

"What?" she said absently, trying to decide between the only two brands of coffee that the small rural grocery store carried, neither of which she had heard of before.

She would have done much better—especially pricewise—to have gone into town. Exhausted from losing sleep last night and from another long day spent unpacking boxes and trying to get their belongings into some sort of order, Jillian had instead opted for shopping at Herb Samples's convenience store, which had been here long before she'd been born. She planned to pick up only enough to tide them over for a few days, and then she would drive into town to stock the pantry and the freezer.

"It's him," Drew said, still sotto voce.

"It's who?"

She selected the more expensive of the two brands, reasoning that cost might be some guarantee of quality, and reminding herself that after Violet's legacy, she didn't have to be quite so diligent about looking for bargains anymore.

As she put the red foil package into the child-seat section of her shopping cart, she turned to look at Drew. His eyes were focused toward the back of the store. With her worries about getting the shopping done and something fixed for supper, his words had barely registered. As soon as she realized who he was talking about, she wished they had.

Mark Peterson was considering the array of items in the freezer cases, his back to them. Like Drew, she recognized him immediately. There was something about the set of his head and the way he carried himself that was unmistakable, despite the changes the years had wrought.

She pulled her gaze away from those broad shoulders, which stretched the chamois-colored twill shirt he wore tightly across his upper back. During that brief examination she had also managed to notice that he was again wearing jeans, either the same ones he'd worn yesterday or a pair that was equally worn and faded. And equally snug across his narrow hips and thighs.

Although she hadn't finished selecting her purchases, she turned and began pushing her buggy toward the front. The decision to put as much space between them as possible was automatic. Unthinking. She was too tired to deal with another meeting. Too proud to put up with his cool disinterest.

"Aren't you going to speak to him?" Drew asked.

Her son hadn't moved. Instead he had raised his voice to carry across the distance she had put between them. She glanced back at him, intending to gesture him to silence. As she did, Mark turned his head, his eyes meeting hers. She felt as guilty as if she'd been discovered in some clandestine act. Maybe running away from the past couldn't be considered clandestine, but it was certainly cowardly.

The hazel eyes held hers for a long heartbeat, and then they moved, without seeming to hurry, to focus on Drew.

Her son's beaming smile of greeting was answered—a little reluctantly, she thought. But it was answered nonetheless. She would have to give Mark credit for that. Just then, his gaze came back to her.

"Shopping?" he asked.

"Just picking up something for dinner."

Noncommittal enough. And the tone had been right, as well. As casual as his, she thought, mentally congratulating herself.

Only then did she remember what Ronnie had told her this morning. About Mark's father and the loans. As she was trying to decide whether or not this would be a good time to ask him if he knew anything about that story, Drew spoke up again.

"Mom always fixes plenty."

The words were so unexpected that it took a second or two for her brain to fit them into context. And not the context of what she'd just been thinking, she realized, but of what she had just said. About getting something for their dinner.

"Don't you, Mom?" Drew prodded.

She met her son's eyes, which were filled with an anticipation she hadn't seen in a long time. Actually, she couldn't ever remember this level of anticipation in their shining darkness about anything. And the frantic mental search she had been making to find a reasonable excuse to rescind his near invitation ground to a halt.

She looked up, over Drew's head, and right into a pair of hazel eyes that seemed to know exactly what she was thinking. The whole sequence of it. They were mocking. Maybe even cynical. Whatever the unidentified emotion in them, it wasn't something that would lead her to believe Mark was expecting or even wanted her to extend an invitation to join them for dinner.

"It'll just be potluck, I'm afraid," she said, goaded both by the mockery in Mark's eyes and Drew's obvious enthusiasm to have him share dinner with them. "But you're welcome to join us."

Had she lost her mind? she wondered. Of course, if she really wanted to get to the bottom of what the sheriff had suggested this morning, then this probably wasn't as bad an idea as it appeared to be on the surface.

"Some other time, maybe," Mark said.

And he said it to her, not to her son.

"Mom doesn't mind," Drew insisted, the words verging on pleading. "Honest she doesn't."

"Drew," she warned softly.

"I've got a run to make this afternoon," Mark said, finally looking at his son again.

"We could wait supper until you get back," Drew told him. "We wouldn't mind waiting at all."

Jillian swallowed against the thickness in her throat, torn between wanting Mark to give in and come, and hoping that she wouldn't have to cope with this tonight. Wouldn't have to cope with him, she amended.

She was worn-out, both emotionally and physically. She was not quite up to having the past thrown so blatantly in her face as it had been last night, not even for Drew.

"Some other time," Mark said.

He turned, opening the case behind him and picking out one of the frozen dinners it contained. Jillian wondered if he was going to carry that with him on that "run" he'd mentioned. She glanced at Drew, hoping that he wasn't thinking what she was.

She hadn't wanted Mark to accept, but she also didn't want him to offer an excuse so flimsy that a nine-year-old would see through it. Angry on her son's behalf, she watched Mark close the case and then disappear into the next aisle.

Almost blindly, she turned, too, reaching out and plucking a couple of cans of soup off the shelf beside her. That would get them through tonight. She already had cereal and milk in the buggy for breakfast in the morning.

Tomorrow she'd postpone the rest of the packing and take Drew into Amarillo. They could have lunch, maybe take in a movie, and then buy a week's worth of groceries before they headed home. It would be a nice break for her and a treat for him. Maybe it would partially make up for...

For what? she wondered bitterly. Make up for the fact that he didn't have a father. Or for the fact that he was apparently so hungry for masculine attention that he had latched on to the first man who showed any interest in him.

Except that wasn't true, she admitted. Drew hadn't had this reaction to Jake's advances. And Jake had tried much harder to win Drew's approval than Mark had. Actually, Mark seemed to have won it without doing any trying at all. And again resentment on her son's behalf burned fiercely in her chest.

She pushed her cart toward the counter at the front, pretending to consider a couple of other items on the way. She deliberately moved slowly enough to give Mark plenty of time to make his purchase and leave.

As she reached the end of the aisle, she was relieved to find that he was nowhere in sight. He must have already gone outside, she thought, taking a steadying breath. She quickly pushed her buggy up to the register and began taking items out of it, placing them on the counter.

"Heard about what happened out at your place last night," Herb Samples said.

Her hand stopped midmotion as she was lifting out the coffee. So much for the sheriff's advice to keep quiet about the incident. The story had to have come from Ronnie, since he was the only one who had known about her visitor. She made her hand set the red foil package on the counter, and then she met Herb's eyes.

"Really," she said, without any inflection in the word. "I wonder how you heard."

"Ronnie Cameron mentioned it when he was in here earlier. I just wanted you to know that not everybody around here feels that way."

"And what way is that, Mr. Samples?" she asked quietly.

His eyes widened, and he had the grace to look uncomfortable. Drew had finally made his way to the front. He was leaning against the counter, examining the display of candy bars that had been arranged enticingly at children's eye level.

"You know. Like whoever left that stuff on your porch feels," the grocer explained vaguely. He picked up the coffee and checked the price on the bottom before he rung it up.

"Why do *you* think someone would have done that?"

There was brief silence, which Herb broke by picking up one of the brown paper bags stacked beside the register and opening it noisily with a practiced flick of the wrist.

"Bad blood, I guess," he said, keeping his eyes carefully downcast as he began putting her purchases into it.

"Bad blood?"

"Folks around here have long memories," he said, still without looking up.

"Mom?" Drew questioned, holding up a candy bar.

As much as she wanted to, she realized this was not the time to discuss that "bad blood." Not with Drew here.

She nodded permission, and he placed the candy bar on the counter. Samples added it to the total without saying anything else. Maybe he didn't have anything to say or maybe he had decided, as she had, that this wasn't the time to say it.

"You want it now or you want it in the bag?" he asked Drew.

"In the bag," Jillian answered for him. "You can have it after dinner."

"Mom," he protested, the word drawn out, rich with disgust.

She didn't bother to answer. Instead, she picked up the single sack that contained her few groceries and turned to leave.

And found herself face-to-face with Mark. She didn't know how much of the conversation he had overheard, but just as she had known he was aware of her frantic mental scrambling to find an excuse to uninvite him to dinner, she could tell by his eyes that he'd heard at least part of it.

"What happened?" he asked.

Surprisingly, Jillian found that she wanted to tell him. Somewhere in the back of her mind, however, Ronnie's warning still echoed. *Don't give them the satisfaction of knowing they succeeded or they might try it again.*

But this was Mark, she told herself. And she knew that he'd had nothing to do with what happened last night, no matter what the sheriff had suggested about his father's animosity to hers.

"Somebody dumped a sack of rotten carcasses on Jillian's porch," Herb said, saving her the trouble of deciding whether or not to obey the sheriff's warning.

"Carcasses?" Mark repeated, a small frown between his brows.

"Roadkill. Mostly armadillos, I think," Jillian explained. "I didn't examine it too carefully."

Mark said nothing for several seconds, simply holding her gaze. "Why?" he asked finally.

She shook her head, not wanting to discuss it in front of Herb. If she did, it would be all over the community by sundown.

"Mom washed the whole front porch," Drew said, making his bid for attention.

Mark glanced down at the child. "Did you help her?"

"No, sir."

There had been a small, shocked silence before Drew answered the question, and his tone had been properly contrite. Despite the resentment Jillian had felt about the sheriff's lecture to her son, she discovered this implied rebuke didn't bother her.

"You should have," Mark said. "Are you all right?"

It took Jillian a second to realize that the question was addressed to her. "Of course," she said.

She took a step, as if she were going to move past him.

"What does your husband think?"

The words froze her because they were so unexpected. *Your husband.* Apparently the small-town gossip mill didn't work quite as efficiently as she had given it credit for. And after all, thinking she was married would be a logical assumption for him to make. She had come back with a different name and a son in tow.

She had assumed Mark would eventually figure out that Drew was his. After all, there were so many things about the little boy that reminded her of him. Not physically, perhaps, but still, putting those together with her phone call...

"She doesn't have a husband," Drew said, sounding totally matter-of-fact.

Thankfully, he had never asked all that many questions about his dad. Not since he was very small. A lot of the kids he went to school with didn't have fathers in their homes. Or they had stepfathers.

Mark contemplated his son's face briefly before he turned his attention back to her.

"Divorced?" he asked, his tone as unemotional as Drew's had been.

"No," she said softly.

She pushed past him, walking quickly toward the door. *Running away.* And this time she didn't bother to deny that's what she was doing, not even to herself.

CHAPTER FIVE

SHE DOESN'T have a husband. That seemed pretty unequivocal, Mark thought.

So was she widowed? Or had she never married? Somehow Jillian didn't seem the type to bear a child out of wedlock. At least she hadn't when he'd known her. The Salvinis were strict Catholics, and Jillian had been raised in the tenets of the church. Of course, people changed in ten years. As did circumstances.

He stepped on the pedal of the garbage can and fed the half-eaten dinner he'd picked up at Samples's into the opening. Whatever potluck Jillian and the kid were having would have beat this. He wondered if the invitation to join them for dinner had been issued after Drew's revelation whether he would have been so quick to turn it down.

She doesn't have a husband. The words had haunted him since this afternoon. After all, it was pretty ironic that both he and Jillian were back in this place. Almost as if fate had stepped in to give them another chance.

Of course, there was always the possibility that Jillian didn't want another chance. She hadn't seemed eager to dwell on their shared past during the two brief encounters they'd had.

She hadn't even wanted to tell him what had happened out at her place last night. He wouldn't have known anything about the incident if he hadn't overheard Herb ask her about it.

And that, too, was ironic, considering Jillian Salvini had once come running to him every time she skinned her knee or got her feelings hurt. Last night somebody had played a vile prank on her, and she hadn't even wanted to tell him about it.

He glanced up at the wall clock and was surprised to find it was almost eight. And already dark, he realized, looking through the windows above the sink. He walked across to pull the curtains shut, just as his mom always had.

When he was growing up, closing the kitchen curtains at twilight had been a ritual. As soon as she finished washing the supper dishes, his mother would draw them over the dark panes of glass, shutting out the night. He had already lifted his hand, then hesitated just before his fingers made contact with the cloth.

Shutting out the night. As if one could shut out the evil that went on in the world during the long, lonely hours between sundown and dawn. And even as he thought that, Drew Sullivan's words echoed in Mark's head. *She doesn't have a husband.*

WITH THE SUPPER dishes done and Drew finally talked into a shower, Jillian carried her electric drill into the den. She had followed the sheriff's suggestion and picked up a dead bolt at the feed and grain when she made her run for groceries this afternoon.

It was a heavy one, the bolt itself almost an inch long, which had seemed like a good idea at the time. Now, considering the solid frame of the old-fashioned door she would have to drill through, the task seemed daunting.

She should have called a locksmith to come out from town. She could afford to pay for services like that now, although the do-it-yourself habits of a lifetime were hard to break.

Surely there was something else she could do to secure the door tonight, and then she would start fresh with the installation in the morning. It probably wouldn't take an hour to complete the entire job, and she was less likely to make a mess of it if she wasn't so tired.

The whole time she'd been talking herself out of putting in the dead bolt, she'd been scanning the contents of the den, looking for a chair that would be suitable for wedging under the knob. Just for tonight, she told herself again.

After all, she had reported last night's incident to the sheriff. And apparently the fact that she had done so had already spread around the community. Maybe whoever had pulled that stunt would think twice about trying something else.

She put the drill and the dead bolt on the small table beside the door and went back into the kitchen to take one of the chairs from under the table. She carried it into the den and, tilting it so that only the back legs rested on the floor, fitted it under the knob of the front door.

Then she reached out and turned the handle, trying to pull the door inward. She couldn't. Pressure from attempting to open the door lodged the chair more firmly into position. Relieved, she turned the lock and stepped back. She'd do the same thing with the back door in the kitchen, and she'd check the windows to make sure they were locked. And then tomorrow—

The knock was so unexpected that she literally jumped, her heart beginning to pound. Which was stupid, she told herself. This was a neighborly community, even if the size of the ranches created a sense of isolation. She had been a little surprised no one had come to welcome her home before now.

"Who is it?" she asked, hearing, despite herself, a faint residue of that initial fright in her voice.

"It's Mark."

Mark. Before she had time to wonder why Mark would come calling at this time of night, her hands were removing the chair she had wedged under the knob and turning the lock.

As the question made its way into her consciousness, she hesitated. Everything Ronnie Cameron had told her this morning came flooding back. Bo Peterson and her dad cosigning loans. Mr. Peterson being furious when he found out her family had left town.

She had never known any of that, but if it was true, then Mark must have lived through it all. And the aftermath. He must have been aware of why his father had lost their ranch. Maybe that was why he had seemed so distant yesterday when he'd brought Drew back. Maybe—

"Jillian?"

She turned the knob, pulling the door inward. It bumped against the kitchen chair. She moved it farther back, setting it out of the way and then opening the door wide enough that she could see her visitor.

Her heart began to hammer again, driven this time by emotion and not adrenaline. Mark had changed clothes since this afternoon. He now wore a navy crew-neck sweater under a brown leather jacket. The omnipresent jeans were newer and long enough that they bunched a little over the instep of his boots. And he had shaved. This afternoon there had definitely been a five o'clock shadow along that tanned jaw line.

"What's wrong?" he asked, his eyes taking in the chair.

"I didn't want a repeat of last night," she said truthfully.

"So you were going to put a *chair* under the knob?"

There was a patent skepticism in his tone.

"For tonight," she said, feeling defensive. "I bought a dead bolt, but..."

She took a breath, not particularly eager to confess how overwhelming that simple task had seemed only a few minutes ago. With the flood of adrenaline his knock had caused, she couldn't seem to remember how washed-out she'd been feeling.

"You want me to put it up for you?"

Any man in this county would have asked that same question. His offer to install the lock didn't mean a thing. So why did her pulse accelerate again?

"I can do it tomorrow," she said. "It was just too late

tonight when I remembered it. The time got away from me.''

"Too late for visitors?"

"I didn't mean that. Did you change your mind about supper? There are some leftovers. I'm not sure…''

There was a subtle movement at the corner of his mouth. She hadn't noticed before, but it, too, had changed. The Mark Peterson she had grown up with was always smiling. This Mark had hardly smiled since she'd been back, except for the almost reluctant return of Drew's grin this afternoon.

"I've had supper. That's not to say I didn't regret turning down Drew's invitation as I ate it.''

"We had soup," she confessed.

Again, they were doing nothing more than making conversation. Very stilted conversation. And she wasn't sure why this was so hard. At one time she could hardly wait to tell Mark about every moment of her day. Every thought. Every experience. Far more than he could possibly have wanted to know.

"Actually, that sounds pretty good," Mark said.

It seemed as if all those years, all those memories, had come down to this—a strained exchange of pleasantries. Commonplaces. But what did she expect after ten years?

"I didn't come for supper, though," he went on. "I came to…to make sure you're all right, I guess.''

She examined the phrase, looking for a hidden meaning.

"Because of last night?"

He nodded. "You have any idea who might have done that?''

She still hadn't invited him in. Despite what happened to her internally whenever she saw him, she wasn't sure she was ready to be alone with him.

"Ronnie Cameron seemed to think that it might have been because of the local animosity toward my father.''

Mark said nothing for a moment. "And obviously he told you about my dad's…animosity. Is that why you were so uncomfortable this afternoon?''

"He mentioned your father," she said carefully.

What the sheriff had said about the loans and Mark's father had played a role in how she'd reacted when Drew invited him to dinner, she admitted, but it hadn't really been what had made her uneasy. It was the fact she kept waiting for him to confront her about their son. Surely by now he must have put the boy's age together with her phone call.

"And that made you think I might have had something to do with what happened out here last night," Mark said.

It wasn't a question. It was a statement. An accusation, although it took her a moment to arrive at that conclusion.

"I didn't say that."

"Hell, Jillian, you know Ronnie Cameron has never had a clue about anything. And he still doesn't. Not even as sheriff. But *you?* You should know better. You should know *me* better. Whatever Cameron told you, I'm not my father."

"Then it's true."

"That my father made no secret about how much he hated your dad? Yeah, it's true. But that doesn't have anything to do with me or you. It never did. I guess I need to straighten Cameron out about some things."

"He didn't say anything derogatory about you. Actually, he didn't mention you at all. And no matter what you think, Mark, I didn't make any connection between your father and last night. Apparently my dad made more than enough enemies around here."

"Then why were you so nervous this afternoon?"

She hesitated, wondering if he could really be that obtuse about the role their relationship had played in her life. Of course, if he really *hadn't* figured out that Drew was his...

Quick roll in the hay brushed through her mind. Followed by the equally obvious possibility that that was exactly why he was here tonight.

"It's never easy to come home," she said. "Especially after this long an absence."

"But it must be nice to be able to come home in state."

"In state?"

"Buying back your family's land."

She could explain Violet's legacy, but it seemed too complicated to go into now. Besides, it wasn't any of Mark's business where the money had come from to buy the ranch. She hadn't flaunted her wealth since she'd been home, despite his comment about coming back in state.

"I thought Drew might do better out here."

He nodded, as if he understood what she meant by that. He couldn't, of course. At least not everything.

"He seems like a good kid," he said.

Her turn to nod. Strained and stilted. Like two strangers. And that was exactly what they were, she realized, disappointment crowding her throat.

You really couldn't go home again. Violet had been wrong about that. About that and everything else, Jillian decided angrily. Maybe she had tried to believe what the old woman had told her because she had wanted to so badly.

"He really is," she agreed. "I guess I'm lucky. Sometimes he's a little…confused about who he is," she said, smiling at the truth of that. "Or maybe about who I am. About our relationship, anyway. Fairly typical for his age, I suppose."

She waited for the inevitable question. Drew's age. Drew's father. Mark might have asked them this afternoon if she had given him a chance. And she would have to tell him the truth sometime. The longer she delayed, the harder it seemed to get the words out.

"You sure you don't want me to put that lock on?" Mark asked. His eyes had found the drill and the dead bolt, still in its packaging, on the table.

"You don't have to. We'll be all right tonight."

"I don't mind."

"I know you don't. It's just that…"

The words trailed. She had run out of excuses. Even she didn't understand why she was so hesitant to let him in the house. It was almost as if she was afraid. Afraid of Mark? Or afraid of the feelings he aroused. Then why the hell had she made this expensive odyssey?

"I didn't know you were here," Drew said, the same undeniable note of pleasure in his voice that she'd heard this afternoon.

She glanced around and found her son standing right behind her. He smelled of soap and shampoo and tooth-paste, those sweet, ready-for-bed smells that made every mother in the world a pushover. His hair was still damp from the shower, and he had on his pajamas. Last year's pajamas, she realized. They were a couple of inches too short, and his bare feet and thin, pale ankles stuck out the bottom of them.

What kind of mother did that make her seem to Mark? she wondered. Then, more rationally, she asked herself why she should care. She was the one who had always been there for Drew, every time he'd needed her since the mo-ment he was born. Every waking hour—and far too many when she shouldn't have been awake—had been spent wor-rying about him.

She put her arm around his shoulders, drawing him against her side, a wave of love washing over her so strongly that her throat went tight. Too damned emotional, she thought disgustedly. She had been since she'd come back.

And she knew why. Her eyes lifted to Mark's face, al-most challengingly. He was looking at Drew's bare feet, and when he raised his eyes to hers, the unspoken question was in them.

"You just get back?" Drew asked.

"Back?" Mark repeated blankly.

"From your run," Jillian said, her tone subtle enough that she thought Drew wouldn't be able to read the sarcasm.

There was a brief silence, and when Mark broke it, his words were unexpected. "I'm afraid that was just an excuse not to accept your invitation to dinner," he said to Drew.

"And it wasn't a very good one, I guess. I apologize for lying to you."

"That's okay," Drew said. "I shouldn't have asked you without clearing it with Mom. I figured you thought you probably shouldn't accept. The horses come tomorrow."

The horses. She had forgotten about that, Jillian realized. So much for the trip into town. She had made arrangements to have a couple of horses delivered to the ranch before she'd left Fort Worth. Not that Drew had shown any enthusiasm for that idea when she told him. Yet, tonight there seemed to be a quiet excitement in his voice over the prospect. It was only when he continued that she realized what had generated it.

"You said I'd like horses—that I'd like riding them," Drew said, still speaking to Mark. "You could come over and check them out. See if they're good ones. Maybe you could go riding with us. If you aren't tied up with work."

She wondered if the convenient out he'd supplied had been deliberate. Drew was no one's fool, and a pretty astute judge of character for someone his age. Of course, he had had to learn to cope with the vagaries of human behavior early, and that had made him more sensitive to atmosphere and attitude than most children.

"I think that's probably another invitation you should have cleared with your mom," Mark said.

Again there was a rebuke implied in the words, but it was gentle enough that it didn't trigger the mother instinct to protect. Still, it had neatly put the ball into her court.

"You'd be welcome to come," she said, a little stiffly. "It's been more years than I care to remember since I've sat a horse. And I was never as good a rider as you. Maybe you could give Drew a few pointers. If you have the time."

She found herself almost as anxious as she knew Drew would be while they waited for Mark's answer.

"I don't ride much anymore," he said.

The delay between the request and the answer had been too long. Jillian had already begun mentally floundering for an appropriate response to that denial, when Mark added the rest.

"But I think I remember enough about how it's done to offer some tutoring if you want it, Drew. Just remember that I'm pretty rusty."

"You've been riding helicopters and not horses," Drew suggested happily.

"Something like that," Mark said, his eyes again on hers.

"Tomorrow afternoon, then," she said. "Maybe… How would around three be?"

Mark nodded. "That's fine. Are you sure about the lock?"

"I'm sure. If I don't get it up in the morning, maybe you can do that while you're here tomorrow."

Mark nodded again. She could almost read his thoughts. He wanted to talk to her alone, without Drew around, and she knew what about. He would ask the same questions about her son's foot and his limp that she had answered innumerable times since Drew's birth. Mark's instincts were right, however. Now was not the time.

"See you then," he said finally. "Sleep tight, cowboy," he said to Drew, holding out his hand. "Sounds like you've got lots to do tomorrow."

The boy's small, almost delicate fingers disappeared into the grip of Mark's long brown ones, and another frisson of emotion brushed through Jillian's body, this one evoked by the too clear memory of those same tanned fingers trailing lightly across her breasts and then moving lower.

Never in a hurry. Never impatient. Displaying the same confident expertise Mark brought to anything he undertook.

"All right!" Drew said enthusiastically.

Involuntarily it seemed, Mark's mouth moved, lifting slightly at the corners in response to the child's eagerness. When he released the boy's hand, his thumb touched quickly on the freckled nose, and then he turned and walked across the porch to disappear into the darkness outside. In a few seconds, they heard the sound of an engine starting.

The lights of the truck he was driving came on, and Jillian was surprised to realize he had parked out by the gate. He hadn't even entered the drive that led up to the house.

That was why she hadn't been aware he was out there until he'd knocked on the door. She must have been in the kitchen getting the chair from under the table when he had driven up. She had heard neither the motor nor the slamming of the door.

She and Drew stood together in the doorway until the pickup's red taillights faded away to pinpoints. She removed her arm from her son's shoulder and closed the door, turning the latch. Then she fitted the kitchen chair under the knob just as she had earlier.

"You think they'll come back tonight?" Drew asked.

"Nope," she said confidently. She didn't. She couldn't have said what that confidence was based on, but she truly wasn't afraid anymore. "But I'm going to put a chair under the back door, as well. Just to be on the safe side. And you can help me make sure all the windows are locked."

"You didn't mind me asking him, did you?"

She turned to look at her son, seeing concern in the dark eyes. Despite the constant attempts Drew made to act as if he didn't care about her opinion, she knew that he really did. He wanted her approval. Maybe even as much as he wanted Mark's.

"It might have been nice to have a little more notice," she said, "but this is your home, too. I guess you have a right to invite your friends over."

"I don't know yet if he's a friend," Drew said.

"But you'd like for him to be."

"Yeah. I'd like for him to be."

"Then…just don't be too pushy," she advised. "If you give him a chance to know you, *really* know you, then I think he'll want to be your friend. If you try to rush things—''

''I know all that, Mom,'' Drew interrupted, the familiar hint of impatience in his voice.

''I know you do,'' she said. ''I'm just trying to help.''

And I don't want you to be hurt, she thought. *Or rejected. We've both had enough of that.*

Again she wondered if she had done the right thing in coming here. The situation suddenly seemed fraught with danger. The emotional kind.

She was more than willing to take that risk herself or she wouldn't be here. What she hadn't fully realized until tonight was that the course she had embarked on when she had bought this ranch put Drew's heart at risk, as well. And now it was far too late to back out.

CHAPTER SIX

"SO WHAT DO you think?" Jillian asked.

They were watching the men unload the two horses. Given Drew's size, she had debated long and hard about the right mount for him, wavering between a pony and a gentle, well-trained horse he could ride for years. In the end, she had opted for a small mare, which had been trained for the youth market. The gelding she had bought for herself had come from the same operation.

"I think they're big," Drew said.

As small as he was, they probably did seem massive. Judging by the ease with which they had allowed themselves to be unloaded, however, Jillian was confident that their dispositions were every bit as good as she'd been promised.

"Big, but not very bright," she said, whispering as if the horses might hear and be offended. "Smarter than cows, of course, which isn't saying much."

Drew's quick grin almost made up for everything that had gone wrong since she'd come home. And despite all the doubts she'd had the last few days about whether or not she had done the right thing, a sense of peace enveloped her. An "all's well with the world" feeling she hadn't had in a very long time.

She was home. There were horses in the barn enclosure. And Mark Peterson was living next door.

She wondered if that last should be cause for serenity. Of course, she had no idea about how he would react when he learned the truth. She had done her part, she told herself. She had tried to tell him ten years ago. She couldn't be held responsible for the fact that he hadn't wanted to listen.

"Mrs. Sullivan?"

She looked around to find one of the men who had delivered the horses standing behind her with a clipboard. "Yes?"

"All I need is your signature, and then we'll be on our way. I think you'll find everything you need in the packet."

He handed her a large manila envelope, which would contain the bill of sale and veterinary records. She opened the clasp and took out the papers, giving them a cursory examination, more for show than substance. She was sure they would be in order. After all, the reputation of the stables from which she had bought these two horses was sterling.

"Looks good," she said, pushing the papers back inside the envelope and stowing it under her arm as she reached for the clipboard. She signed where he indicated and then looked up to smile at him. "Thanks."

"Enjoy them," he said.

It had been obvious to him that the horses were for pleasure. Equally obvious this wasn't a working ranch. At least not yet. The place still had that unlived-in look that a property took on after a period of sitting vacant.

"One of them's for you, I'd guess," the man said to Drew. As he did, he pushed his hat onto the back of his head with his thumb, revealing a line of untanned skin along his hairline.

"Yes, sir."

"Which one?"

"I'm not sure."

"The mare," Jillian said.

"Good choice. You take care of her now," he said to Drew before he looked up to meet Jillian's eyes again. "You have our number, ma'am, if you need to get in touch?"

Jillian nodded.

"Well, okay then. I guess that's it."

He smiled at Drew again before turning to walk back to the truck, his rolling gait making it obvious that he spent more time in the saddle than behind the wheel. His cohort was already in the passenger seat. They both waved as the truck pulled out of the yard. Gradually the sound of the engine faded away into the distance, leaving a cold, windswept silence behind.

"Want to go take a look at them?" Jillian asked.

"Sure," Drew said.

Despite his observation about the size of the horses, he didn't seem to be afraid or intimidated by them. Together they walked over to the corral fence. She leaned against it, and Drew stepped up on the bottom slat, putting his hands around the top rail to hold himself in place.

The horses were exploring the parameters of their new home, including the metal tank at the far end of the corral. A tank that was dry, Jillian realized belatedly.

She looked up, shading her eyes with her hand. Only now did she understand why it had seemed a little too quiet out here since they'd moved in. She had been missing the familiar, omnipresent creak of the old wooden windmill.

Long before her family had moved here, it had been erected to pump water for use in the yard and the barn. According to her father, it had been constructed by one of the itinerant builders who had plied their trade before the turn of the century, and it had been in continuous use since then. The previous owners must have locked the mechanism when they sold off the stock. With water so precious, no one in this country was wasteful.

"What are they doing?" Drew asked.

"Looking for water, but the tank's dry," she explained, still gazing up. "I guess we'll have to fix that."

"What's wrong with it?" Drew asked, his eyes following hers to the top of the tower. The huge wheel was unmoving, although the wind was strong enough to cause it to turn.

"If you don't need water out here, you lock the blades, which keeps the pump from working."

"You know how to unlock it?" he asked.

"I think I can figure it out," she said, smiling down at him. "Want to help me?"

"Sure."

She led the way over to the windmill, which was on the side of the stock enclosure away from the house. Just where she had remembered it to be, she found the brake release at the foot of the tower, and it seemed fairly obvious how it worked.

She felt relieved that her unthinking error could be fixed so easily. As soon as the wheel began to turn, the pump would bring up cool, clean water from deep below the surface of the earth. It would flow out of a pipe at the foot of the windmill to fill the tank beneath. All she had to do was to release the brake and allow the ever present wind to put the wheel into motion.

Using both hands, she applied enough pressure to slip the lever away from the notch that held it. She eased it back and then looked up, expecting the newly freed wheel above her head to turn. Nothing happened.

She waited a few seconds, but there was still no movement. The chill breeze that was whipping dust across the yard was more than strong enough to cause the blades to spin. She looked back down, meeting Drew's questioning gaze.

"Was that the brake?" he asked.

"Well, I thought so," she said, smiling at her earlier confidence, which had just been flattened.

"Then why isn't it working?"

"Maybe there's something else I need to turn," she said.

After a careful search, she realized there was absolutely nothing down here but the brake release. Just to be sure she had done it correctly, she grasped the lever again and slipped it back into the slot, then released it again. Still nothing.

"Maybe it's rusted," Drew said, looking up.

The wheel remained frustratingly still. If the pump was intended to be off for a long time, as the previous owners had known it would be when they had packed up and left, maybe there was a safety brake at the top that could also be set. To find out would mean climbing the tower.

She had never been up it before, but she remembered her father climbing it many times so he could repair the mechanism or add oil. That was another possibility, she realized. Drew might be right. Maybe something was rusted up there. And there was really only one way to find out.

With luck, all she would have to do was get to the top and find another release that would unlock the wheel. The fact that she hadn't even realized the pump wasn't working until this morning indicated how long it had been since she'd been involved in the day-to-day operation of a ranch.

Even during the years she had lived here, her father had never allowed her to help with the outside chores. Her jobs, other than gathering eggs, feeding the hens or working in the garden, had been mostly indoors, helping her mother. Her dad had been the one who had kept the machinery operational.

She could do it, she reassured herself, fighting a nagging sense of failure. Once she was up there, she could have the windmill and the pump working in a matter of minutes. Despite their long journey, the animals would be all right until then.

A metal ladder, which had at some time replaced the original wooden one, ran up the center of the tower. Just below the wheel itself was a flat platform from which her father had worked on the mechanism. She guessed that the release for the safety brake she was looking for would be accessible from there. At least that seemed to make the most sense.

She glanced at her watch. The horse trailer had arrived later than scheduled, and it was almost three o'clock, which meant Mark would be here very soon.

She wasn't eager for him to find out that she had forgotten to get the windmill operational before the horses arrived. If she was going to own stock, then she should get her act together and look after them.

She moved over to the ladder and stood at the foot of it,

looking up. The platform and wheel seemed to loom impossibly high above her. She couldn't remember exactly how tall the structure was, but right now it seemed a lot higher than she wanted it to be.

"What should I do?" Drew asked.

She resisted the urge to say "Pray," and glanced away from the top of the windmill, almost gratefully, to smile at him with a confidence she was far from feeling.

"You can tell me if the pump starts. *When* it starts, I mean," she corrected, trying to build her own self-confidence.

"Okay," he agreed.

Glad she was wearing gloves, she reached out and put both hands on the thin metal rung just above her head. She stepped up onto the bottom one with her right foot. She had on riding boots, which were probably not the best footwear for this job. And she realized from just that first step that the spacing between the rungs had been designed for someone with longer legs.

"It looks awfully high," Drew said uneasily.

Understatement, she thought, glancing up. The clouds seemed incredibly distant, and their drifting movement bothered her. It made her feel as if the tower were moving rather than the clouds.

She focused on her fingers, which were wrapped tightly around the metal bar. *Death grip.* As soon as the words popped into her brain, she banished them, concentrating on getting the job done. Her stock. Her responsibility.

I can do this, she told herself grimly. *Just don't look up. And don't look down.* The classic advice, and in this case…

She shifted her weight from the foot that was still on the ground onto the one that was on the bottom rung of the ladder and began to climb. She forced her eyes to watch her hands as they reached upward for the next rung, trying to focus on her gloved fingers and nothing else.

And she was doing all right, she realized with a sense of accomplishment. There was a strong pull on the muscles of her upper arms and each step was a bit of a stretch, but she didn't make the mistake of looking up again. If she banged her hand on the platform at the top, it would be better than watching that mesmerizing pattern of clouds that had almost disoriented her while she was still firmly anchored to the ground. She couldn't imagine what that disorientation would feel like halfway up.

"Mom?" Drew called.

She hesitated, refusing to look down at him, but she did halt her upward motion. She took a deep breath and decided that she could answer him without any danger.

"What is it?"

Don't look down. Don't look down. Before today she would have said that she had no fear of heights. But somehow she knew that if she looked down now, she'd be panicked by how far from the ground she was.

"You okay?"

She smiled at the unaccustomed concern in Drew's voice, although she understood it. She wouldn't have let him come up here for all the money in the world. Yet here she was, acting like some intrepid mountain climber, simply because she didn't want Mark to find out she'd had stock delivered without making provisions to water them. Talk about a greenhorn blunder.

"I'm fine," she said.

"Okay."

End of conversation, apparently. And time to climb again. Her legs were becoming a little strained from the reach she was having to make between each step. Nothing she couldn't handle, she told herself as she continued to move upward. Just tremor from muscles she hadn't used in a while.

"Mom?"

Drew's voice sounded much farther away this time. Again she stopped, concentrating on willing away her tension.

"What?"

"He's here."

He. That could only mean…

Involuntarily Jillian looked down and knew in an instant it was a mistake. She closed her eyes, leaning against the ladder to steady herself. The ground had seemed incredibly far below, as had the figure of her son, who was staring up at her.

Despite what Drew just said, she hadn't seen Mark's truck in that split-second downward glance. And then, almost subliminally, she heard the steady sound of the hooves of a horse, traveling at a fast canter.

Not by truck. Of course not. Given the way Drew's invitation had been couched, she should probably have expected Mark to arrive via horseback. A wave of nostalgia for the sight of that flawless communication between man and animal swept through her. The sight of Mark on horseback had always given her pleasure. Especially that last summer...

She took another breath, doggedly resisting the urge to look down again. Not allowed. Not even to see Mark.

She needed to concentrate on finishing the job she'd started. Climb the rest of the way up and find out why the wheel wasn't turning. She reached upward to the next rung.

She was waiting for Mark's shout. As soon as he realized what was going on, she expected him to order her down. It was a demand her father would have made, and while she was growing up, Mark had been almost as protective of her as her dad had been. He would offer to fix the mechanism himself, just as he'd offered to install the dead bolt last night.

At least that job had been done. And successfully, too, she thought, feeling a surge of gratification. That should be some comfort, even if she couldn't fix the problem up here.

As she moved upward again, she was aware of the murmur of voices from below. The shout she had been expecting didn't come, however. Although she didn't dare look up to gauge her progress, she felt intuitively that she was very near the top of the tower.

She put her right foot on the next rung and began to shift her weight onto that foot. As she did, she heard a faint creak. Although she didn't consciously associate the noise with the placement of her foot, her mind must have made the connection.

Her left hand, the one that was highest on the ladder, tightened reflexively around the metal bar it was resting on. Her right, which had been stretched upward as she shifted her weight, instinctively reached out and grasped the same rung.

Almost before she had time to realize what was happening, the thin metal bar on which her right foot rested gave way, tearing loose from the side rail to which it had been attached. The foot that had been supporting most of her weight slid sideways. As the rung broke free of the rail, her body was jerked to the right, her foot sliding completely off the support.

Like a miracle, the instep of her right boot caught on the next rung down, the same one on which her left foot had been resting. The momentum of her downward motion, short though it was, caused her right knee to buckle, sending it forward into the hole where the broken bar had been.

The front of her body slammed into the ladder, but her boot heel was long enough to catch and hold. Both hands clung desperately to the rung above her head, but the strain on her fingers was terrifying. If she had been an inch shorter, they would have been pulled off the bar by that sudden wrench, and she would have fallen.

She lay against the ladder, taking short, almost sobbing breaths and fighting her panic. The voices she had heard below had disappeared from her consciousness, along with everything else.

There was only the ladder, the strain on her overextended muscles, and the unwanted knowledge, assimilated from that earlier downward glance, of how far from the safety of the ground she was. And right now, it seemed she was incapable of doing anything to reach it.

"Jillian?"

Mark's voice. She closed her eyes, feeling the burn of tears at how dearly familiar that tone was. She had heard the same deep timbre of concern when she had come back to consciousness the first time she'd been thrown from a horse. The time the flat of her dad's hand had left a mark on her cheek, and Mark had noticed it. And she had heard just that same tone when she had cried out that summer night under the stars—

"Jillian."

It was a demand this time. *Tell me you're all right. Tell me you aren't going to fall.*

"I'm okay," she said, as much to reassure Drew as to reply to Mark's demand for information. She wasn't okay, of course. Her whole body was trembling.

"I'm coming up," Mark said.

And she wanted him to. *Come get me. Rescue me. Protect me.*

That had been Mark's role through most of her childhood. Maybe he hadn't wanted her tagging along at his heels, but he had been the one who was always there to pick her up and dust her off when she fell. And she had always hidden her pain and her tears, pretending to be as tough as he was.

"I can't," she breathed, arguing with her own desire to hide her fear from him.

The whispered words were not loud enough to reach the bottom of the tower where he stood, a million miles below. They weren't an answer to him, anyway, but an admission of her own failure. So damn many failures.

She felt the ladder move, and knew that Mark was doing what he'd said he would do. He was coming up to try to talk her down. If one of the rungs had given under *her* weight...

"No," she yelled, a different fear strengthening her voice. "The bolts are rusted away. Don't come up here."

She could still feel movement communicated upward through the metal rails of the ladder. She should have known that the possibility of being in danger wouldn't stop Mark. It never had.

"If another rung tears away," she said, trying to think of anything that might deter him, "I won't be able to get down. And you're shaking the ladder. Don't come up here."

"Then you come down," he said unequivocally.

No choices. No options. If she didn't force herself to climb down, then she understood Mark well enough to know that he would come up after her, no matter what argument she made.

"Jillian?"

"Okay," she called. "Just—just stay down there."

She opened her eyes, still feeling the small vibration of the ladder, which she hoped signaled his return to the ground. Cautiously she lowered her right foot, searching for the next rung down. At the same time she forced the fingers of her right hand to uncurl, moving it to the bar beside her face.

Then she had to let go with her left hand, releasing the hold that had stabilized her from the moment she heard that first ominous creak. And she didn't think she had ever done anything so difficult in her life.

"Again," Mark demanded when she paused. "Next step, Jilly. Take the next step, damn it."

No choice. So she repeated the process, successfully negotiating her body downward through the next set of rungs. It should have been easier this time, but it wasn't. And she was still trembling, from both muscle fatigue and residual fear.

"Okay," Mark said calmly, "now you're at the missing rung. You're going to have to use the side rails."

She understood the concept. She had to remove her fingers from the rung and fasten them around the sides of the ladder. The gap made by the missing rung was too wide to allow her to reach down and grasp the next one.

"Do it, Jilly. Use the side rails."

She closed her eyes and took another deep breath, preparing to obey. Then she slid her right hand out to the end of the rung and forced her fingers to release it and grasp the side. It was thicker than the thin cross bars and seemed harder to grip.

"Now the other hand," Mark prodded.

She slid it outward, finding the side rail on the left. Without her conscious volition her eyes had followed the movement of her hand. As her fingers unfurled to release the rung, her eyes locked on what was revealed.

Each metal rung was flattened on the end and bolted to the side rail. A gap had opened between the top of the one she had been holding and the rail. A telltale space, as if this rung, too, were about to pull away. She could still see the head of the bolt, however, which didn't look particularly rusted. So how could the part that was inside, protected from the weather, be rusted enough to give way? It didn't make any sense. But if two of them were in this same condition…

She tightened her grip on the sides and reached downward with her right foot, feeling for the next rung. She couldn't find it, and for a panicked two or three heartbeats, she thought that it, too, must have fallen off the ladder.

"An inch farther down," Mark instructed.

The absolute calm in his voice was reassuring, but he hadn't seen what she had. He didn't really understand the condition of the ladder she was trying to negotiate.

She allowed her hands to slip a little lower on the rail, stretching her leg until her foot made contact with the next rung. Cautiously, she lowered part of her weight onto it, still holding tightly to the sides of the ladder with her hands. The bar beneath the instep of her boot felt secure. She could feel no play in the metal that would indicate another weakened bolt. She eased downward with her left foot and then paused again.

"Come on, Mom," Drew encouraged. "You can do it."

And the faster she did it, the faster she would reach him, she told herself, and the safety of the ground. And the less cowardly she would seem to the two of them.

She eased her right foot off the rung and moved it downward. As she lowered her body, she examined the rung below the one that had broken. Both bolts seemed tight, with no sign of rust or damage. She didn't test that conclusion, however, feeling more confident now in grasping onto the side rails.

She wondered briefly if she could hold on if the bar under her feet suddenly gave way. She had before, she told herself. Besides, these were rungs that had already borne her weight and not failed. Surely they would hold until she got down.

Repeating that like a mantra, she lowered herself again, and then again, knowing that each step brought her closer to the ground. Closer to safety. Closer to Drew and to Mark. And with each step the subtle sway of the ladder lessened. Felt steadier. Nearer to the precious, solid earth. And although she was still careful, she began to move faster as her confidence increased.

"Almost here," Mark said.

His tone was conversational, and her heart jumped at how near he sounded. She fought not to look down to judge how accurate that assessment was.

Just keep doing what I'm doing, she told herself. *Just keep—*

His hands fastened around the outside of her thighs, offering support. As she lowered her body, they moved upward—to her hips and then her waist. And finally, the toe of her boot made contact with the ground.

She turned into Mark's arms without hesitation, and they fastened around her, holding her tightly against his chest. Despite how calm he'd sounded, she could feel the pounding of his heart under her breasts, and the tears she had denied at the top of the ladder welled upward again, in gratitude this time.

She rubbed her face against the smooth cotton of his shirt. The feel and the smell of him was like a long-forgotten dream, so sharp and so clear she wondered how she could ever have forgotten it.

Laundry soap. A brand she knew, but couldn't have named right now to save her life. Underlying that was the fragrance of his body. She would have been able to recognize him in a crowd of a thousand men. There was a hint of the soap he'd used this morning. The pleasantly clean, slightly salt-tanged aroma of a working man's perspiration. Subtle horse smell. Oiled leather.

She closed her eyes, letting the pleasure she felt wash over her in a wave of security. She was safe. Just as she had known her whole life long, in Mark's arms she was safe.

After a moment, he put his hands on her shoulders, pushing her away. She resisted at first, wanting nothing more than to cling to the rock-solid feel of his body. And then the import of his hands' urging registered. In obedience she took a step back, looking up to meet his eyes, which were suspiciously bright.

"You okay?" he asked, his voice very gentle.

She nodded, not trusting her own. Drew laid his head against her side. She reached out to pull him close.

"What the hell happened up there?" Mark asked.

She bent to put her cheek against the gloss of her son's hair, shutting her eyes in thankfulness that she could do that. After a second she opened them and looked back up to answer him.

"I forgot to turn on the pump before the horses arrived."

"I mean with the ladder."

So much for her confession, which he obviously didn't need or want to hear.

"The bolts must be rusted," she said. "One of them broke or pulled away."

Mark looked up, his eyes tracing up the length of the ladder. She had no inclination to let hers follow. She didn't need to know exactly how high up that missing rung was.

"I'll take care of the horses," he said after a few seconds, finally lowering his gaze to her face. "Why don't you take Drew inside? Make us some coffee."

Inventing something for her to do to get her out of the yard? Even if he was, it didn't seem like a bad idea. Drew needed reassurance that everything was all right. And the way her knees had begun to tremble again, she could use a chair.

So she nodded. She began to move toward the house, talking quietly to Drew the whole way, her arm around his shoulders. Her legs were still shaking when they reached the back door.

She opened it, directing the boy inside with her hand on his back, before she turned to look at Mark. He was standing beside the ladder, his fingers busy with one of the bolts on the eye-level rung, working it out of the hole.

"Mom?" Drew said.

She turned to smile at him, and then she, too, entered the house, closing the back door behind her.

Mark had said he'd take care of the horses, and Jillian had absolutely no doubt he would. The horses and anything else that needed taking care of. Judging by his ongoing examination of that ladder, right now, "anything else" apparently included her.

CHAPTER SEVEN

"NONE OF THE other bolts seem rusted," Mark said into the phone. "Not enough to fail, at any rate."

"But the one that *did* fail might have been," Ronnie Cameron said. "Hard to tell if you don't have that particular bolt to look at."

"I'm telling you, somebody tampered with that ladder."

"And I'm telling you that you don't have any proof of that. What you think, what I think, don't matter a hill of beans to the law. You got to have proof. Besides, why would anyone want to fool with the ladder on that windmill?"

It was the question Mark realized he didn't have a satisfactory answer for. Not unless he wanted to believe what the sheriff had suggested about the vandalism—that someone was holding a ten-year-old grudge against Jillian's father. A grudge strong enough to make them try to hurt her.

"Maybe for the same reason somebody dumped dead animals on her porch," Mark said. "You suggested that was because her father disappeared owing money to a lot of people around here."

"I can buy that for somebody pulling a prank, but there's a big difference between that and what you're saying. Tampering with those bolts could have had serious consequences."

A hell of an understatement, Mark thought, remembering the rush of terror he'd felt watching that rung give way. He still didn't know how Jillian had managed to hang on.

"Consequences like murder," he said aloud.

There was a long, pregnant silence on the other end, and

then the sheriff's voice, quieter and more serious, said, "I think maybe you better slow down. That's quite a leap from somebody harassing Jillian to somebody trying to murder her."

"Somebody was going to climb that ladder eventually. If the bolt had been tampered with, then whoever it was would be in danger of falling."

"*Whoever* it was," Cameron repeated, emphasizing the pronoun. "There was no way to know who would be going up that ladder first. It could have been anybody. If this was supposed to be directed at Jillian, then loosening those bolts seems a pretty haphazard way to go about it."

"Maybe it was just more vandalism," Mark agreed. "Directed at discouraging her from staying. Even if it wasn't Jillian who fell, an accident like that would have to be disheartening for a new owner. Maybe she would even have some legal liability if a workman tried to fix the windmill and was injured."

There was another brief silence.

"That place has been vacant for months," the sheriff said. "Anybody could have gone out there and done anything—*if* the ladder was tampered with in the first place. From what you've told me so far, you don't have any real proof that it was. This could have been a simple accident."

"The wheel wouldn't turn," Mark reminded him.

"You go up there to see why?"

"If there's one thing I learned in flying, it's not to push your luck. Jillian said that on the way down she noticed other rungs where the bolts are loose."

Another silence, protracted this time. "I'll ride out there and take a look," Ronnie said finally.

Grudgingly, Mark thought.

And then the sheriff added, "It would have been better if Jillian had called me herself."

"Why the hell should that make any difference?" Mark asked, irritated with what he perceived to be procedural foot dragging. It wasn't as if Ronnie was normally a stickler for how things were supposed to be done. "I'm just reporting what happened out here this afternoon. An incident *I* witnessed."

ʻ "Jillian's the property owner. It should be her call on whether she thinks anything looks suspicious at her place."

"You come check out that windmill, and then you can decide how suspicious it looks."

"I'll be out as soon as one of the deputies gets back into the office. Can't leave it unattended."

"We'll be here," Mark said shortly.

He replaced the receiver and stood a moment thinking about what Cameron had said. It was true that no one could guarantee Jillian would have been the one to climb that ladder. Of course, it was more than likely, given the situation. She was the owner. And she had grown up on the ranch, so she knew how things worked. There were no hands on the place, at least not yet. Given the way gossip spread around here, he imagined that most people in the county were aware of those things.

"Is he coming?" Jillian asked from behind him.

Mark turned and found her watching him from the doorway that led from the den into the kitchen. Her cheeks had more color in them than when she'd stepped off the ladder onto the ground.

And the tears were gone, thank God. It wasn't like Jillian to cry. Seeing that had frightened him almost as much as watching her make that harrowing descent.

"As soon as he gets someone in to cover the office."

She nodded, as if that made sense. "The coffee's ready. If you really wanted a cup," she added.

"I want it," he said, smiling at her. "I'm an addict."

"I thought maybe you were just giving me something to do with my hands. Considering how much they were shaking, I make no guarantees that I measured it right."

"Whatever it tastes like, it'll be better than Stumpy's."

"Stumpy Winters? Don't tell me he's still around?"

"He works...with me."

He had almost said "at the ranch," but she might interpret that to mean he still owned the place. After all, they hadn't yet gotten into all the ramifications of what had gone on between her father and his. He wondered if Jillian even understood that his dad had lost his land because Salvini had run out on him.

Of course, that was water long under the bridge, and as he'd told her before, it had nothing to do with her. Nothing to do with what had once been between them.

"You both work for the co-op," she said.

Which pretty much answered that question, he thought.

"Like most everybody around here. At least everybody who's still trying to run cows."

She said nothing for a moment, although it was a natural opening for an explanation of her intentions. Even as devalued as this ranch had been by the cattle market and the ongoing drought, the purchase price represented a good-size investment.

"I can't seem to manage taking care of a couple of saddle horses," she said.

"They're all right. I hand pumped enough water to fill the trough and gave them some grain. The journey doesn't seem to have fazed them. They look like good animals."

"I've almost forgotten what to do with a horse."

"It's a lot like riding a bike. You never really forget. Your muscles may take a little reminding, though," he said.

His had. He had avoided the saddle since his return, both to protect his back and because he'd learned quickly that an overindulgence in nostalgia wasn't conducive to a good night's sleep.

Even if he would pay the price later, he had enjoyed the ride over this afternoon. At least he *had* been enjoying it, until he'd arrived just in time to watch the rung slip out from under Jillian's foot.

"Mine will take more than a little reminding," she said. "That's one reason I wanted you here the first time Drew saddles up. I guess we'll have to postpone that for a while."

"Let's see what the sheriff says."

"I'm still not sure why you called him."

"Considering the incident the other night, I just thought it might be the smart thing to do. To report what happened."

"Do you really believe somebody tampered with the ladder?"

She had apparently listened to more of his conversation with Ronnie than he'd realized. Of course, Jillian was bright enough to put two and two together on her own.

"I don't see how some of those bolts could have rusted through and the rest of them look as good as they do." He held up the one he'd removed from the bottom of the ladder as proof.

"Harassment," she said softly.

"Maybe," he agreed. "But whatever it was, it seems serious enough to me to get the sheriff back out here to take a look. It can't hurt to be sure."

"So what do you think?" Jillian asked, coming up to the men.

Their conclave had gone on long enough, so she'd decided to join them. It shouldn't have taken this much time to look at a few bolts, she reasoned.

"I think we need to find the bolt that pulled loose before we jump to any conclusions," Cameron said.

They had already looked for it. Even from inside the house it had been obvious to Jillian that that's what they were doing.

"I can't believe somebody would have purposely removed it," she said, "if that's what you're thinking."

"I don't know what I'm thinking," Ronnie said. "Not yet. And I won't until I see that bolt."

"Maybe part of it's still in the hole," Mark suggested.

"I would have noticed it on the way down," Jillian said, her gaze shifting from the sheriff's face to Mark's.

His features were tight. Whatever had been said out here while she was in the house, he hadn't liked it. Of course, he

probably wasn't happy about the sheriff's wait-and-see attitude either, but she could hardly blame Ronnie for his reluc-
tance to believe that someone was trying to kill her.

She found the idea a stretch in logic as well. She had just
moved back here a few days ago, hardly long enough to make
enemies. The notion that someone would hold a grudge
against her father for ten years and then try to take it out on
her seemed pretty far-fetched.

"Then how about examining the one on the other side of
the bar that came loose," Mark said. "They should be rusted
the same. *If* they're rusted at all."

"No proof they would be," Ronnie said. "All kinds of
things could have come into play."

"So what stopped the wheel?" Mark asked. A muscle
knotted and released in his jaw as he waited for the sheriff's
answer.

That was a sure sign of his tension, Jillian knew from
experience. Mark had once been as hot-tempered as his father, and only his self-restraint had kept that hair-trigger temper from costing him friends as they'd grown up.

"I thought there must be some sort of safety brake at the
top," Jillian said. "That's why I was going up."

"Not on a windmill this old," Mark said decisively.
"There would only be the brake at the bottom."

She looked at Ronnie Cameron for confirmation of that
information. His lips pursed as if he were thinking about it.
Finally he tilted his head and lifted his eyebrows as if he
couldn't really disagree.

"There may be a ladder in the barn," Mark said unexpectedly. "If there is, I'm going up there to see if the wheel's
been blocked—since you seem to need more proof than
this."

He handed something to the sheriff and then turned on his
heel, heading toward the barn. Jillian looked at the object he
had given Ronnie, which was lying on the sheriff's outstretched palm. It was the bolt Mark had removed from the

rung at the bottom of the ladder. The one he had shown her inside.

She had to admit it looked solid enough. So how could one in the same ladder, exposed to the same winds and rains, be so corroded as to disintegrate under her weight?

"You see anybody suspicious out here since you moved in?"

Surprised by the question, she glanced up, straight into Ronnie's eyes. Apparently he'd been watching her.

"Suspicious?" she asked. "Suspicious how?"

"Somebody who shouldn't be out here."

Actually, she realized, there had been very few people on the ranch since she'd moved in. Until today at least.

"Only whoever dumped that garbage bag on the porch. And I didn't *see* them."

"So who's been out here who had a reason to be?"

"The movers. You. The men who delivered the horses today. And Mark," she added belatedly. "I think that's about it."

"You tell anybody about that delivery? That it was going to be made today?"

She hadn't. Of course, she had bought grain for the horses at the same time she'd picked up the dead bolt, but she hadn't mentioned to anybody at the feed store when the horses were scheduled to arrive.

She hadn't been keeping it a secret, but with the move, Drew's attempt to run away and then the vandalism, she had lost track of the days. Actually, she had forgotten that the horses would be arriving today until—

The realization of exactly when she'd remembered it produced a frisson of unease. Drew had told Mark the horses were going to be delivered this afternoon. Just before he had invited him to come over.

Surely she couldn't be thinking Mark had had anything to do with sabotaging the windmill? Mark, whose calm direction had gotten her off that ladder without injury, she reminded herself.

"Jillian?"

"No," she said, her voice too soft.

Suspiciously so? But it wasn't a lie, she told herself. Drew had told Mark about the horses, so technically...

"So no one's been out here between the movers and the deliverymen?" Ronnie asked. "No one except me."

Mark had been. Last night. But no one could have tampered with the windmill at night, she reasoned, even as the thought formed. She mentally shivered at the idea of trying to climb that ladder in the darkness.

As she did, some part of her intellect acknowledged that someone familiar with the ranch, someone with a small but powerful flashlight would have had little trouble making that climb. Especially if that person had no fear of heights.

And as soon as she made the natural progression to the next thought—that a pilot would have no fear of heights—she deliberately pushed the idea out of her mind.

It would have been easy to tamper with the mill. All anyone would have to do was to climb that ladder, block the action of the wheel, and then come part of the way back down and cut through or loosen some of the bolts. After that, the saboteur could climb the rest of the way down the ladder and take off in the darkness, with no one the wiser. The windmill was far enough from the house that she would never have been aware of what was going on.

"Just the people I told you about," she said.

"If Peterson's right," Ronnie said, holding her eyes, "then you realize that you and your boy could be in danger. We could be dealing with somebody who's got a very sick mind."

"I can't imagine why anybody would want to hurt me or my son," she said, coldness coiling in the pit of her stomach.

She *couldn't* imagine that. And she especially couldn't imagine it about Mark.

"Some people have never forgiven your father for what he did. Not the folks who got hurt the most by it."

Like Mark's father? And ultimately Mark himself? His bitterness over the loss of the ranch had been evident in his voice when he had talked about working for the co-op. The ranch next door should have been his. It would have been, if not for her father. At least that's what Ronnie Cameron would have her believe.

"I just can't buy that someone would do something this dangerous because they were angry with my father ten years ago."

"You'd be surprised at what people will do to get revenge."

"Revenge? That's just it, Ronnie. That's what doesn't make sense. How could they think that doing something to me would get revenge on my father?"

She and her father hadn't even spoken to each other in years. Of course, no one here could know that, she admitted.

"Maybe you're the only target they can get to."

He glanced up, his eyes focusing on Mark, who was coming out of the barn. Without a ladder.

"No luck?" Ronnie called.

Mark shook his head, looking up at the tower as he walked. For the first time Jillian's gaze also considered the windmill and the ladder that led to its top. She could see the gap where one side of the rung had pulled away. The metal bar itself hung down, still connected to the rail by the bolt on the left side.

Her instincts had been right. She had been very near the top. She suppressed another shudder, pulling her eyes away from the tower to watch Mark's approach.

"I know there's a ladder back at the ranch," he said. "I'll put it on the truck and bring it over in the morning. Then we'll see what's going on up there."

"You seem mighty interested in proving this theory of yours," the sheriff said.

"Jillian needs water for her animals. I'm just as interested in getting the pump working as I am in examining the condition of the wheel. Unless you plan to come by every day and pump enough by hand for their needs."

The sheriff considered Jillian's face briefly before he turned to Mark. "I guess I'll leave that up to you. Let me know what you find at the top."

"You'll be the first to know, I promise you," Mark said.

The sheriff nodded, his lips lifting a little as if Mark's assurance amused him. Then he touched his hat to Jillian in an obvious gesture of farewell.

Standing together, she and Mark watched Ronnie walk over to the cruiser and get in. He repeated the radio ritual Jillian had noticed before, and then he backed the car into the yard, heading it out toward the road. As he drove close to them, he stopped the vehicle and lowered the window.

"You get that lock for your door?" he asked.

"It's already installed," Jillian said.

"Make sure you use it," he ordered.

Then the automatic window slid upward, and the sheriff adjusted his sunglasses more securely on his nose before he put the car into gear. Mark waited until he had pulled out of the yard before he spoke again.

"Son of a bitch refuses to believe somebody would tamper with the ladder, but then he warns you to lock your doors."

"He wanted to know who knew about the horses' arrival," she said, throwing caution to the winds. Apparently the sheriff's questions bothered her more than she had been willing to admit.

It took a second for the implication of what she'd just said to penetrate Mark's anger. He turned his head, his eyes leaving the departing patrol car to focus on hers. "And who did?" he asked.

"Nobody," she said softly. *Nobody but you.*

She found herself unwilling to put into words the doubt that had been created by the sheriff's question. She had told no one when the animals would be delivered. No one except Mark. He was the only person who knew for sure that she'd need water from the windmill pump today.

Of course, that didn't prove anything. Even if the ladder

had been sabotaged, there was no way to know when it had been done—hours, days, or weeks ago.

"You told *me*," he said, still holding her eyes.

She could feel the heat seep into her cheeks. She hoped the betraying rush of blood wasn't visible, but even if it were, she couldn't do anything about it.

"You can't think *I* had something to do with this," he said.

Could she? She knew that if she had told the sheriff the truth, that was almost certainly the conclusion he would have come to. The conclusion most people would reach, given the ill will between their fathers and the fact that Mark was the only local person who had known the horses would be delivered today. *And* the only person who she knew for a fact had been on her ranch last night.

"Jillian?"

"I think that's what Ronnie was implying."

"I don't give a damn what Cameron was implying. I want to know if *you* think I'm the one who tampered with that ladder."

The seeds of doubt the sheriff had planted prevented her from making an outright denial.

"You do, damn it," Mark said, taking hold of her upper arms.

His fingers bit into the soft flesh. She flinched, trying to pull away from him, but he refused to release her.

"You're hurting me," she said, gritting her teeth against the pressure and her own growing anger.

"If I was responsible for that ladder giving way, then why the hell would I be the one pushing the sheriff to find out what happened?" he asked. "Cameron's perfectly content to think that broken bolt is the result of natural wear and tear. And if I had had anything to do with that rung pulling loose, I'd be breaking my neck to agree with him."

"Maybe you figure that's the best way to divert suspicion from you."

His eyes changed, growing hard and cold in a way she had

never seen before, but he didn't deny the possibility of what she said. And she wanted him to.

"You lost your ranch because of what my father did," she went on. "Or you seem to believe that's what happened."

"That's what my father believed. I'm not my father."

"And I'm not mine. I had no idea why we were leaving that night. He never explained. He just packed us up and we left."

"Leaving *my* father holding the bag."

That was the same expression Cameron had used. *Holding the bag.* She had wondered then if it were supposed to be a metaphor for what had been dumped on her front porch.

"I had nothing to do with what my father did," she said.

"And no idea what was going on. Your dad just decided to move you all in the middle of the night. And you bought that."

The sarcasm stung, more than she would have believed possible after all these years. "I thought he'd found out."

His eyes narrowed slightly, a small crease forming between them. The pressure his fingers had been exerting on her arms had eased, no longer painful but still controlling.

"Found out what?"

"I thought he'd found out what we'd done."

Her words stopped him because he believed her. She could see it in his eyes.

"You thought your dad had found out we'd made love."

Made love. He had used the very words she had been avoiding. Deliberately avoiding, because the memory of that night was still so powerful.

Mark was the only man she had made love to in her entire life, as difficult as that would probably be for him to believe. And now, being this near him again, seeing him interact with his son, she realized that every emotion she had once felt for him had returned with all the raw, painful intensity of a first love.

Except she was no longer seventeen years old and terrified. She was a woman now. With a woman's needs. And this was the only man who had ever touched her with passion. Whatever she knew about love between a man and a woman, Mark had taught her.

That one night they had spent together had branded her. It was as if every stroke of his hands and caress of his lips over her skin had burned so deeply that the feel of them could never be erased.

Maybe that's what she had been trying to do with Jake. Erase the memory of Mark. And Violet had somehow known that.

Eventually, however, she had been forced to admit that she still belonged to him as much as she had that night. That's why she had come here. Not for Drew's sake, despite everything she had tried to tell herself, but for her own.

"Jilly?" He questioned her continued silence.

"He told me I could never see you again. And to never try to call you."

"So you didn't." Again the bitterness was as thick as smoke, lying under the quiet words. "You were such a good little girl, weren't you? You always did whatever he told you to do."

"He was my father," she said, controlling her own bitterness over having to defend herself. "And I was seventeen years old."

"Old enough."

"Old enough to make love to you?" she asked mockingly, stung by the criticism that she should have rebelled against her father's authority. She had—later, of course—but by then it had been too late.

"I didn't force you," Mark said.

He hadn't. He would never have done that. *Never.* It had been her decision, made with her eyes wide-open.

And the night they had made love, she had wanted him as much as he could possibly have wanted her. Wanted his mouth, sliding hot and open over hers. Wanted him with a desperation that had as much to do with her fear that she might lose him as it did with her undeniable and lifelong adoration.

She had lived through the year he'd been away at college absolutely terrified that Mark would fall in love with someone else before she could work up nerve enough to tell him how she felt. The fear had haunted her that he would meet someone beautiful and sophisticated. Someone whom he hadn't seen through every awkward phase of growing up. A woman who would be mysterious and enticing in ways she knew she could never be.

And when he had come home that summer, she had done everything she could to bring herself to his attention. Not as Jilly, whose scrapes and bruises he had doctored, but as Jillian, who could be as sexually daring as anyone he had met at college.

She had succeeded too well. She had gotten in way over her head before she had even realized what was happening between them. Her pseudosophistication had not extended to birth control, despite what she had told Mark.

Besides, the night they had made love, she had never intended to let things go so far. Of course, she had never imagined that she could feel the way she had, either. Never imagined that his hands and his mouth could make her react like that, inhibitions spiraling away in the star-touched darkness.

And ironically, the very fate that she had been told awaited girls who didn't remain pure had happened to her. She had not even been surprised when she'd discovered a few weeks later that she was pregnant and that the man whose baby she carried could not be found. Her father had quickly made her feel as if she had gotten exactly what she deserved.

"I didn't know what I was getting into," she said, the dark despair of those days coloring her voice even now.

"You sure as hell acted like you did."

"*Acted.* I think that's the operative word."

"Are you telling me you were acting that night?"

She couldn't truthfully tell him that. She hadn't been. She

had simply been swept away by what had been happening between them.

"No," she said, willing to leave it at that.

"Then just what the hell *are* you saying?"

"That...I wasn't ready for what happened, I guess. I wasn't prepared."

He studied her intently a long time. Finally he released her arms. His hands fell to his side, fingers curling inward.

"And you regret it," he said. Statement and not question.

But of course he was unaware of all the tangled issues inherent in regretting what had happened between them that night. She could never regret having Drew. He was her life. An enormous part of it anyway, and the extent to which he was had a lot to do with the circumstances surrounding his birth.

She opened her mouth, knowing it was past time to tell Mark the truth. Long past time. The longer she delayed, the worse it would be when he found out. Maybe now that he had met Drew—

The sound of the screen door slamming drew his attention toward the house. She turned, and watched as Drew limped toward them.

"Jake called," he said. "I told him you were outside. He said to call him back. He said it's important."

"Thanks," she replied, seizing the excuse almost gratefully.

She turned back to meet Mark's eyes. They hadn't changed. They were still as hard and as cold as they had been when he had asked her if she regretted making love to him. Too difficult a question, she thought. At least too difficult for her to answer completely right now.

"I need to return that call," she said to him.

"*Jake's* call?" There was an edge of the same mockery in his question that she had used against him earlier. "And who the hell is Jake?"

"A friend from Fort Worth."

"A *friend,*" he repeated. He held her eyes, daring her to

tell him the truth. Daring her to answer the question about that relationship, which hadn't really been a question at all.

"Aren't we going riding?" Drew asked.

Neither of them answered for a few seconds. And neither broke the connection between their locked gazes.

"I'm coming back in the morning," Mark said. "Maybe we'll take the horses out then. We'll see how things go."

"I thought that's why you came over here," Drew protested.

Jillian looked down at her son. He was obviously disappointed. But she was relieved to find he was suffering no ill effects from having witnessed her near accident. Actually, he seemed pretty much back to normal, even whining a little since he wasn't getting his way. She wished she were as resilient.

"We got sidetracked when your mom nearly fell," Mark said.

Again the rebuke was only implied, but Drew got the message.

"But she's all right now. Aren't you, Mom?"

"I'm fine," she said. *Just fine,* she thought bitterly. *Other than the fact that I've got about ten years' worth of regret to sort through.*

"So, you still want to go riding?" Drew asked her.

"I'm going inside to call Jake. Maybe tomorrow," she said, meeting Mark's eyes once more.

He nodded without speaking. At least he didn't ask any more questions. Maybe by tomorrow she would have figured out answers to the ones he should have asked, and hadn't, ten years ago.

CHAPTER EIGHT

"YOU AND Mom have a fight?" Drew asked.

Mark realized he had just been standing there, watching Jillian walk away from him. Watching and remembering. A dangerous combination, considering how Jillian looked from this angle. And considering the kinds of things he was remembering.

"What makes you think that?" he asked.

"I'm not stupid."

"No, you're not," Mark said, finally looking down at the child at his side. "So, who's Jake?"

"Some rich guy who wants to marry Mom."

There wasn't a single word in that sentence that didn't make him sick to his stomach, Mark decided.

Especially after what Jillian had just said. He had been forced to come to terms with a lot of unpleasant things about his life lately. Finding out that Jillian had always regretted giving him her virginity ranked right up at the top of the list.

Maybe he should have understood that when he hadn't heard from her after that night. Instead, he had been perfectly willing to blame her father for keeping them apart.

And he had done everything he could to try to find the Salvinis. To no avail. Tony Salvini, his wife, and Jillian had disappeared, seemingly without a trace. Faced with his own father's nearly mindless fury at Salvini's desertion, Mark had assumed Jillian's dad would do anything to prevent her from making contact with him again.

"What'd you fight about?" the boy asked.

His eyes, locked on Mark's face, were so much like Jillian's had been when she was a child that it was eerie. And a constant reminder of their shared past.

"Nothing that's any of your business," Mark said succinctly.

He turned and started around the corral fence. While they had been waiting for the sheriff to show up, he had unsaddled the gelding he'd "borrowed" from the co-op and let him out into the enclosure with Jillian's horses.

"If you tell me, I'll tell you about Jake," Drew called after him.

Which was tempting as hell, Mark admitted. He didn't think it would be smart to let the kid get away with that kind of blackmail this early in their relationship, however.

"What makes you think I want to know about Jake?" he asked.

He didn't look back, although he was aware the boy was now following him. Mark didn't slow his angry stride, but it didn't take long for Drew to catch up. The boy moved quickly, despite the limp.

The glimpse he had gotten last night of that small, slightly twisted foot had bothered him more than he would have believed possible. And it wasn't pity. He had had enough of that offered by friends after the crash to understand how little Drew would welcome it from him.

The day the kid had run from the helicopter, Mark had attributed his limp to some temporary injury. Now that he knew better, he was curious as to what had caused it.

Jillian obviously hadn't wanted to explain, not with Drew there. And Mark could understand that. It might be better to give the kid an opportunity to tell him himself, especially since Drew had apparently decided they were going to be friends.

"I guess that's not a blister like I thought," he said as they walked together around the fence.

"It happened before I was born. Something went wrong."

The kid said the words with as little emotion as if he were

explaining the freckles on his nose. Or as if he had said them a hundred times. Which he probably had, Mark realized.

"Yeah?" he said, glancing down at the upturned face and carefully keeping his voice free of surprise or concern. Aiming for a "no big deal" tone.

"Mom said it wouldn't keep me from riding."

The concern Mark had denied in his own comment was very obvious in this one. For a different reason, of course.

"I can't see why it would," Mark agreed, "but I thought you didn't like horses." He smiled as he said the last, just to make sure the boy understood he was teasing him.

Drew's answering grin was unabashed. When he saw it, the slight tension Mark had felt at asking about his limp eased.

"I said they smell, but...they're okay, I guess."

They stopped while Mark unfastened the gate to the enclosure. He stepped in, holding it open for the boy, who had hesitated just outside. "You coming or not?" Mark asked.

The brown eyes shifted to the three horses standing peacefully at the far side of the corral. Then he looked back up at Mark, who didn't add any encouragement, although that seemed to be what the boy expected. After a few seconds, Drew came through the gate, and Mark closed it behind them.

"So tell me about Jake," he said, giving in to his curiosity as they crossed to where the horses stood.

"He's okay, I guess. A lot older than you. He's got gray in his hair. And he's not as tall."

And rich. You forgot rich.

"What does he do?" Mark asked aloud.

"I don't know. Works at a bank or something. He hired Mom to decorate his office. That's when they started dating."

"How long ago?"

"A couple of years, maybe. I was at my same school."

A couple of years. Mark realized he had been hoping for less. If they had been involved for two years, then chances were good they were sleeping together.

And what the hell did you expect? That she'd been in a

nunnery since her father dragged her away in the middle of
the night? The proof that she hasn't been is right beside you.

"Is your mom thinking about it? About marrying this
guy?"

Mark took hold of the lead of the borrowed bay. His lips
felt stiff as he posed the question. Despite what his head
understood about the chance that he and Jillian would ever
mean anything to each other again, his heart was beating way
too fast as he waited for the boy's answer.

"I guess so."

Drew reached up to run his fingers, a little tentatively,
down the long velvet nose of the gelding. Placid as a sheep,
the horse lowered his head, snuffling Drew's hand. A grin,
wide and spontaneous, lit the thin face, and the image of a
skinny little girl with dark, wild curls suddenly filled Mark's
mind.

Jillian Salvini had tagged at his heels most of his life, and
the idea that she had eventually come to regret that hero
worship—and to regret what it had led to—ate at his pride
like acid. And he sure didn't have all that much pride left.

"What's his name?" Drew asked.

It took a second for Mark to realize he meant the gelding.
At least it was something else to think about, something besides Jillian lying in the arms of some rich bastard named
Jake. He dredged around in his brain for the horse's name,
trying to remember what Stumpy had told him. He didn't
think it had anything to do with the gelding's color, but
something—

"Tumbleweed," he said, the word popping into his head
in one of those unexpected flashes of memory.

"Tumbleweed," the boy repeated, his caressing fingers
bolder.

"You named yours yet?"

The dark eyes widened with surprise. "Don't they already
have names?"

"You can rename him. Call him anything you want to."

"Her. Mom said mine's a mare."

"Good choice," Mark said, considering the two horses.

"Which one's the mare?"

Mark laughed, putting his hand against the back of the narrow shoulders, covered today by a down-filled jacket that bore the Cowboys' logo. "Why don't we go meet her?" he suggested.

"You think she'll be friendly like this one?"

"I'm sure of it," Mark assured him.

"Jake wanted to buy Mom some kind of fancy horse. An Arabian, I think. She wouldn't let him. She said she just needed a good old quarter horse."

Mark could almost hear Jillian saying that. Of course, if she was rich enough to buy this place with her own money, then she didn't need somebody buying her an expensive Arabian. She could do that for herself. The fact that this Jake guy was able to make that kind of offer rankled, though. Right now Mark would have had a hard time affording any kind of horse. Hell, he would have had a hard time affording a piece of tack.

"He's always trying to give us stuff," Drew continued, adding fuel to that fire. "He took me to a football game before we came up here, and when he showed up at our apartment, he had this jacket for me to wear to the game. He didn't even ask if I wanted it. He's always doing stuff like that. For Mom, too."

There was no denying the lack of approval in Drew's voice, but somehow it didn't quite destroy the surge of jealousy Mark felt.

"You think Storm would be a good name?"

The question pulled Mark's attention back to the boy and the mare, who was good-naturedly allowing Drew to rub her neck, the movement of the small hand still a little hesitant.

"Good as any," Mark said shortly, and then immediately felt guilty about the lack of enthusiasm. He didn't want his bad mood to interfere with Drew's pleasure in his first horse. "Why Storm?" he asked, trying to sound interested in the naming process. After all, he was the one who had suggested it.

"She kind of looks like one of those really dark clouds. And…it was storming the day I met you," Drew added, his attention still ostensibly on the mare.

After a second or two, however, the brown eyes cut up to consider Mark's face. The look was brief, but there was undoubtedly some emotion in their dark depths.

Concern that the name he had suggested might evoke ridicule? Or had it been something else? Mark wondered, still trying to evaluate what had been revealed so briefly in that glance. A request for approval? Or an invitation to friendship?

Surprisingly, Mark's throat tightened. Rather than risk making a fool of himself or saying the wrong thing, he simply nodded, reaching out to squeeze the thin shoulder covered by the expensive jacket another man had provided. A man who was obviously very interested in winning the approval not only of Jillian, but also of her son. A man who had the financial means to do that.

Of course, at one time Jillian Salvini's love hadn't been for sale, Mark thought bitterly.

Yeah, and at one time she thought you hung the moon. It's pretty obvious she doesn't think that any longer. Times change, and so, apparently, do people.

"So you think Storm's a good name?" Drew asked again.

Mark looked down once more, realizing the boy was studying him more openly this time. Obviously seeking his approval. And although Mark couldn't quite figure out what he'd done to deserve that accolade, he gave it.

"I think it's perfect," he said, and was rewarded by another of those endearingly wide grins. *Just about perfect.*

THE DISTANT CLANG of metal pulled Jillian out of a too deep sleep. She opened her eyes, knowing it was late by the brightness of the sunlight filtering through the closed blinds.

The first part of the night she had jumped at every creak

of the old house as she replayed over and over in her head her conversation with Jake. Gradually, she had relaxed enough to doze, although she had jerked awake periodically to listen to the surrounding stillness. Finally, sometime before dawn, she had fallen into an exhausted slumber that this as-yet-unidentified noise had just destroyed.

As she listened, trying to decide exactly what she'd heard, she realized there were other noises coming from outside. None of them was as distinct as the first, but they were not the familiar sounds she had always associated with the ranch.

She pushed the covers off and, slipping her feet into her slides, walked over to the window. There she lifted one slat of the blind and, eyes narrowed against the glare, scanned the yard.

There was a dusty black pickup parked out by the barn. When she saw it, her pulse quickened. She had already begun to turn, intending to use the bedside phone to call the sheriff's office, when a motion caught her eye, bringing her back to the window.

A man was standing at the foot of the windmill, looking up. Her gaze searched the tower, and only then did she become aware of the second man, halfway up a ladder that had been propped against the center structure.

Mark. She made the identification as her eyes followed his ascent. He had said yesterday that he was going to bring another ladder over and check out the windmill.

She again considered the figure of the man at the foot of the second ladder, trying to place him. She couldn't, but she was sure from his size and build that it wasn't the sheriff.

She allowed the slat to fall into place and hurried across the room, pulling her nightgown over her head as she moved. She threw it onto the bed and grabbed a pair of jeans and a sweatshirt from the drawers of the bedroom chest, not bothering with underwear. After rummaging in the bottom of the closet for shoes, she settled on a pair of loafers.

As soon as she was dressed, she hurried down the hall, through the kitchen, and out the back door. She heard the screen slam behind her and headed across the yard. As she walked, she looked up, shading her eyes with her hand against the glare of the morning sun.

Mark was no longer climbing. He had stopped just below the platform and seemed to be doing something to the original ladder. She fought the urge to call out to him, afraid she might startle him. She was uneasy about him being up there, maybe simply because of her experience yesterday. Mark knew what he was doing, she told herself as she approached the windmill. After all, he'd grown up doing this kind of stuff, and his physical reflexes had always been quick as a cat's.

"Morning, Jilly."

Surprised by the childhood nickname, she lowered her gaze to find that the man at the foot of the tower, whom she had seen only from the back, was looking over his shoulder to smile at her. She recognized him immediately, of course.

"Mark rope you into helping him, Stumpy?" she asked, returning the smile.

"Didn't have nothing better to do. If I'da stayed at the ranch, somebody mighta put me to work."

"A fate worse than death," she teased.

"Got it down to an art after all these years. Avoiding work. I'd hate to spoil my record."

He turned his head to spit an arch of brown juice into the dirt. When he turned back, he apologized, although she couldn't imagine Stumpy without that ever present wad of chewing tobacco.

"Beg your pardon, Jilly. Mark said you been having some trouble over here."

"Minor vandalism," she said, lifting her eyes again to the man at the top of the ladder.

If Mark had been wearing a jacket against the morning chill, he had discarded it before he'd begun the climb. He was wearing jeans again and a sage-colored shirt.

"Bad business," Stumpy said. "Any idea who done it?"

She shook her head, still looking up. "The sheriff thinks it might be somebody with a grudge against my father."

She lowered her eyes in time to catch the older man's expression. Obviously another person who wasn't an admirer of Tony Salvini.

"Even so, ain't no call to take it out on you," he said.

"If you figure out who this is, Stumpy, would you tell them that, please?"

Her eyes were drawn back to the ladder by its movement. Stumpy stepped forward, putting steadying hands on the side rails. Mark had moved out of sight, up onto the platform, which was designed to provide a place to work on the mill mechanism. After only a few seconds, the massive wheel began to turn.

A minor victory, perhaps, but there hadn't been many victories of any kind since she'd moved out here. Jillian admitted that it felt good to finally be watching those massive blades turn around and around in the ever present Panhandle wind.

"Well, looky there," Stumpy said. "The boy got that fixed in record time."

She and Mark would always be children to Stumpy. She smiled, though, hearing the same genuine pleasure she had just felt at Mark's success reflected in the old man's voice.

"There must not have been much wrong with it."

"Guess not," Stumpy agreed. "Once you could get up there to look at it. Mark said somebody had tampered with the ladder."

"One of the rungs came loose as I was climbing it yesterday. The bolt on the right-hand side broke or had rusted away. At least that's what the sheriff thinks."

Stumpy turned his head and spit again. Jillian wondered if that was an editorial comment on Ronnie Cameron's opinion.

The ladder vibrated and both of them glanced up. Mark was making his way down. They watched each step he took as if his descent were the most interesting thing they'd ever seen. As he reached the bottom, Stumpy stepped back to give him room to step off onto the ground, and she followed suit.

When Mark turned around, his eyes fastened on her face. For a split second she wished she'd taken time to comb her hair and put on some makeup before she came out. It would probably have looked ridiculous if she had, but it would have been nice to face that intense appraisal without the dark circles caused by her sleepless night being quite so clearly revealed.

"You got it fixed," she said unnecessarily.

The words sounded thready, almost breathless. For some reason, however, she felt unnerved by his scrutiny. Maybe because whatever doubts she had about her bedraggled appearance this morning, she couldn't find any fault with Mark's.

His eyes were clear, almost green in the morning light. The lean cheeks were freshly shaven, and his sun-streaked hair was being ruffled by the same wind that was turning the wheel above their heads. A sweet, hot flood of desire stirred in her lower body, just as it had all those years ago.

And she knew why her conversation with Jake yesterday afternoon had left such an unpleasant aftertaste. She could never marry Jake Tyler. Not feeling the way she did about another man.

"Somebody had shoved a two-by-four between the blades."

"I seen that done before," Stumpy said. "Folks gonna be away awhile and didn't want to chance having the brake thrown."

"That's possible, isn't it?" Jillian asked, her eyes still on Mark's. "The last owner knew this place was probably going to take a while to sell."

"Maybe," Mark conceded. "Except for this."

Long brown fingers fished in the pocket of the wool flannel shirt he wore in lieu of a jacket. She couldn't see what they brought out. He held whatever it was out to her, and automatically she opened her hand to receive it.

As he placed the object on her outstretched palm, a jolt of reaction seared along the same nerve endings that had just burned with the heat of sexual awareness. The feeling was so powerful that she wondered how he could have avoided feeling it, too.

His face was expressionless, however, as he released the object and raised his eyes again to hers. She was so disoriented by the intensity of her reaction that it took a long heartbeat for her to force her eyes downward.

A bolt lay in the center of her hand. There was no rust on it, just as there had been none on the one Mark had taken from the bottom of the ladder yesterday. There was, however, a deep, shining groove just beyond the head. It was obvious by the brightness of the metal within that it had been cut.

"Sawed almost through," Mark said, his voice low and tight.

She looked up into his eyes again, only now identifying what was in them—sheer raw fury, carefully controlled.

"I don't understand," she said, almost too shocked by what she was seeing to take in all the implications.

Obviously Mark had been right yesterday. Someone had sabotaged the ladder that led to the top of her windmill. A windmill that had been blocked from turning by the simple expedient of sticking a board between the blades.

"Put enough pressure on that," he said, nodding at the object on her palm, "and eventually it's going to break."

"But...this isn't the one that broke," she said, speaking that realization aloud.

"There are several cut like that, all of them near the top. A couple of them held as you climbed past them. The one that didn't..." He stopped, a muscle tightening in his jaw.

"Mighty lucky you didn't fall, Jilly girl," Stumpy said. He had come over to look at the bolt. "Can't imagine how you managed to hold on when that rung gave way."

She shook her head, still trying to take in the unbelievable concept that someone had deliberately tried to hurt her. Her gaze lifted again, finding the gap in the ladder where the bolt had broken under her weight. Like Stumpy, she couldn't imagine how she had managed to hold on. And if she hadn't—

The distance might not have been enough to kill her. And the idea that murder was the intent of whoever had sawed through those bolts was pretty melodramatic, she supposed. The distance was enough, however, to make sure that if she fell, she wouldn't walk away unscathed.

"What now?" she asked, trying to keep her voice steady.

"For starters, we give that to Cameron. Maybe it will make him start taking this seriously."

"This?"

Mark hesitated before he answered. "Vandalism. Harassment. Attempted murder."

"Do you honestly believe someone is trying to kill me because my father ran out on some loans a decade ago?"

"You know another reason?" Mark asked quietly.

He was right, she realized. If this wasn't tied to her father and what had happened before they'd left this community, then…what the hell was it about? She had no enemies. There was nothing in her life that should have led to this kind of animosity or hatred. There was absolutely no reason for anyone—

"Violet's money." She breathed the sudden thought aloud.

Was it possible there was some clause or provision in Violet's will that would give the money to someone else if anything happened to her? She had never thought to ask Dylan Garrett that question.

She had assumed from what he'd told her that the money was hers, free and clear. And she would have assumed, had she even thought about it, that if anything happened to her, the money would go to Drew. But she hadn't asked.

She had Garrett's phone number somewhere. She tried to think where she had put the papers Violet's lawyers had sent her about the inheritance. Of course, with all her belongings in such a jumble after the move—

"Violet?" Mark asked. "Who's Violet?"

"A friend," Jillian said. "A friend who left me...a lot of money."

For some reason she felt awkward saying the words. But it *had* been a lot of money. Of course, a good portion of it was tied up in this ranch.

"A...friend?" Mark questioned, skepticism in his voice.

"I see the horses have arrived," someone said from behind them.

As soon as she recognized the voice, Jillian's fingers closed over the bolt Mark had brought down from the top of the ladder. Then, moving almost in unison, the three of them turned, staring at the man who was coming across the yard.

Just what I need, Jillian thought, watching the dust settle on Jake Tyler's highly polished dress shoes as he walked toward them. *Just exactly what I need to insure that this will turn out to be one of the worst days of my life.*

CHAPTER NINE

"THEY LOOK GOOD. Obviously none the worse for the journey."

The man crossing the yard was looking Jillian's horses over with a proprietary air that for some reason annoyed the hell out of Mark. And when he approached her, without any hesitation that might have implied he needed to ask permission, the guy put his arm around Jillian's shoulders, pulling her against his side.

"How are you, sweetheart?"

He bent his head and kissed her. Granted, it was only on the temple, but the gesture was even more proprietary than his comment about her horses had been.

"I'm fine, Jake," Jillian said stiffly.

By then, of course, Mark had already figured out who this must be. And to give her credit, it appeared Jillian was trying to ease away from his embrace and put more space between them. Tyler's big hand tightened around her shoulder, holding her firmly in place.

"These your boys?" he asked, smiling at Mark and Stumpy.

There was a small awkward silence, which lasted until Jillian broke it. "These are friends of mine," she said. "Mark Peterson and Stumpy Winters. Meet Jake Tyler."

Her eyes met Mark's as she said the name, and he wondered if what he felt was reflected in his face. *Some rich guy who wants to marry Mom*, Drew had said. And here he was in the flesh.

Tyler held out his hand, which at least forced him to let

go of Jillian. Since Stumpy was nearer, the old man responded first, putting his gnarled fingers in the manicured
grasp of Jillian's suitor. By the time that handshake had been
completed, Mark had gathered enough control to be able to
offer Tyler his hand instead of punching him in the nose.

Which would have been a real shame, he thought, assess-
ing the face that arrogantly sculpted nose dominated. As he
did, he realized how misleading Drew's description had been.

Of course, to a kid his age, we probably all seem ancient,
Mark thought. Jake Tyler was maybe five or six years older
than Mark. And he was undeniably handsome.

Prematurely gray at the temples, he was also nicely tanned.
The smooth, even kind of tan that came from lying around
a pool or the beach. Not the kind that came from working,
in any case.

"Nice to meet you both," Jake said easily.

He made it sound as if it really was. Of course, this guy
couldn't possibly be viewing him or Stumpy as rivals, so
Mark knew that the insecurity he was feeling wasn't churning
in Jake Tyler's gut. Nor was the fear.

Rival, he thought again, examining the word as he allowed
his fingers to tighten over the ones extended to him.

There was nothing weak about Tyler's handshake. The
blue eyes seemed a little surprised at the strength with which
Mark returned it, but not surprised or interested enough to
remain focused on his face for more than a couple of seconds.
Tyler's hand uncurled, and he turned to smile down at Jillian.

"What are you doing here, Jake?" she asked.

Good question, Mark thought. From his perspective at
least.

It meant that she hadn't been expecting Tyler. That this
visit was not part of some arrangement the two of them had
made together during that telephone conversation yesterday.
He was obviously not here at her invitation.

"Thought I'd surprise you. Come out and take a look at
the place. Try to figure out what the attraction is."

Tyler's smile broadened as he said the last.

"The attraction is that it's home."

The slight chill Mark heard in Jillian's voice allowed his heartbeat to slow. And it allowed him to take a breath, which in turn made him realize how long it had been since he'd remembered to do that.

She wasn't pleased to see the bastard. The surge of relief from that realization was so strong it made his knees weak.

"It used to be home," Tyler corrected, still smiling.

It was obvious from his tone that he hadn't taken offense at Jillian's bluntness. Or maybe he was a good enough actor that he could hide whatever he was feeling. Which was something Mark had never been any good at. He was pretty much a what-you-see-is-what-you-get kind of person. And maybe that had been a mistake.

"It still is," Jillian said.

She held Tyler's eyes almost challengingly. After a moment, the banker broke the contact, still showing no signs of annoyance at the way their reunion was going. He looked up at the wheel turning above their heads. The steady creak had been background noise during Mark's and Jillian's childhood.

"Haven't seen one like that in a while," Tyler said.

"We just got it working this morning," Stumpy interjected.

Jake's eyes considered the old man, and then they lifted again to the top of the tower. "Is that a fact?"

"Yes, sir. Shore did," Stumpy expounded, obviously pleased to have found a topic on which they could comfortably converse.

"What was wrong with it?" Tyler asked.

He looked back down at Stumpy, eyebrows raised in inquiry. There was another awkward silence, which Jillian again broke.

"The previous owner had blocked the wheel before he left. Probably concerned about wasting water. Someone had to climb up and take out the block."

"Looks like there's a rung missing." Tyler walked over

to the metal ladder and wrapped his fingers around the rung that was at waist level. He shook it, testing the stability, before he turned back to smile at Jillian. "You better get that fixed before somebody gets hurt. Want me to get someone out here to take care of it for you?"

"I'll take care of it," Mark said.

The offer was clipped and ungracious. Tyler's eyes considered him with the same lack of interest they had just displayed when he'd looked at Stumpy.

"I'd be much obliged if you would. Mark, was it?"

"Why don't we go inside?" Jillian suggested.

Mark didn't know if Tyler had picked up on what he was feeling, but Jillian and Stumpy both understood him well enough to know that the tone the guy had just used was guaranteed to set his teeth on edge. And it had.

"Mark Peterson," he said. "I grew up next door."

There was a flare of something in the banker's eyes, which he quickly controlled, leaving Mark to wonder exactly what the reaction had been and what had provoked it. Had Jake recognized his name? Had Jillian mentioned him? Or was the banker as attuned to the possibility of a rival as Mark himself was?

Of course, according to Drew, Tyler had already staked his claim and therefore had a reason to be wary of competition for Jillian's affection. Mark didn't. Other than the spontaneous hug when she had finally reached the safety of the ground yesterday afternoon, Jillian had given him no reason to believe she felt anything for him. Nothing except regret that she once had.

"It was nice to have met you two," Tyler said.

Neither Mark nor Stumpy returned the courtesy. Jake Tyler's eyes touched again on Mark's face before he put his arm around Jillian's shoulder, directing her toward the house. As they walked away, Stumpy spit a stream of tobacco juice that splattered in the dirt approximately where the banker had been standing.

"What's she see in him?" the old man asked.

"According to the kid, enough money so she won't ever have to worry about anything ever again."

"Hell, she had enough of her own to buy this place. That's more'n you or me got. More'n we got together."

It was only the truth. Yet Mark was surprised how much hearing it could hurt.

"I'm taking that bolt in to the sheriff," he said. "I'll take you back by the ranch on the way into town."

"You think Cameron's gonna figure out who sawed into those bolts?" Stumpy asked derisively.

"No, but at least he can't say there's nothing to this now."

"Oh, he can say it all right. He may not believe it, but he's capable of saying whatever he thinks will keep folks happy."

"You heard any talk about what's going on out here?"

Stumpy was bound to be more connected to the local grapevine than either he or Jillian. After all, the old hand had lived here all his life, without any side trips into the rest of the world.

"Not a word. I'll ask around, though. Won't say you told me to. Somebody may be bragging about what they've done. Surest way for a criminal to get caught," Stumpy pronounced, "is not being able to resist the urge to tell somebody how smart he is."

"Maybe we'll get lucky," Mark said, his eyes on the back door of the house, through which Jillian and her visitor had just disappeared. "Maybe somebody *didn't* resist."

"I TOLD YOU," Jake said. "I just wanted to see what the place looks like. I had to fly to Denver for a meeting yesterday, and I decided to stop off on the way home and look it over. See if you got your money's worth."

The teasing lilt that she had found so attractive the first time she met Jake was in his voice, and he was smiling at her. It was even possible he was telling the truth. Jake used the company plane a lot, and having the pilot set it down in

Amarillo for a few hours while he rented a car to come out to the ranch would be just like him.

And he had been protective of her since the day he'd met her. That old-fashioned, gentlemanly kind of protectiveness that was rare now. After years of struggling to support herself and Drew, she had found it undeniably appealing.

She had occasionally wondered after they'd become engaged if that had been the prime appeal Jake had for her. If so, she found she didn't particularly like the type of woman that would make her.

"So did I?" she asked.

"I don't think this purchase was really about getting your money's worth," he said. "Or am I wrong?"

"I told you what it was about."

"About Drew. About doing what was best for him."

"Among other things."

"And I suspect I just had the pleasure of meeting one of those...other things."

She didn't deny it. She wondered, almost despising herself for it, what he had thought about Mark.

And what can it possibly matter to me what Jake thinks?

"Is he the one?" he asked after a moment.

"I don't believe that's any of your concern," she said.

"I put a ring on your finger, Jillian, and you took it off to come out here on this...crazy, cockeyed mission to rediscover the past. I think that makes it my concern."

Maybe it did. But even before Violet had died she had begun to wonder if she had done the right thing in accepting Jake's ring.

"I'm sorry, Jake," she said softly.

"You don't have to be sorry, sweetheart. Not unless—" He stopped, his lips closing firmly over the rest of the sentence.

He reached out instead and put his fingertips against her cheek. She had to force herself not to turn away.

And her mind made the inevitable comparison to that moment out in the yard when Mark's fingers had accidentally brushed against her hand, sending molten sensation roaring through every nerve ending in her body. The feel of Jake's fingers, familiar and pleasant though it was, produced nothing like that.

Maybe the other was sheer sexual reaction. She wouldn't be surprised if that was the case, given the way she had responded to Mark's every touch that summer. As an adult, however, she couldn't afford to put much stock in the viability of a relationship that was based strictly on physical attraction. There had to be more to a relationship than great sex.

Like friendship? her memories mocked. Shared values. Shared experiences. Nearly a lifetime of being in love. Whatever that means.

Infamous words, but ones she had thought about a lot since she had met Jake. What exactly *did* it mean to be in love?

"I'll admit I was pretty furious when you handed me back my ring," he said, "but after I had a chance to calm down, I realized that I want you to be very sure, Jillian. Before you put it back on again. And if this…excursion into the past is what it takes for that to happen, then I'll just have to trust that you'll make the right decision."

"Right for *me?*" she asked, smiling at him for the first time. Remembering all the things that had attracted her to Jake Tyler. Like his common sense and his maturity. His sense of balance. "Or right for *you?*"

"I hope right for both of us."

She couldn't ask for anything fairer than that, she acknowledged. Jake had always been fair. Considerate of her feelings. Even patient with her doubts. Most people would think she'd lost her mind if she let him slip through her fingers.

"So where's Drew?" he asked, rather obviously changing the subject. Apparently he had said all he thought needed saying. "I brought him something."

"Maybe still asleep," she guessed, glancing at the clock on the microwave. It was after ten. She had slept even later than she thought. "Or maybe not," she amended. "I didn't realize how late it is. Of course Drew can always find something in his room to entertain himself with. The computer. His PlayStation.''

Even as she said the words, she thought how unusual it was that he hadn't come out into the yard to look for her when he woke up. Especially if he had looked out his window and realized Mark was there.

She crossed the kitchen and walked into the den. She took a perfunctory look around, but it was obvious he wasn't here, either. She went on into the hall, fighting a growing sense of unease. It was ridiculous to be nervous because Drew overslept. After all, so had she. It was just that so much had happened around here lately—

She knocked and then opened the door to his bedroom without waiting for a reply. Drew was lying in bed, eyes open. His head turned at the sound of the door, and he smiled at her.

"What's up, sleepyhead?" she asked, returning the smile. "I figured you'd be out and about by now."

"I couldn't sleep. I kept listening for stuff."

She walked over to the bed and sat down on the edge, her fingers toying with the top sheet as she examined his face.

"What kind of stuff?"

"I don't know. Somebody outside, I guess."

She had moved them here, several hundred miles away from everything Drew had ever known. And part of her reason for doing that, at least in her own mind, had been so her son could have the same kind of idyllic childhood she had had. Instead...

"You should have come and crawled into the bed with me."

"I'm too old for that," he said scornfully.

"I guess you are at that," she agreed. She didn't really feel he was, but that was not something Drew would want to hear.

"Were you talking to Mark?" he asked.

"Just now?"

He nodded. He had probably heard their voices coming from the kitchen. That might even have been what awakened him. Or maybe the sound of Mark's pickup leaving had done that.

"He came over to check out the windmill, but he didn't come inside."

"I thought we were going riding."

Mark hadn't even mentioned the promised lesson. Actually, he hadn't asked about Drew at all, but she knew he would be disappointed if she told him that.

"Jake's here," she said instead. "And he's got something for you."

"He's always got something for me."

Drew's tone was not anticipatory. Obviously, changing the subject hadn't worked.

"It must be nice to know that someone is always thinking about how to please you," she said evenly, ignoring that less than enthusiastic response.

"Mom, the only person Jake is trying to please is *you.*"

"Well, then he's succeeding. It does please me that he's good to you. There's nothing wrong with that, is there?"

"I guess not," Drew conceded. "Has Mark already gone?"

"I don't really know," she hedged. "He had a friend with him, so he probably didn't intend to stay long."

Drew turned his head toward the window, but he made no move to get out of bed to check.

"Are you okay?" she asked, reaching out to brush the hair off his forehead.

He put his hand up, blocking the gesture. Obviously too grown-up for that, too, she thought.

"Why don't you get some clothes on and come into the kitchen," she suggested. "Find out what Jake brought you."

"Can I call Mark to see if we're still going riding?"

"I don't think I have his number."

"We could find it in the phone book."

"I'll look for it while you get dressed."

She would look, she told herself, since she had promised him she would. Mark didn't own the ranch, so she suspected that if the phone was listed, it wouldn't be under his name.

"Okay," he said, but again there was a decided lack of enthusiasm in his voice.

"It might be something you'll like," she said, almost amused by how clearly his loyalties had changed.

Although Drew had never seemed to hero-worship Jake, he had never been reluctant to interact with him. Again she wondered at that almost instantaneous bond that had formed between her son and his father. As if blood had called to blood. *And you can't get much more fanciful than that,* she admonished herself.

Jake had called what she was doing a mission. Maybe it was, but she needed to be careful that she didn't impose her own hopes on the other two people involved. Very careful.

"Maybe," Drew said, "but I doubt it."

"There's only one way to find out," she said. "I'll meet you in the kitchen."

Again Drew's gaze moved toward the window. "Did he ask you where I was?"

He didn't mean Jake. And Mark hadn't even mentioned the boy. To be fair, Mark had had more serious, and more sinister, things on his mind this morning than a riding lesson. But that cut bolt wasn't something she wanted to discuss with a child who had just admitted he hadn't slept last night because he'd been listening for people moving around outside.

"He was fixing the wheel on the windmill so the horses could have water. And I told you he brought a friend over to help him. I suspect that's why he didn't wait until you were up."

"Maybe he's coming back."

"Maybe," she said.

Like a motherly "We'll see," that seemed noncommittal enough for any situation. She had no idea whether Mark had remembered the promised riding lesson. Or, if he had, whether he would come back now that he knew Jake was here.

"You don't think he will," Drew said, reading her too well.

His voice held disappointment and maybe even a tinge of bitterness. But judging by what had been in Mark's eyes when Jake had hugged her, she really didn't think he'd come, she realized. Maybe that primal male possessiveness she had glimpsed should have given her hope, but she couldn't be sure it was anything other than that. *Possessiveness.*

"Jake's waiting," she said quietly. At least *he* never forgot a promise.

There were far too many things she couldn't protect her son from anymore. That was part of growing up, of course. But protecting him from hurt had been one of the things that had brought her back to the ranch.

One of them, she admitted. Only one of them.

"So WHAT do you say? Your mom said you were going to be starting school here on Monday. This will be kind of a last fling for us. You game?" Jake asked, reaching out to ruffle Drew's hair.

The child refrained from evading Jake's hand as he had hers, but Jillian could see by the stiffness in his small shoulders that he had to forcibly prevent himself from dodging away. At least the politeness she had tried so hard to instill seemed to be holding up as Drew approached adolescence.

"I guess," he said.

"I thought you'd be thrilled about going to another Cowboys' game. We had a good time before, didn't we?" Jake asked, bending down to balance on his toes, eye level with the boy.

"I guess," Drew said again.

Jake glanced up at her, obviously hoping for an explanation about the change in response to tickets to a pro game.

"I think Drew was hoping to do some riding this weekend," she said.

"Is that right?" Jake asked, turning back to the boy and infusing enthusiasm into his voice. "I think we can arrange that. Remember that Arabian I wanted to get your mom? How about you and I go check him out? See if he's as good as they claim."

"Jake," she began to protest.

"I can't really ride," Drew said, his words falling on top of hers. "Mark was going to give me lessons."

Again Jake's eyes lifted to meet hers, but this time Jillian knew they weren't seeking an explanation. They seemed to be making an evaluation instead.

"Why don't we give you a head start," Jake suggested, looking back down at the boy. "Then, when Mark gets around to it, you'll be able to surprise him with how well you do."

She could sense the wheels turning inside Drew's head. That idea would appeal to him, of course. He never wanted to appear inept at anything. That was one thing that had made him work so hard at school as well as at physical therapy.

"Cool," he said softly.

Jake's smile was blatantly triumphant. "Then as soon as your mom can get you packed..."

He let the suggestion trail, his eyes meeting Jillian's again. She didn't suppose she had any option. An invitation had been issued and surprisingly accepted.

Some part of her would rejoice in getting Drew away from the ranch. Away from whatever was going on out here. She knew Jake would look after him. Or at least Consuelo would, and Drew truly adored Jake's Hispanic housekeeper.

And he would have a good time at the game. Jake would see to that. It had been obvious to her what the deciding factor in the boy's accepting that invitation had been. The chance to impress Mark with his riding ability had outweighed anything else Jake had offered.

Blood to blood, she thought again, remembering that same competitive streak in another boy. That same desire to be the best at everything he did.

That had been the boy she had known a long time ago. A boy she had lost. A boy she had come back ten years later to take a chance on finding.

Taking a chance. That was all this amounted to. All she was doing. Taking a chance that there was something left of what they had once had. And if there wasn't—

"Mom?"

She looked down to smile at Drew. His loss of sleep last night was reflected in his eyes, which were a little red-rimmed. At least he'd be able to sleep soundly at Jake's, she thought. And as much as she knew she would miss him during the next three days, she would sleep more soundly knowing that.

"Okay, then," she said. "I guess that's decided. Let's go see about getting you packed."

CHAPTER TEN

"VIOLET'S MONEY is yours, free and clear. No strings attached," Dylan Garrett assured her.

"And if something happens to me?" Jillian said into the phone, the image of that missing rung on the ladder in her head.

"Something?" Garrett repeated. "Like what?"

"What happens to Violet's legacy at my death?"

He probably thinks I'm some kind of nut, Jillian thought, almost wishing she hadn't called to ask Dylan her question.

Other than this possibility, however, she hadn't been able to come up with any reason someone might want to harm her. Actually, this seemed less far-fetched than someone holding a ten-year-old grudge against her father and trying to take it out on her. At least it had until she had put the idea into words.

"The same thing that will happen to the rest of your assets. Whoever is named in your will as your heir will inherit it." Garrett's tone was quizzical, as if he couldn't figure out what had prompted her to ask something that must seem obvious to him.

Whoever is named in your will as your heir...

Which was Drew, of course. He had been since she'd first made a will several years ago. And he certainly wasn't trying to do her in to inherit her sudden wealth.

"Is something wrong, Jillian?" Dylan asked, that note of puzzlement still in his voice.

"No," she said quickly.

She'd made a big enough fool of herself for one day. Even

given the rapport they'd established the day Dylan had told her about Violet's role in his own life, she couldn't see the point of unburdening herself to him about what was going on here.

"I guess I just wanted to clarify the situation," she said.

"Well, the bottom line is that the money is yours—and then your heirs—to do with as you wish," Dylan said, sounding slightly relieved at her disclaimer.

The knock on her back door came at the same time Garrett said the last word of that sentence. Jillian tried to move toward the window, but the spiral cord on the old-fashioned phone wouldn't let her get near enough to see out it.

"That's good," she said. "Sorry to have bothered you."

"No bother. Call me at any time if I can be of help. Any friend of Violet's and all that," he said, a gentle amusement replacing the disquietude she had heard before.

The knock sounded again, but they were so near the end of the conversation that she didn't see any need to tell Dylan there was someone at her door. It would only sound as if she were making an excuse to hang up.

"Thanks again for the information," she said, trying to hurry the conversation to a natural end. "And be warned—I may take you up on the offer someday."

"Anytime. I'll look forward to hearing from you."

"Thanks, Dylan."

She put the receiver back on the cradle and hurried over to the door. Her hand hesitated before it closed over the knob.

"Who is it?"

The inquiry was fairly pointless since she hadn't locked the door when she'd come inside with Jake this morning. Locking doors was a habit she was going to have to acquire, she acknowledged, in light of what was going on around here.

"It's Mark."

He hadn't forgotten the riding lesson after all. A wave of relief washed through her that he hadn't changed. At least, not that much.

She opened the door, stepping back to allow him to come into the kitchen. Instead, he stayed where he was, standing on the back stoop, his eyes examining the room behind her.

"Jake's gone back to Fort Worth," she said, interpreting that look. "He was only here for a couple of hours."

"I thought you might be heading back with him."

"I don't live in Fort Worth."

He nodded, his eyes returning to assess her face. This time she was more prepared, and more willing, to have him do that. After Drew and Jake left this morning, she had showered and put on makeup—maybe more as a morale booster than anything else.

The house had seemed too quiet without the familiar background noises of Drew's games. She had straightened his room and unpacked the last of the boxes before she had remembered to call Dylan, which said something about her state of mind.

"Where's Drew?" Mark asked.

She hesitated, knowing instinctively that he wasn't going to like her answer. Actually, as the hours had passed since Drew and Jake left, she'd found she liked it less and less herself. She had thought that sending Drew to Fort Worth would be the smart thing to do, the safe thing. Instead, she was worrying more about him as the afternoon progressed. At least when he was here, she could see him and know he was all right.

"Jake had tickets for the Cowboys' game this weekend."

Mark's eyes changed, hardening as they had before, but his voice was almost without inflection.

"I guess Drew must have been looking forward to that."

"To be honest, I'm not sure he was. He didn't appear eager to go. But…Jake promised him a head start on the riding lessons. That's what really convinced him."

"A head start?"

"I think Drew's afraid of appearing inept in front of you."

"Why in the world would Drew…?" Without finishing the question, Mark shook his head, his brow furrowed.

"Drew's worried about what I'll think about his riding ability? That doesn't make much sense—since I'm supposed to be teaching him."

"It does if you know Drew. He's a perfectionist, and not just about things at which he could be expected to excel. He wants to do *everything* well." She hesitated and then added, "That can be really hard if you don't have a lot of physical attributes on your side. And Drew never has."

"His limp?" Mark said, cutting through her convoluted explanation to reach the heart of what she was telling him.

She nodded, wondering how much more to say and how much would be better left unsaid. This came too close to a lot of the other things she knew she needed to tell Mark. And hadn't. Not yet. It didn't seem that any of them should be discussed out on her doorstep, in any case.

"Would you like to come in?" she asked. "I could make us some coffee."

He didn't seem eager to accept, and all the doubts about the wisdom of what she was doing here, doubts that Jake had brought to the surface this morning, reared their ugly heads.

Finally, without verbally acknowledging her invitation, Mark stepped across the threshold. As he did, he turned and hung his Stetson on one of the pegs by the back door.

She closed the door behind him, and he walked across to the kitchen table to pull out one of the chairs. Before he sat down in it, he looked up at her.

"You need some help?"

"Not to make coffee," she said.

He sat down, watching as she rinsed out the glass carafe and dumped this morning's grounds and filter into the trash.

"Cameron seemed willing to take things a little more seriously after he saw that cut bolt," Mark said.

She looked at him over her shoulder. "That's good, I guess." It was almost a question.

"And Stumpy's going to ask around. Find out if anybody's been talking."

"About the windmill?"

"That. Or the roadkill. You coming back after all these years. Anything that might relate to what's been going on."

"I just can't believe this is about my dad, no matter what Cameron says." Her hands went through the motions of the familiar task as she talked: inserting the filter, spooning the coffee into it, measuring the water. "I mean, if they sold off everything," she said as she poured the water into the back of the coffeemaker, "then most of the people he owed must have gotten part of their money back. Isn't that the way it works? They divide whatever comes from the sale among the people you owe."

"The bank probably got most of it."

"Who in the world did he owe besides the bank?" she asked, turning around to face Mark and leaning back against the counter as she waited for the coffee to brew. "I have to admit, I don't quite understand what my dad and yours thought they were doing. They mortgaged their homes and their land. And then they borrowed additional money? What in the world for?"

"It takes capital to operate a ranch. Times were hard."

"Harder than now? Harder than they'd been through before? It doesn't seem to me like we ever had enough money around here. Ever. But my dad had never borrowed through those times. He hated to owe anybody anything. I just can't imagine him doing what Cameron said."

"Exactly what did Cameron tell you?"

She tried to think, but after the sheriff told her about her father mortgaging the ranch, she really hadn't paid all that much attention. It had been so contrary to everything she had always believed about the reason for their leaving.

"That your dad and mine had signed loans together. Loans beyond the mortgages they had taken out. He said that your dad wanted to experiment with hybrids because he thought they'd have a better chance up here."

"He talked about that some," Mark agreed.

"With all the money they supposedly borrowed, they must have done something other than talk about it."

"Not that I'm aware of."

"Then…what happened to it? What happened to the money?"

"Probably the same thing that happens to any money in the ranching business. It just got sucked down into that black hole of ongoing needs."

She shook her head. "Those needs were still there when we left. No improvements. No new stock. No new equipment. As far as I can remember, nothing at all to show for those loans."

Mark's shoulders lifted as if he couldn't explain that. And he couldn't be expected to. Not after ten years. No one could.

She turned around to check the coffee, alerted by the rich dark smell that it was through brewing. She reached over her head, stretching on tiptoe to get two mugs from the cabinet above the coffeemaker. She poured the steaming coffee into them and then carried both cups over to the table, setting one in front of Mark. As soon as she released the handle, his fingers closed around her wrist. Startled, she jumped, her own coffee sloshing out over the rim.

"Ow," she said, hurriedly setting the mug down on the table.

She shook the scalding liquid off her fingers and put them in her mouth as her eyes sought Mark's face. Despite her inarticulate protest, he hadn't released her arm.

"What the hell do you think you're doing?" she demanded.

"Trying to figure you out."

"Figure me out?"

"What you're doing here. Why you really came back."

She swallowed, feeling her heart rate accelerate. She supposed she had known these questions were inevitable, but she wasn't sure she was prepared to answer them. Not yet.

"I thought this might be a better place than the city to raise Drew," she said. And that *had* been part of the reason.

He held her eyes, apparently trying to evaluate the truth of that claim from whatever was in them.

"I'll buy that," he said after a moment. "What else?"

She thought about denying that there had been anything else. Or asking him why he thought there was. For some reason the rock-steady regard in those hazel eyes required, or maybe deserved, better than that. And after all, she had known from the first that this moment would come.

"A friend reminded me that you can't really move forward into the future if there are unanswered questions in your past."

His eyes narrowed slightly, as they always did when he was thinking. His thumb had begun to move against the sensitive skin inside her wrist. His fingers were still controlling, long enough to hold her securely without that slowly caressing thumb.

"And are there?"

"A few," she said.

She didn't know what her eyes were telling him. Or her pulse, which, she realized belatedly, he was in the perfect position to read. She tried to keep her face expressionless, but she had never been very good at hiding things from Mark. He knew her too well. *Had* known her too well, she amended. Whether he did now or not—

"And some of them involve what happened between us," he suggested.

…*what happened between us.* Was that phrasing a little cold? Maybe even…clinical? Or simply a natural masculine evasion of a more emotional description?

"Drew says Tyler wants to marry you," he went on. "Did you come back so you could decide what to tell him?"

A denial had already formed in her brain when she realized that, too, was part of the truth. If there had been nothing here, nothing left of what had once been between them, she would probably have said yes to Jake eventually.

The problem was there *was* something still here. Something so powerful that the merest brush of Mark Peterson's hand could make her blood run hot and hungry through her veins. Something so compelling that his thumb moving against her pulse was even now creating a sweet, aching emptiness within her body.

She nodded slowly, not trusting her voice. Not with the tumult that was going on inside. That tremulous swell of desire was so strong that she was surprised he hadn't sensed it.

His eyes didn't change however, still holding on her face. And then his fingers tightened, urging her nearer. She put her left hand flat on the surface of the table for balance, bending from the waist and allowing herself to be pulled toward him.

He held her eyes until the last possible second before he lowered his head, away from hers. His lips found the thin, blue vein that ran along the pale skin inside her forearm instead.

For a moment, he simply pressed the warmth of his mouth against its pulse. And then his lips opened, the hot, wet heat of his tongue sliding along the length of that vein, tracing its journey from her wrist to the inside of her elbow. As if she stood outside her body, an onlooker to what was happening, she heard her breath catch in her throat, the sound escaping through lips that had parted of their own accord.

He suckled the tender skin in the bend of her elbow, and then his mouth trailed upward again, moving hot and demanding onto the soft flesh of her upper arm. And as it did, his fingers, still fastened around her wrist, pulled her nearer and nearer. Her left forearm, from palm to elbow, was resting on the table now, as were her stomach and her breasts.

Mark, too, had shifted position. He was still seated, but he was leaning across the surface of the table, his face lowered against her arm. Their positions should have been awkward. Uncomfortable. Something. And yet she was not aware of anything beyond the feel of his mouth moving against her skin. And of the resulting tremors of sensation that ran through her nerves like the shimmer of summer lightning.

Nothing had changed. Not about this. And even as she made that discovery, he lifted his head, so that they were face-to-face. Eye to eye. Breath to breath.

And his was as ragged as hers. Uneven. Disturbed.

He held her eyes as his mouth inexorably approached hers. His lips were open, prepared to fasten over her own. Her head tilted, automatically aligning her mouth to fit under his. And when it closed over hers, it was as if she had finally really come home. *Home*...

Whatever doubts she had had about what she was doing here melted under the searing heat of his kiss. And her body's response felt exactly as it had when she was seventeen.

She was suddenly mindless with need. Unable to think about anything beyond the feel of Mark's mouth moving, urgent and demanding, against hers. And the stronger, deeper urgency it had begun to evoke within her body.

Except she was no longer seventeen. When she had been, she had given in to this mindless clamor. She had blocked out everything except Mark's kiss. Mark's touch. As a result she had allowed what she felt for him to move them from attraction to fulfillment, without any time for plans or preparation.

And if she wasn't careful, she realized with a sense of shock, the same thing would happen again. Her mouth opened, breath coming in gasps against his. As yet, she had told him nothing. Explained nothing. And if she didn't...

She lifted her head, breaking the contact between their lips. Without resistance now, she was able to pull her wrist free from the grip of his fingers.

With her left hand pressed against the table, she pushed upright, looking down on his still bowed head. After a second or two, as she shudderingly drew air into her lungs, he raised it, looking up into her eyes. And within his, control was reasserted, replacing a need that seemed as raw and powerful as her own.

Gradually, his breathing eased, slowed, evened. His lips closed tightly, as if he feared the words that might come through them if he didn't exert the control she had just watched him struggle to regain.

"We need to talk," she said.

It took a second to identify the harsh sound he made in response to those words as laughter, perhaps because there had not been any trace of amusement in it.

"About what?" he asked. "If you're going to tell me that I had no right to do that—"

"About Drew," she said, her words interrupting the sharp staccato rhythm of his.

There was a brief silence. "Okay," he said, his tone modified. No longer expressing anger. Maybe simply curious.

And now that she was here, she had no idea how to say this to him. It had become very obvious during the last few days that despite her long-ago phone call, Mark truly had no idea Drew was his son. It was even possible, she conceded, that Mr. Peterson had never even told him she'd called. And all the years she had assumed Mark hadn't wanted to get in touch with her...

"What about Drew?" he demanded.

What would she be able to tell from his reaction? How accurate that assumption had been? Or how much responsibility she would have to bear for her misjudgment in making it?

"He's yours."

The words were soft, and they had been said seemingly without emotion. Maybe that's why it took so long for any reaction to be reflected in that cold hazel stare. And when it finally appeared, she had no idea what she was seeing.

Disbelief? For perhaps a heartbeat. And then slowly, as he continued to search her face, that changed.

At least he believed her, she had time to think before he stood, moving so abruptly that the chair he had been sitting in toppled backward, slamming into the wall. His hands closed painfully around her upper arms, pulling her to him.

Off balance, she kept herself from falling by putting her hands down on the surface of the table. Again they were leaning toward each other, its scarred wooden top between them. Their faces close. Eye to eye.

"What the hell are you talking about?" he demanded, his voice low and intense.

"I called you." There was accusation in those words, just as there had been in his question.

His eyes revealed that he had heard it. And had identified it. "*Called* me? About that? About Drew."

"As soon as I knew."

He shook his head, the movement slight enough that he never released her eyes. "No," he said softly.

"As soon as I knew," she said again. "I left a message with your father. I didn't know what else to do."

"My *father?*"

She nodded, feeling the sting of tears at the back of her eyes and fighting them. She was determined not to let him see her cry.

She could still remember that terrible sense of panic, that sense that this couldn't be happening to her, that it somehow wasn't fair. It was an old pain now. An old betrayal. One she had dealt with long ago. Long before she had made the decision to come back here.

The burning in her eyes now was for what was happening in his. Mark was only now learning about the pain of that kind of betrayal. And in spite of what his father had done, even in spite of what it had meant to her life and to Drew's, she was sorry that she was the one who had to teach him.

"You told my father you were pregnant?"

How many times through the years had she dealt with that particular what-if? And in how many ways had she answered her own question? If Mark had really cared, he would have called, no matter what message she'd left. If he had wanted to get in touch with her, he would have called. After all, he must have known, given the timing of her call, that pregnancy was a possibility.

"I told him I had to talk to you," she said. "I gave him my number. I told him it was very important that you return my call. *Very* important."

Again his eyes assessed her face. And this time she hid nothing of the feelings that these memories evoked.

"That stupid son of a bitch." His voice was low and harsh.

And then he released her so suddenly that she might have fallen had she not been braced. He turned, moving almost blindly, and stumbled into the chair he had overturned. With the same volatility she remembered from his adolescence, he kicked out at the chair, slamming it once more into the wall. There was the sharp crack as something broke, but he kicked it again, the movement accompanied by a low string of profanities.

Watching him, she straightened away from the table, crossing her arms almost protectively in front of her chest and running her hands up and down them, as if the room had become chilled. In actuality, the display of his anger made her blood run cold.

She should have known he had never gotten her message. She should have trusted that if he had, he would have called her back. Never in all the years she had known him had Mark let her down. He had never once failed to take care of her. Why would she have believed that he would then?

She realized that the low noise of his cursing had stopped. She raised her head, blinking to clear her vision.

Shoulders hunched in a posture that was obviously as much a defense against pain as her own, Mark's back was to her. His forehead was pressed against the wall, and his hands, still clenched into fists, were above his head.

"I'm sorry," she whispered. "I'm so sorry."

She saw the depth of the breath he took, so deep it lifted his broad shoulders. And then he turned to face her, pushing away from the wall almost wearily. Whatever she had expected to find in his eyes—accusation or bitterness—wasn't there. They were touched with moisture, and when she saw it, her own blurred again.

He shook his head, his mouth tightening as he swallowed. The movement was visible all the way down the brown corded column of his throat.

"Why should *you* be sorry?" he said. "What the hell do you have to be sorry about?"

"I thought you didn't care," she said. "I thought…I thought you didn't want us."

"He never told me you called, Jilly. I swear he never said a word. I tried to find you. God knows how hard I tried, but it was like you had just disappeared off the face of the earth."

"My father didn't intend for anyone to find us. He even changed our name. I thought he was determined to keep me away from you, but…" She paused, trying to understand what had happened. Trying not to make the same wrong assumptions she had made back then. "Ronnie implied that we had to leave because my dad had lost the ranch. Because of all the people he owed. And that really makes a lot more sense. The idea that he was running from something rather than trying to hide me from you."

"Whatever his reasons, the effect was the same."

She nodded, wondering why she hadn't known there was more to that sudden midnight exodus than her father's discovery of a teenage love affair. Maybe because she had been as self-absorbed as any other seventeen-year-old? Or because her whole world, at least that summer, revolved around Mark? She had been totally oblivious to anything else.

Looking back now, she knew that there were signs she should have picked up on. Her father's moods, for one, although they had always been unpredictable. That spring and summer the fuse on his rage had been extremely short. And then later, when he had found out she was pregnant… She shivered, remembering the terrible night her mother had finally told him.

"Why didn't you call again? You must have known I'd come."

Mark's voice was quiet, still free of indictment. And it was a legitimate question. That message had been too important to trust to one phone call.

"The next time I tried, the next time I *could* try, they told me the number was no longer in service. I know this sounds stupid, but…I thought your father had it changed so I couldn't call you.''

"We were probably gone by then."

Gone. The Petersons had lost their ranch, too. She knew that now, although she had had no inkling of it back then. Ronnie had told her that Bo had been able to hold on to his place a little longer, but inevitably the bank had foreclosed on his property, too. So even if she had made it back here on that desperate journey that had ended instead in Pinto—

"We had a blowup," Mark said, his voice tinged with bitterness, which was obviously not directed at her. "One of several we had in those days. He said some things about you that were…unforgivable. So I left. Packed up and just walked out. I had no money to go back to school, and I couldn't see myself doing those same backbreaking jobs I'd done for my father all those years. So I enlisted. The military seemed to offer more opportunity than this place ever had."

She nodded, as if that made sense, but she wondered—and somehow knew from his voice not to ask—why he had eventually ended up back here. Just as she had, she realized. Full circle. They had both come back. Drawn by the passion that had flared so strongly—and so briefly—ten years ago?

Whatever had happened that summer, whatever had driven her father to pack up his family and disappear in the middle of the night, had irrevocably changed their lives. And Drew's.

Especially Drew's. Drew had never had a father's love and guidance. She hadn't been cruel enough to say that to Mark. She couldn't do that to him. Not after the pain she had seen in his eyes when he'd learned of his father's betrayal.

Mark wasn't a man who revealed his emotions. And as long as she had known him, she'd never before seen him cry. That, for her, had been the most telling aspect of his reaction by far, and the most revealing of what he truly felt when he realized Drew was his.

Between them, their fathers had managed to destroy what had sprung to life during those long, hot days and even more heated nights. And now, after all these years, she finally understood that its destruction had not even been deliberate. She and Mark had simply been the unwitting victims of events neither of them had been aware of at the time.

"I need to know," she said softly.

"Need to know what?" Mark asked.

"I need to know what happened that summer. If those debts were what drove my father to run away, then…I need to know what he used that money for. I need to know why they did what they did. I need to understand."

"You're going to ask him?"

That was a logical question, especially since she hadn't yet told Mark everything. Why not just ask her father what the money he and Bo Peterson borrowed had been spent on?

"My father and I haven't spoken in almost ten years," she said. "I'm not sure I could get in touch with him now, even if I wanted to."

"And you don't want to?" he asked, reading her tone.

"He—he never forgave me," she said.

And I never forgave him. That was the real truth that had kept her from contacting her mother and father all these years.

"Then…I don't see how we'll ever know what they were doing," Mark said. "And, frankly, I'm not sure it's all that important. Knowing where that money went won't change anything."

"Maybe not, but…we're both here again. And things are happening again. Somebody is trying to drive me off this ranch. Maybe they did the same thing to my dad. And maybe he let them get away with it, and it changed everything. For all of us."

"Jillian—"

"They aren't going to make me run, Mark. Not until I know what's going on. Not until I understand what this is all about."

"This may have nothing to do with what went on back then."

"You don't really believe that," she challenged.

He said nothing for a long time, and she waited through the silence.

"You're right," he said finally. "I *don't* believe that."

They hadn't talked about Drew. Or about anything that was really important. Maybe the other—this old mystery— offered an excuse to avoid dealing with something that was still too raw and painful to discuss.

Their fathers, and whatever had been going on that summer, had kept them apart for ten years. It had also deprived their son of the family he deserved. And eventually, they would have to deal with the implications of that. Eventually.

"So what do we do about it?" she asked.

"We find out what happened then," Mark said. "And maybe if we do, we'll understand what's going on now."

CHAPTER ELEVEN

"HOW DID YOU find all this?" Jillian asked, looking at the papers Mark spread out over her table the following afternoon.

"Bankruptcies are a matter of public record. All I had to do was go to the county courthouse and pay to have these copied."

She pushed a few of them around as if she were scanning their contents, feeling a little overwhelmed by the sheer volume of the material. She wondered if Mark could possibly have read all of this. After all, he couldn't have found delving into his father's finances pleasant.

"None of these tell us much," Mark said.

He pulled out one of the kitchen chairs and turned it around so its back was to the table where the papers lay. He sat down, long, jeans-clad legs straddling the seat backward. It was something she must have seen him do a thousand times while they'd been growing up. Another memory. One that joined all those that had been stirred up yesterday.

And they had been powerful enough that she had lost sleep again last night. Of course, she could probably blame part of that insomnia on being alone in this house. She had lain awake for hours, breathing suspended, trying to identify every unfamiliar noise. Between those episodes, the conversation she and Mark had yesterday had replayed endlessly through her brain.

She didn't know what she had expected to happen after she told him about Drew. Certainly not that the separation of the last ten years would simply disappear. Or that they could go back to where they had been the night their son was conceived.

She had to confess that she had expected *something*. Questions about Drew or about what their lives had been like. A discussion of where their relationship might head from here. Or what role Mark would have in Drew's life from now on. Something.

"What, exactly, did you expect these to tell us?" she asked.

He glanced up from the papers, surprise in his eyes.

"I thought I'd find out who my dad owed. Who got paid off and who didn't."

"And who was left holding the bag," she said softly, thinking how many times that metaphor had been used.

It might have been applied to her relationship with Mark all those years ago. After all, she was the one who had been left, alone and pregnant, to bear her father's wrath.

"And who was left holding the bag," he repeated.

His voice was equally as soft, his eyes seeming to echo her thoughts. Which was absurd, she admitted, since he couldn't possibly know what she had been thinking.

"So...did you find out who that was?" she asked.

"You were right. Most people got something. They figured the paybacks as a percentage on the dollar. The bank got the land and the equipment. After everything else was sold, the other creditors were paid in proportion to what they were owed.

"And there doesn't seem to be any one individual you could point to as the big loser," he went on. "Most of those loans were from old friends, and not for particularly large amounts. I guess Dad had used up everything he could offer as collateral. The last loans were penny-ante. Desperation kind of stuff."

"Trying to stave off the bank's takeover of the ranch?"

"If that's what he planned, he never acted on it."

"I don't understand."

"He didn't *make* the payments to the bank. Not any of

them,'' Mark said, his hand almost aimlessly moving the papers around.

"But he still kept borrowing?"

He nodded.

"That's…" She paused, unable to come up with a description that fit.

"Crazy?" Mark's laugh was bitter. "Maybe they both were."

"Both? Are my father's records like this?"

"In his case, there was no bankruptcy, so they aren't public. When your family disappeared, the bank just took over. I'm not even sure they tried to find your dad. I'm assuming his creditors, if there were any other than the ones he and Dad co-signed loans with, presented their claims to the bank and took what they could get after the ranch was auctioned off."

"So who are the people the sheriff was talking about? The ones who are supposedly holding a grudge over that money?"

"There are probably a few. Friends who felt they got cheated. But as far as coming up with one name—" he shook his head "—it's just not there."

"I guess we should have known it wouldn't be that easy. Nothing ever is."

"It might not hurt to talk to some of these people. Most of them didn't have all that much to begin with. It would have taken a pretty good story to pry money from them."

She nodded, trying to remember if her father had said anything at all about borrowing money or owing people. Of course, he hadn't felt that the way he ran his ranch was anyone else's business. Certainly not hers.

"Now what?" she asked, feeling a sense of letdown. Nothing had gone as she'd expected since she'd come home.

"I thought I'd do that. Talk to some of them, I mean. Stumpy's still feeling people out, but so far he hasn't turned up anything."

"It seems like a waste of effort," she said.

"You have a better idea?"

"I didn't mean that. But…nothing's happened here the last couple of nights. Maybe they've decided enough's enough. Maybe they got the ill will out of their system."

"Or maybe they're just waiting to hear whether or not you've fallen off that ladder yet and broken your neck," he suggested.

Which put things into perspective in a hurry, she supposed. She didn't really have much option about pursuing this. Someone had tried to hurt her, maybe even kill her, and if she were serious about staying—

"You talk to Drew today?"

Despite the casualness of Mark's question, she was glad he asked it. The fact that he had gave her more hope than anything that had happened since he'd told her she had nothing to be sorry for. It almost made up for their lack of discussion about their son yesterday.

"I tried. Jake's housekeeper said they'd gone to the stables to look at an Arabian."

"Must be nice," Mark said.

There had been no inflection in the words, but she knew him too well to let it go. "What must be nice?"

"To have enough money that you can give a kid everything his heart desires."

"Are you talking about Jake?"

"You, too, I guess. Stumpy reminded me that you aren't exactly strapped for cash. Not if you can afford to write a check for this place. He heard that's how you managed to get the deal through so quickly."

The tone of *that* was easy enough to decipher.

"It *is* nice to have enough money so your child doesn't want for things," Jillian said. "Especially since he frequently has. Throughout most of Drew's life I've been in a very different financial situation, I can assure you."

Her comment was intended to stop the direction in which she thought this conversation might be headed. She didn't want the money Violet had left her to become a barrier between her and Mark. She was sorry now that she had even mentioned it yesterday. Maybe it had sounded as if she were boasting about her sudden wealth. At the time, she had simply been grasping at any straw that might explain what was going on.

"I tried to find you," Mark said, his voice intense. "I didn't know about the baby, but...I swear to God, Jillian, I did everything I knew to track you down."

"I didn't mean that," she said quickly. "I wasn't blaming you. I was stating a fact. Maybe trying to explain why what Jake offered us was so appealing at one time."

"Was?" The question, spoken softly, deserved an answer. Maybe this was what Mark had been waiting for.

"I told you about Violet. The money she left me gave me more than the opportunity to come home. It gave me freedom. Freedom from having to make that decision based on anything other than what I feel about Jake Tyler as a man."

"And how do you feel?"

"As if he's dependable. Stable. Someone I can count on to be there if I need him."

All of which might be construed as criticism of Mark, but it was only the truth. She had been able to send Drew off with Jake yesterday without worrying about whether or not he would be taken care of. She had always known that Jake would take care of Drew. And of her. If only she would let him.

"Is that what you want, Jilly? Still looking for someone to bandage the scrapes and wipe away the tears? Someone who'll set you on your feet if you stumble? Is that why you came back?"

Is that why you came back to me? He didn't say the words, but he might as well have.

"I don't need someone to pick me up and dust me off. I haven't in a long time. I've had friends through the years who did a lot for me. I'll always be grateful for the help they gave me when Drew was a baby and I was struggling just to make ends meet. But...that was a long time ago. And I survived. I don't really need anyone to take care of me, Mark. I'm not looking for someone to do that."

"I guess that's good. For me at least. Because I'm not in the knee-bandaging business anymore. I guess I just needed to understand what you were looking for when you came back here."

"I wasn't looking for anything," she said, knowing even as she said it that it wasn't the whole truth. "I thought you deserved to know about your son. That maybe...he deserved to know about you."

"You knew I was here *before* you came back."

She had, of course. As soon as she had been given Violet's check, as soon as she had decided that the old woman had been right about those unresolved issues in her past, she had hired someone to track Mark Peterson down. And the path his life had taken had led right back here. The place where whatever was between them had all started.

"I knew," she admitted.

"So...this wasn't an accident. Our showing up here at the same time."

"No," she admitted.

No accident. She had come here to find him and to find out if the intensity of the emotions she'd felt at seventeen had faded.

He nodded slowly, as if he were thinking about that.

"So was this trip home really about Drew? Or was it more about you and Tyler?"

"I don't understand," she said.

She didn't. She didn't have a clue what he was asking her.

"Were you looking for some kind of...proof that it's over?" Mark asked. "Proof that what we had, what we were, isn't here anymore?"

She had wanted to know if there was anything still between them, but the way Mark phrased his question was a subtle reversal of that. She hadn't needed to know that it was over. She had wanted to verify that it didn't have to be.

"That's not exactly how it was," she said, knowing she sounded defensive.

"Then how was it?"

"I needed to know what was left."

"And do you?"

Desire. Need, she thought. *And love. Just as there was ten years ago. And a little boy who is like you in too many ways to allow me to ever forget.*

"I know there's something left between us," she said.

Surely he wouldn't try to deny that, not after that kiss yesterday.

"So what are you going to do about it?" he asked.

"What do you want me to do?"

"This is your play, Jillian. You came back here, knowing I was here. You're the one who's got something to prove."

She had already proved it, at least to herself. Mark wasn't making it easy, however, for her to confess that her feelings for him hadn't changed. Was that because he wanted to punish her for becoming involved with Jake? Or because *his* feelings had changed?

The ringing of the phone was an intrusion, shattering the waiting silence that had fallen after his challenge. She let it ring twice, holding his eyes, before she finally moved to answer it. The only reason she did was that it could be Drew, calling in response to the message she had left with Consuelo this morning. She walked over to the counter and picked up the receiver before it could ring again.

"Hello."

"Jillian?"

Jake's voice sounded strained. And immediately her mother instincts, already on edge, interpreted that as meaning bad news.

"What's wrong?" she demanded.

"We have...a problem."

Despite the lack of any real information in those words, her knees went weak. She sagged against the counter, head down, eyes clenched, as she fought to keep panic at bay.

Too much had happened lately. Too many things she hadn't expected. Now, because of them, she was preparing for the worst.

"What kind of problem?" she managed to ask, grateful that her voice still sounded almost normal.

She was aware that Mark was moving. She listened to his footsteps cross the floor as the slow seconds ticked off while she waited for Jake's reply.

"It's Drew."

And this was, of course, the thing she had feared most. Dreaded most. Her heart stopped and then began to hammer. Mark's hands closed around her shoulders, and she welcomed their strength, as she leaned back against him. An old reflex.

"It's his appendix," Jake went on, his voice calmer in the face of her own careful control. "They think it's hot."

Hot. Inflamed. Dangerous. Operation. She opened her eyes as the words formed in her head. Not nearly as terrible as what she had been imagining.

"They need to operate right away," Jake continued.

"I'll be right there," she said, taking the phone away from her ear. He must have known that's what she'd do because he spoke quickly and loudly to stop her.

"They need to do it now, Jillian. There isn't time to wait for you. Apparently this has been going on for a couple of days. For some reason Drew didn't say anything about being sick."

The image of her little boy lying listlessly in bed the morning she'd sent him off with Jake flashed through her mind. She had known there was something strange about his lethargy, but she had had other things to think about. She had ignored the unease she'd felt at his uncharacteristic behavior, and now—

"They need your permission," Jake said. "I have the surgeon standing right here. He's the best in the state, sweetheart. One of the best in the nation. I promise you that."

"Are you saying they're going to operate on Drew without me being there?"

"They feel they have to, Jillian. If his appendix ruptures, we're talking about a very different situation. A far more dangerous situation. As it is now, this is a very minor procedure. Very safe. I'll let the doctor explain it to you."

"I need to be there, Jake," she said fiercely. "At least when he wakes up. I need to get there as soon as I can."

"I'm sending the plane for you," he said. "I've already checked on that. It's not here right now. One of the vice presidents had to go to Atlanta, but they're going to send it to Amarillo as soon as he gets back. I'll get you here just as soon as I possibly can, Jillian. I promise you that. In the meantime, you need to talk to the doctor."

"Of course," she said, closing her eyes again, this time in prayer. A brief silence stretched over the lines as Jake transferred the phone to the surgeon.

"Mrs. Sullivan?"

"I'm here," she said, fighting her panic so she could concentrate on every word. "I'm listening."

She was. She needed so desperately to know everything that was going on. And when she did, when she understood it all, she knew Jake was right. She had no choice. No choice but to give them permission to go ahead with the operation before she could get there.

And despite understanding the urgency of the situation, despite wanting what was best for her son, she still found that saying the words was one of the hardest things she had ever done.

MARK HAD KNOWN the call was bad news the instant he'd watched the blood drain from Jillian's face, leaving her complexion almost gray. Actually, listening to her side of the conversation, he had feared something much worse than an emergency appendectomy. Much worse.

"He'll be okay," he said reassuringly as he held her.

She had hung up the phone and turned immediately into

his arms. Exactly as she had when she'd stepped off the bottom rung of that damaged ladder. And in spite of the circumstances that had led her to do that in both incidents, Mark celebrated the knowledge that she still felt safe here. Safe in his arms.

"Jake said the surgeon is one of the best."

Her voice was slightly muffled against his shirt. He put his hand on the back of her head, smoothing her dark, tumbled hair as he held her.

It must be nice to have the financial means to arrange that, he thought for one bitter instant—before he reminded himself just how much he owed Jake Tyler. This was *his* son Tyler was taking care of. Despite his personal feelings, he was grateful that Jake was in a position to see to it that Drew had the best possible care. Something Mark wouldn't have been able to ensure.

"That's good. Great surgeon for a very simple operation."

Please, God, let it be simple. Please, God, don't let anything happen to Drew. To my little boy. Emotion ached in his chest, and he fought to control any expression of how frightened he was.

He had discovered only yesterday that he had a son, a fact that had been deliberately kept from him by his father. Instead of sleeping, he had spent most of last night tossing and turning, thinking about everything Jillian must have gone through. And she had had to do it alone—from the birth of a baby with special needs to dealing with the normal growing-up rebellion of a preadolescent boy. And he hadn't been around for any of it. If anything happened to Drew...

He held her, thinking about that almost fragile little boy with the wide grin, the dusting of freckles and the rather obvious hero-worship in his eyes. He desperately wanted to tell her not to worry. To reassure her that he would take care of everything. But even as he thought it, he realized how ill equipped he was to make that promise.

Besides, Jillian hadn't given him permission to take care

of her or Drew. She hadn't suggested that he have any role in their lives. Or that she wanted him to.

That was something he had needed to hear, he admitted. Especially with Jake Tyler hovering in the background.

"I need to be there," Jillian said, pushing far enough away from him so that she could look up into his face.

"I can take you."

Her eyes widened. Obviously she was thinking about the offer. Evaluating it. "Jake said he'd send the plane to Amarillo as soon as it gets back from Atlanta."

"The helicopter's ready to go now."

"This isn't exactly co-op business."

"They'll understand."

It was the right thing to do, since they had the means at hand to get Jillian there quickly. And Shipley was a decent man. Mark didn't have any doubt he'd agree to the flight.

"Are you sure?"

The hope that he was was apparent in her voice. And in her eyes. Maybe he couldn't see to it that Drew had the finest medical care money could buy, but he could get Jillian to Fort Worth, and long before Jake's company plane could do it.

"Positive."

"Then...yes. I would really appreciate it. Give me time to pack a bag?" she questioned, sounding relieved.

"I'll call Stumpy and tell him we're on the way."

And he would ask the old man to check the latest weather reports. According to the radio, there was another storm brewing, but it shouldn't affect a flight south. Once they lifted off, they'd be heading away from whatever weather was rolling in.

"You can't know how much this means," Jillian said.

"I know I'm pretty new at this, but...I want to be there, too. I really need to be there."

Drew is my son as well as yours. He didn't say the words, because they were new. So much so that he would have been uncomfortable saying them aloud.

And he wasn't sure that he had the right to make that claim, given that he had had no part in Drew's upbringing. It hadn't been his fault, but he wasn't sure Jillian had completely absolved him of all blame. The only hopeful signs that she might were that she had come back home, knowing he was here, and that she had finally told him the truth about Drew.

Jillian nodded. Despite the fact that neither of them put it into words, it was clear she understood.

He hadn't been there all the other times when things had gone wrong. This time, he vowed silently, he would be. For Drew and for Jilly.

"THEY'RE SAYING it's gonna get nasty," Stumpy warned, "but not for several hours. At least according to the latest bulletins. You'll be fine," the old man added reassuringly.

"Thanks, Stumpy," Mark said as he settled his gym bag and Jillian's small suitcase into the space behind the seats.

Despite Stumpy's assurance that the storm wasn't imminent, the sky had darkened, and clouds loomed threateningly above the horizon. Once the bags had been safely stowed away, both of them turned to look northward, toward the roiling sky.

"Won't amount to much," Stumpy said confidently.

Mark turned to consider the weather-beaten face of the man beside him, who was still busy studying those clouds. If Stumpy thought this blow would be minor, then no matter what the meteorologist was forecasting, Mark decided he wasn't going to worry about the storm. He'd put the old man's bones up against the weathermen and their sophisticated instruments anytime.

"Would you keep trying to get in touch with Shipley for me?"

Although he had phoned the co-op owner from Jillian's ranch while she was packing, and then again when he'd gone up to the ranch house here to throw a few of his own things into a bag, Mark hadn't been able to get through.

"I'll track him down," Stumpy promised. "Not that he'll make no fuss if I don't."

Mark nodded, reassured that the old man read the situation as he had. Transporting a sick child was the kind of thing the owners would normally offer the chopper for, despite the cost.

"I tried Jake's cell phone," Jillian called, "but I couldn't reach him. Either he has it off, or he's out of range."

They both looked up, watching as she hurried across the last few yards toward the waiting chopper. While Mark handled the preflight, she'd stayed inside his parents' house to try to reach Jake and let him know they were on the way.

She had taken time before they left her place to throw on a navy blazer. Under it she wore the same short-sleeved white sweater and charcoal slacks she'd had on when Mark knocked on her door this morning. Her cheeks were slightly reddened, either from the cold or from the exertion of that run from the house.

"I left a message with Jake's housekeeper that we were on the way," she added as she reached them. "She's going to try to get in touch with him and tell him not to send the plane."

The last sentence was breathless. Mark held out his hand as she reached him, waiting to help her up into the passenger seat.

"Them boys got enough moola that it won't matter if they go ahead and send it," Stumpy said. "You got enough on you without worrying about that kind of stuff."

"Thanks, Stumpy. And thanks for checking on the weather."

"No trouble. You want me to keep trying to get Mr. Tyler?"

For a second or two, Jillian looked as if she were tempted to let him. Then she shook her head, reaching out to give him a quick hug. "It's okay. You're right. It won't matter if Consuelo doesn't stop him. We'll be there in a few hours."

"Okay, then," the old man said, his voice holding a trace

of embarrassment, maybe over Jillian's show of affection or because he wasn't comfortable with her gratitude. "You two get on along now. I'll hold down the fort here."

The slightly rheumy eyes met Mark's before they again considered the distant clouds. He wasn't sure what message the old man intended to convey with that look. Maybe that they needed to get a move on if they intended to outrun the storm.

He handed Jillian up into the seat, remembering with an unwanted tightness in his throat the day Drew had scrambled in on his own, refusing help. The boy's face, aglow with excitement, was suddenly crystal clear in his mind's eye. He closed his eyes, fighting an unexpected sting of tears.

"Mark?" Jillian questioned.

"Buckle up," he ordered harshly.

He reached out to touch the harness on her seat. Before he could move his hand, she laid her fingers on top of his. He looked up, straight into her eyes, and realized that she understood exactly what he was feeling.

"He's going to be all right."

She was comforting him, he realized. And the hell of it was, he needed comforting.

For a second or two, their gazes held as they drew strength from each other. Mark knew there had probably been other times in Drew's life when Jillian had been this concerned. For him, this feeling of helplessness and gut-chilling fear was a first, and Jillian needed neither from him right now. She needed his strength and his comfort. It wasn't supposed to be the other way around.

"I know," he said, the words barely audible.

It had been almost impossible to push them past the knot in his throat. *His* son. Their son, he amended. And he hadn't had nearly long enough to get to know him.

But I will, Mark swore grimly as he shut the door. Through the window, Jillian's eyes held his a moment before she turned and began buckling the harness.

Just hang on, cowboy, Mark urged his son silently as he

walked around the nose of the chopper. *Your mom and I are on the way. You just hang on until we get there, and I promise you I'm going to make everything right for all of us. Everything.*

CHAPTER TWELVE

"HOW LONG?" Jillian asked.

They'd been in the air for what seemed an eternity. In fact, it had probably been less than fifteen minutes, although she hadn't looked at her watch when they'd taken off.

Mark turned to study her a few seconds, evaluating. Finally, his lips tilted into a smile.

He was amused over her childlike question, she realized. She forced herself to return his smile, although her mouth felt stiff with tension, the movement forced.

"I sound like Drew," she admitted. "Any trip we ever take, he asks that same thing every five minutes."

"You always did, too," Mark said, his tone nostalgic.

"I'd forgotten that," she said, remembering only now how her father used to tease her about it. "I guess most kids don't have much patience when it comes to long trips."

Mark said nothing in response, and after a second or two, he turned his attention back to the instruments. He glanced at his watch, which made her think he might be working out an estimate of their arrival time in Fort Worth.

She took a breath, trying to relax. Holding on to all the positive things Jake and the surgeon had told her. *Minor procedure. Very little danger.* She glanced at her watch, wondering if the operation might be over. If she could know—

"Son of a bitch." Mark's voice hadn't been particularly loud, but the expletive was heartfelt. And compelling.

Surprised, she turned to look at him. He appeared to be totally focused on the instrument panel before him, so focused that her own eyes were drawn there, too. What she saw was pretty meaningless, just a jumble of knobs and dials and lights.

One of which was blinking, she realized. She glanced back at Mark and saw that he was watching the gauge beside that light with an intensity that was almost frightening.

"What is it?"

"Oil pressure," he said tersely.

Her gaze went back to the dial beside the light, which had stopped blinking, but gleamed balefully yellow like a cat's eye. Despite her lack of knowledge about the chopper's instrumentation, even she could see that the needle on the gauge beside it was moving. Dropping rapidly.

"What's happening?" she demanded.

For a moment Mark didn't answer her. His eyes were scanning the ground beneath them.

"Mark?"

"I have to set it down," he said.

Set it down. The helicopter? Land the helicopter? As soon as she made the mental connection, her gaze followed his. When she looked out through the windshield, a fear almost more powerful than her worry over Drew stirred in her heart.

Spread out below them, in all its terrifying ruggedness, was one of the deep canyons that bisected the High Plains. Like those more well-known, this one had been cut through the escarpment by a million years of water erosion. Irregular rock formations dotted its floor, which stretched out before them, sandwiched between forbidding sandstone and gypsum cliffs.

She couldn't imagine a place less conducive to an emergency landing. Of course, she told herself reassuringly, a helicopter wasn't like a plane. The landing area Mark used at the ranch was tiny. All he needed was a relatively small area of level ground.

As that thought formed, there was a sharp bang behind and above her. She ducked, instinctively hunching her shoulders to protect her neck and head from whatever had caused it. At the same time she heard the explosion, the chopper jerked to the left.

The expletive Mark rasped this time was one she had never heard him use before. One she could never have imagined him using in front of her. Shocked, she glanced toward him again, but his concentration seemed total. His feet moved on the pedals. One hand guided the stick between his legs, while the other pushed a handlelike thing downward, toward the floor of the chopper.

And he was talking, she realized belatedly. Not to her, but into the mike of the headset he was wearing. Although his voice was perfectly calm, there could be little doubt about the message. And as soon as she had grasped the gist of it, she again considered the terrain beneath them.

She fought the urge to close her eyes and the equal urge to demand some answers. Answers Mark didn't have time to give.

She hadn't immediately understood the significance of the bang she'd heard. Not as he obviously had. If she had known then what had caused that noise, she might well have echoed his profanity. Only gradually had she become aware of the absence of that high-pitched whine coming from the jet engine behind them. The noise it had made throughout the flight had been loud enough to make conversation difficult. Now the only sound in the chopper was the steady thump of its rotor, which was still turning over their heads.

Mark was moving the stick, making the same minute adjustments she had watched him make during the first part of the flight. Despite the failure of the engine, he must still have some control over the aircraft.

Enough to avoid the rocks scattered across the surface below? A surface that sickeningly seemed to be rising to meet them all too quickly.

She stole another glance at Mark's face. It was perfectly composed, his concentration absolute. If he was terrified about their situation, his features gave no evidence of it.

His hand, the one not on the stick, moved again, this time pulling upward on the lever he had previously pushed to the floor. As he did, the nose of the chopper began to lift. There was a slight corresponding decrease in the rate of their descent, noticeable enough that she gave a small sigh of relief. Maybe they weren't going down after all.

"Brace yourself," Mark warned, shattering that illusion.

His tone was almost conversational. Of course, with the noise of the engine missing, it wasn't necessary to shout as it had been before. And that was *not* a good thing, she acknowledged.

She tried to comply, preparing herself as well as she could for the hard landing he seemed to be anticipating. And she realized that as they descended, he was trying desperately to steer the chopper to avoid the more prominent features of the canyon's bottom.

The problem was that all of it was rough. Even the surfaces that appeared relatively level were strewn with small boulders and rubble. Finding a perfectly flat location on which to land was going to be impossible. All they could hope for—

The chopper touched down, far less violently than she had been anticipating. She had time to take the breath she'd missed as she'd watched that descent, and then realized that, although they were on the ground, they hadn't stopped moving.

The area where they had landed was slightly sloping. The chopper bumped against the ground and then continued to slide forward down the incline. As it did, it tilted a little to Mark's side. She held her breath, willing it not to turn over.

Instead it slid into one of the rock formations Mark had taken such pains to avoid. The collision was hard enough to jolt the entire ship, its metal skin crumpling against a sandstone outcropping on the pilot's side. She was thrown forward and to the side with the force of the impact. Her body strained against the harness before she was slammed just as sharply backward.

It took a second or two after the collision before she realized that the chopper was finally motionless. Only the blades were still moving above their heads. They were down. And they were both still alive.

Actually, she thought, turning her head carefully to verify that supposition, they were not only alive, but they seemed to be uninjured.

"You okay?" Mark asked.

She nodded, and then realized he wasn't looking at her. His head was against his seat, eyes closed, mouth tight set.

"I'm okay," she said.

For several heartbeats, the only noise was the gradually slowing thump of the rotor and the settling of the smaller rocks they had disturbed outside. As she listened to them, she waited for Mark to tell her what to do next.

A dozen questions formed in her head. Since she couldn't decide which, if any, were vital, neither of them said anything for what seemed to be a very long time. Long enough for the blades to quit spinning and the last of the pebbles to roll to a stop around the skids. And when Mark finally did speak again, it wasn't to her. It was into his headset mike.

As he talked, she licked her lips. They seemed incredibly dry, probably because she had been breathing too rapidly through her mouth. And her hands had begun to shake. Delayed reaction now that the worst was over. At least she *hoped* it was.

She looked out the window on her side, which was canted upward at a relatively steep angle. The cliffs that surrounded them, with their brilliant red, pale lavender and chalky white strata, would have been beautiful at any other time. Now they were simply desolate and forbidding. And too damn isolated.

"Son of a bitch," Mark said again, his voice no longer quiet.

Actually, the anger she heard in it sounded more normal, given their situation. She turned her head again so she could consider his face. His skin seemed gray under the bronze of his tan, and despite the temperature, there was a fine dew of perspiration on his upper lip and at his temple.

Of course, all of those might be the result of the harrowing descent he had just brought them safely through. She suspected there was more to it, though, simply because he had seemed so utterly composed while that had been going on.

To an outside observer, the same might have been said about her. Now that it was over, she was sick to her stomach. And she doubted her legs would support her if she tried to crawl out the door on her side, which seemed to be the only means of exit.

Just as she was about to suggest they should do that, the images of a hundred exploding planes from the movies in her head, Mark spoke.

"Radio isn't working."

She turned to face him, but he was staring out the windshield, seeming to study the desolation around them.

"But you got through to somebody before, so...somebody knows where we are," she suggested hopefully, a rise in inflection unwillingly attached to the end of the sentence.

"At least they know as much about where we are as I did."

"What does that mean?"

"That there are a lot of these canyons. A lot of arroyos to search. It could take a while for them to find us."

A couple of seconds ticked by as she thought about that. About the vagueness of it. "How long a while?"

Again her lips felt stiff, unwilling to form the words. And she had begun to shiver. The cold or shock?

Mark shook his head, his gaze still directed outside, but he didn't offer anything further.

"What happened?" she asked.

Whatever had gone wrong hadn't been Mark's fault. It had been obvious by his reactions that something very unexpected had occurred.

"Rapid loss of oil pressure," he said.

"What would cause that?"

He shook his head again, but this time he turned to face her. His eyes held hers, and despite the fact that she was shaking with reaction, shivers running through her body like a chill, she tried not to let her face reveal what she was feeling. Apparently she wasn't completely successful.

"I'm sorry, Jillian. God, I know how much..."

"It's not your fault," she said when he stopped, shaking his head wearily. "That noise I heard, that...explosion? Was that what caused the loss of pressure?"

"The result. The engine seized up. Apparently a turbine locked up and came apart."

"But...the blades kept turning," she said.

"Thank God," Mark said. "That's the beauty of rotary wing."

"That was a good thing?" she guessed.

"The fact that the blades keep turning lets you set it down. It would have been nice to have done it with a little more finesse, but given the conditions..." He paused again, his eyes going back to consider the terrain.

"We're alive," Jillian said. "And you told them we were going down, so...somebody will find us eventually." She wasn't sure to which of them she was offering that solace.

"But not in time for you to be there with Drew."

"He won't know whether I'm there or not," she said. It was nothing less than the truth. "At least for a while. And I *will* be there eventually. I mean, there's not much chance that they won't find us, is there?"

"Not a snowball's chance in hell," he said decisively, and she took comfort from his surety. "I gave them the general vicinity. They'll have searchers out here as soon as they can."

"Before nightfall?" she asked.

Again, too many seconds drifted by before he answered. Enough that she knew he was going to give her the best case scenario, although she suspected it would not necessarily be what he really thought would happen.

"Depends on the impact of the storm we were outrunning."

She had forgotten the impending storm. As Mark said, they

had been running ahead of it. Away from the ominous clouds that shrouded the horizon back at the ranch. Now, however…

"I guess we need to prepare for the possibility that we might be stuck here a few hours," he added. "We've got a thermos of coffee and sandwiches Stumpy made, so we'll be all right in that respect. You have anything warmer than what you're wearing in your suitcase?"

She tried to remember what she had packed. She had been in such a hurry that she hadn't given it much thought. Her nightgown, of course. And a couple of changes of day wear, slacks and sweaters. Nothing particularly cold-worthy, since she had anticipated that she would be spending most of her time during the next few days at the hospital or at Jake's.

"Nothing warmer, really, but…I guess I could add a couple of layers to what I have on."

Suddenly, his lips moved, one side quirking upward in a gesture that was heart-stoppingly familiar. It was the look Mark had always gotten when he intended to tease her about something. An expression that meant whatever he was about to say was designed to get some kind of rise out of her.

"I could use a good joke right now," she said. "Even if it's on me."

The smile broadened, creasing his lean cheeks in a way that sent a frisson of need—and memory—through her body.

"I figured that the next time we were alone, I'd be trying to convince you to take off a few layers of clothing instead of encouraging you to put more on."

She found she had no idea what to say in response to that blatant sexual innuendo. As the silence grew and expanded, Mark's eyes, locked on hers, didn't change. And he made no effort to retreat from the invitation he had just issued.

There was no doubt in her mind that it was an invitation, no matter how it had been phrased. An invitation she wasn't quite ready to accept, she realized.

Not quite ready, despite the fact that she had been the one who had sought him out. Despite the instant connection that had formed between him and Drew. Despite her conviction that Mark had been telling the absolute truth about what his father had done to try to keep them apart.

Ten years was a long time. A lot of days and hours and minutes stretched between then and now. Between who they had been back then and who they were now. And no matter how much she had once loved Mark Peterson—and God knew she had—there was no denying the existence of that gap.

Whatever she eventually decided to do about the feelings that were obviously still between them, it was a decision she didn't want to make under these conditions. There was too much going on that made her vulnerable to what Mark had just offered. To what he had always offered her.

Still looking for someone to bandage the scrapes and wipe away the tears? he had asked. But she wasn't. Not anymore. She wasn't going to fall back into those old habits.

"I need my suitcase," she said. "And privacy to change."

The smile slowly disappeared. His lips tightened, although that movement was more subtle than the invitation had been.

"I think your door's the only one that still works," he said, his voice revealing nothing.

She knew she could trust that whatever he was feeling, the emotion would be decently hidden until they got out of here. Whatever was going to happen between them would be up to her. Her choice. Her move. Just as it had been all those years ago.

"WARM ENOUGH?"

She was still awake, although she wasn't sure how Mark could have known that. Her head had been back, resting against the rear bench-type seat they'd climbed into because it offered more room for the night.

She opened her eyes and turned toward the sound of his voice as if she would somehow be able to see his face. She couldn't, of course. The interior of the chopper was almost totally dark. Mark was simply a silhouette, a shape set against the surrounding blackness of the night and the howling storm.

It was rare that the Panhandle got snow in November, but it happened. There had even been blizzards this early, one she remembered from when she was a little girl. Despite that experience, she had never taken seriously the idea that this storm might contain significant snowfall. She'd been wrong.

"I'm fine," she lied. Actually, she was cold and miserable, but sharing that information with him would serve no purpose. There wasn't anything Mark could do about it.

"I guess I'm going to have to stop depending on Stumpy's bones for my forecasts," he said, his voice touched with humor.

Despite the discomfort, despite the situation, her own lips tilted into a smile. She had reconciled herself hours ago to the fact that she wasn't going to be able to reach her son's bedside tonight. And somehow, with that almost stoic determination she had developed through the years, she had managed to convince herself that Drew would be fine, even if she wasn't there.

The operation was long over, and given that her son was normally healthy as a horse, there was no reason on earth for her not to assume it had gone well. So she had locked that worry away in the tiny corner of her mind to which she relegated all the worries she couldn't do anything about.

Then she had tried to concentrate on anything other than the surgery. And she had been surprisingly successful in the attempt. She had examined again what Mark had told her about their fathers' financial dealings. Taken some time to try to deal with her bitterness over the fact that his father had never delivered her message and to imagine how different her life might have been if he had. And that had led her to reexamine the depth of emotion she'd heard in Mark's voice as he had sworn that he'd tried to find her—even though he hadn't known she was pregnant.

And then, with all that out of the way, she had considered what else he had said. His invitation. In light of all the time she'd just spent thinking about it, she was very grateful that he had finally introduced another topic of conversation.

"So what did Stumpy predict about the weather?" she asked.

Her voice had seemed as relaxed as his, and she congratulated herself. After all, they didn't have any choice but to make the best of their situation. They couldn't leave the chopper, not only because it offered protection against the wind, but because it represented their best chance of being found when the rescue efforts were finally able to get underway.

"That this storm wasn't going to be bad. I think I'd hate to see what Stumpy considers 'bad.'"

She laughed, although the sound was barely audible. "Well, I wouldn't want to be caught out in it."

"We could always cuddle," Mark said. "Shared body warmth and all that."

She laughed again. It was another invitation, but this one was very different. The sexual undertone was clearly missing.

"I don't think I have any left to share. Besides, I might hurt your back," she added.

The comment served to keep the conversation away from a subject that seemed too dangerous. It also gave her an opening to question something she'd been concerned about since they'd scrambled awkwardly out of the tilted chopper.

They'd gotten the extra clothing out of her suitcase, and after she'd added another sweater to what she was wearing, Mark had helped her crawl up and into the back seat. Although he'd said nothing, it had become obvious during those maneuvers that he was favoring his back.

She had been jerked around hard enough during the landing to know that every bone in her body would be sore tomorrow. Yet the real force of the collision had been on his side. Throughout the hours they'd spent side by side on the cold vinyl seat, she had been aware that Mark had shifted positions, obviously trying to find one that was more comfortable. The last time, that careful movement had been accompanied by a soft, involuntary grunt of pain.

"Old football injury," he said, voice deliberately light.

"You didn't play football."

"I battered my tail bone against a few broncs instead."

She couldn't tell from his tone if he were serious, although the events he'd competed in could have led to back problems. Maybe reminding her of his rodeoing days was simply his way of diverting attention from whatever he'd done to himself when they'd hit.

"And you did permanent damage to it back then?" she asked skeptically. There was a long moment of silence.

As she waited for his voice to come out of the darkness again, she felt distanced from him. Almost alone. Not being able to see another person's face was isolating. As if you weren't really together. And yet, in a strange way it also seemed freeing. Maybe because you couldn't see the impact of whatever you said on the other person's face or in his eyes.

"It's not the first time I've done this," Mark said finally. The amusement that had been in his voice before was missing.

Done this. She examined the phrase, trying to decide exactly what "this" referred to.

"The last time..." His voice faded, and then strengthened to finish. "Not everybody was so lucky."

Crashed. This was not the first time he'd crashed, she realized finally. And if they hadn't been as lucky, then...

"Someone got hurt?"

"Yeah," he said softly.

"Including you."

"I was the pilot."

She knew him, so she understood what he meant, although it certainly hadn't made much sense in context. Mark had been the pilot, so he would take responsibility whether it had been his fault or not. Whether he himself had suffered from it or not.

"What happened?" she forced herself to ask.

Not because she wanted to know. She didn't. It seemed

obvious, however, that Mark wanted to tell her, maybe even needed to tell her, or he would never have brought it up.

"We had a pilot shot down. Flying recon. The bastards said he had broached their no-fly zone, but that was nothing but an excuse to shoot at him. They got off on doing that. This time they got lucky. We knew he'd ejected, but we also knew that if they got to him before we did..." Again his voice faded.

"You were the one sent in to get him."

"As soon as we got his signal. It was supposed to be a quick touchdown. Pick him up and then get back into the air. Get the hell out of there. The problem was they'd picked up that locator signal, too. They got there about the same time we did."

The silence built again, and this time she waited through it. She didn't even know what questions to ask. Besides, Mark wanted to tell her this. Eventually he would get around to the rest. And it would be better to let him do it in his own way.

"We got the pilot, but a couple of rounds hit the tail rotor. I didn't have enough altitude yet to do much with it, and...we went down. A lot rougher than today. They got to us. Our guys, I mean, but not before...they shot my copilot. And one of the guys who came down to pull us out."

His voice died, and although she waited a long time, he said nothing else. "It doesn't sound as if there was much you could have done to prevent any of that," she said finally.

"Maybe not. There was no official reprimand. No one suggested pilot error, but...I guess I'll always wonder. If I'd been quicker," he said, his voice very soft, "or a little better. A little more skillful..."

"Is that why you got out of the military?"

He laughed, the sound short and harsh.

"They wouldn't let me fly anymore. Couldn't pass the damn flight physical. According to them, I was 'medically unfit.'" The phrase was caustic. "I didn't figure there was any reason to stay.'' His voice had lightened a little on the last.

Relieved, she smiled, thinking how much like the Mark of old that sounded. Bullheaded. *If I can't do it my way...*

''I've never loved anything in my life except you and rodeoing as much as I loved flying,'' he said, the tone no longer mocking, not even of himself. ''Maybe that's why I took the job the co-op offered. Just trying to hold on to one of them.''

Trying to hold on to one of them. As romantic admissions went, it wasn't spectacular. Jake would have said it better. His words would have been polished, the implications crystal clear. Hearing Mark's words whispering through the darkness, she felt her throat tighten and fought a losing battle against the sting of tears.

However it had been phrased, there was no doubting the emotion behind what Mark had just said. Just as there had been no doubt about the impact when he had learned about his father's betrayal. No doubt about his response to the knowledge that Drew was his son. Mark Peterson wasn't a man who willingly exposed his feelings. Or his vulnerabilities. Tonight, deliberately, he had done both.

I've never loved anything in my life except you... Just trying to hold on to one of them. He still was. Which was why, of course, he had told her this.

She understood that, and because she understood him so well, she knew he believed there was some kind of competition between him and Jake. She had never meant to make him feel he had to compete with Jake to win her and Drew.

But since he thought this was a contest, Mark believed this was all he had to offer. The fact that he loved her. The fact that Drew was his son and he had never had a chance to be a father to him. The fact that he would welcome that opportunity.

I love you. I want us to be together again. I want us to be a family. Me and you and Drew.

He would probably never manage to say those words to her. And in all honesty, she didn't need them. She knew what was in Mark's heart. She had seen it in his eyes when she'd told him about Drew. And she had heard it in his voice, in those halting words coming out of tonight's cold, lonely darkness.

She had taken Jake's ring off her finger because she had known marrying him wasn't the right thing to do. Not right for her or for Drew. And she had come back here because deep down inside she had been hoping that Mark would want them, her and his son. And now that she knew he did...

She straightened in the seat and reached across it to lay her hand against his chest. She couldn't see his face, but despite the darkness, she could tell he had turned toward her. His hand, hard and strong and warm despite the frigid air surrounding them, settled over hers, pressing it closely against his heart.

A heart that was beating heavily enough that she could feel it, even through the sweater and the leather jacket he wore. Again her lips slanted upward. She knew she had been right. His confession that he loved her had been no offhand remark.

"Jilly?" he said softly.

"There's probably as much room here as there was in your daddy's pickup, but I feel I should warn you. I'm a lot older now than I was then."

The silence lasted through a few more heartbeats. And she felt, quite clearly, their sudden increase under her palm.

"Me, too," he said softly, his voice incredibly intimate in the darkness. "And a whole lot stiffer."

"You promise?" she asked, letting him hear her genuine amusement at the unintended double entendre.

And when he laughed, the sound of it chased away the ghosts and shadows they had let come between them. She knew then it was going to be all right. Whatever else had happened, this, at least, had not changed.

"I think you can safely count on it," he said, pulling her into his arms as if she had never been away.

This, too, she realized, was just another way of coming home.

CHAPTER THIRTEEN

THEY HAD REMOVED only the clothing that was absolutely
necessary. With the cramped conditions, accomplishing that
had proven another interesting challenge. Interesting and, she
admitted, arousing.

As soon as Mark had touched her breasts, now bare under
the double layer of sweaters she still wore, she had been
seventeen again. Virginal. Excited. Terrified. She closed her
eyes, inhaling sharply as the hard masculinity of his hands
closed over their softness.

"What's wrong?" he asked, lips moving against her
cheek.

"Nothing," she whispered. "It's just…"

"Just what?" he demanded.

"It's been a long time."

"Maybe," he said, his voice sounding lazily amused, "but
I doubt we've forgotten how this is done."

She leaned forward against his chest, forcing his hands to
give up their possession. Uncomplainingly, he put his arms
around her, holding her close. She turned her head, the
leather of his jacket cold under her cheek.

"Speak for yourself," she said, the words very soft.

She could hear his heart, beating steadily. After a couple
of seconds, she felt him draw breath, his hands stilling their
comforting movement up and down her spine.

"You want to explain that?"

His chin moved on the top of her head as he spoke. And
despite her recent disclaimer about not needing anyone to

kiss her bruises and make them well, she had to admit it felt good to be held. Protected. Sheltered.

"Not particularly."

Again she waited, listening to his heart. Knowing that if she could sleep against his chest every night for the rest of her life, lulled by the comforting sound of his heartbeat, she would ask for nothing else. Not for herself, in any case.

This was right—being in Mark's arms. It *felt* right. As if she belonged here. And that was what had been missing with Jake. This sense of belonging. Of being at peace.

"I know I have no right to ask—" he began.

"No, you don't," she agreed, interrupting that tentative probing. "Absolutely no right at all."

He not only had no right to ask, he had no right to expect. After all, she wasn't asking him what he'd done during the last ten years. Times had changed. The so-called double standard no longer existed, not even in rural Texas. Not even for good Catholic girls from devout homes.

"Okay." He lowered his head, putting his mouth against her hair, his breath warm over her scalp. "Then I won't."

And with his agreement, perversely, she found she wanted to tell him. She wanted him to know. She *needed* him to understand what her life had been like.

"At first, if I had wanted to date, if I'd had energy enough, I couldn't have afforded a baby-sitter," she said, thinking about the endless difficulties of those days. The abject loneliness of them. "Even if there had been anyone interested in an unmarried mother with no money and a demanding toddler in tow. And there wasn't," she added truthfully.

"And later?" he asked after a while. His hand had begun to smooth up and down her back again. Unhurried. Caressing.

"Later…" A harder question to answer. "There just never seemed to be enough time for a relationship. School and work and Drew took up every minute."

"Until Tyler," he said, his voice flat.

"Jake asked me to marry him."

His hand hesitated. To give him credit it was only for an

instant. Then it returned to that slow stroking of her spine. She smiled, the movement of her lips hidden against his body.

"And because I thought Drew needed a father, I accepted. It seemed the smart thing to do. The sensible solution. And then Violet convinced me that I was settling for second best, when what I really wanted…"

His breathing hesitated as her words had, and his heart rate accelerated again. But he didn't ask. He simply waited through the pause, his heart pumping strongly under her cheek.

"When what I really wanted was you," she confessed. "You were the only man I ever wanted. In this way. And in every other."

"Are you saying…" He took another breath, the leather of his jacket creaking gently with the force of it.

"I'm saying exactly that. There's never been anyone but you. A ridiculous confession for a twenty-eight-year-old woman to make these days, but…there it is."

There was another long pause, and when he spoke again, the words were not what she had been expecting. "I wanted to kill the son of a bitch."

"Jake?"

"Of course Jake. That sanctimonious bastard."

She laughed, lifting her head from its comfortable position against his chest. She touched his cheek in lieu of being able to look into his eyes, amused by his sudden transformation from resigned acceptance if she had slept with Jake to this vehement confession. "You were jealous," she accused.

"Damn right. I didn't like the way he touched you. Putting his arm around you like he owned you. Hell, I didn't like the way he pronounced judgment on your horses. And I damn well don't like the idea of him palling around with my son."

"Well, why don't you just get it all out in the open. Don't hold anything back now," she said with a touch of amused sarcasm.

Secretly, she was flattered over the strength of his reaction to Jake. His jealousy was pretty heady, actually.

In response to her teasing, he lowered his head, his mouth finding hers, his kiss swallowing the last word of her jibe. She didn't resist.

"We ought to try this in a bed sometime."

His breath feathered against her temple. He put his mouth over her ear, and she turned her head to accommodate its touch. His tongue laved the small, concentric circles of the rim before it dipped inside, sending a shiver of reaction through her.

"Why mess with success?" she said, shifting the position of her body so her hips straddled his.

He had suggested earlier that she sit on his lap. She didn't believe this was what he had meant, but given the constraints of space, as well as her concern for his back, this seemed the most practical way to accomplish what they both wanted.

And as she slowly lowered over his erection, she decided she might like being in control. Enough that it could become addictive, she thought, smiling at the realization.

Her head tilted as his mouth continued to explore, trailing hot and moist over the fragile, sensitive skin of her neck. Nuzzling aside the top of her sweater to find the soft hollow formed by her collarbone.

She lifted her hips and then lowered them again, millimeter by millimeter. Savoring each slow, erotic one of them. Savoring the shuddering breath he took. Even savoring the small pain evoked by the sudden clenching of his hands over her buttocks.

"Slow down," Mark whispered.

His face burrowed against her neck, his breath warmly sensual over the sweat-dampened coolness of her skin. She closed her eyes, feeling a surge of satisfaction that he was this aroused. This ready this soon.

Although outwardly she obeyed, she began to move over him in a different way, tightening the muscles that surrounded his arousal, caressing him internally. His gasp against her throat was all the encouragement she needed to continue those efforts.

Again she tensed and then slowly released. His reaction this time was more forceful. His hips moved, lifting into hers, as his hands, cupped over her bottom, pulled her closer.

The resulting gasp was hers. In response, he repeated that movement, filling her more completely than she would have dreamed he could. An almost painful fullness, which ironically caused her to want more. Something more. Something that she knew lay just beyond her reach. Barely beyond...

She lifted again and then again. This time he made no protest. Instead his hands and his hips moved in unison with hers. Encouraging. Answering. Encompassing.

And she began to lose the capacity to think, becoming one with the feelings that were building in her body. Becoming sensation. Becoming need.

Her movements grew more frantic, fueled by the promise of whatever waited beyond. Something outside her experience. Outside her expectations.

Her breathing was as harsh as his, their bodies straining together in a frenzied duet. A dance as old as time. And as new each time as the dawn.

When the spiraling heat began, searing along nerve pathways whose existence she had never before been aware of, she wasn't even sure what was happening. All she knew was that this was what she had been waiting for. What she had been straining to reach.

She felt the hot, jetting pulse of his release a fraction of a second before her own began. And she closed her eyes against the force of it. It swept through her body in a wave of molten heat. It shimmered along muscle and bone and nerve, exploding with power in the bottom of her stomach and then roaring into her chest and lungs, sending her heart hammering.

His body strained under hers as the last shivering flicker of ecstasy eased and then retreated. Draining slowly downward, following the same paths of sensation it had traveled before, until it was gone.

Leaving her breathless. Boneless. Mindless.

She slumped against him, and once more his arms tightened around her, moving under the sweaters, squeezing her hard against his chest. Their breathing mingled in the frigid air, the ragged sound of it the only noise in the still darkness. Gradually it, too, eased. Slowed. Faltered to normal. He breathed once, very deeply, his arms tightening reflexively.

"If I didn't know better..." he said, his voice teasing.

"What?" she asked obediently, willing to play straight man to whatever he wanted to say. Willing at this moment to do anything he asked of her.

"I'd think you'd been practicing."

She laughed, snuggling closely into the warmth of his body.

"Just think what it might have been like if I had," she whispered, letting him hear her own amusement.

"I can't even imagine."

"You won't have to. Imagine, I mean. If practice really does make perfect..."

"Any more perfect, and I'm a dead man."

"How's your back?" she asked, feeling guilty that she had forgotten the need for caution.

"Numb. All those other nerves were screaming so loud, they kind of beat the ones in my back into submission."

"This probably wasn't a good idea."

"Speak for yourself. Or were you?" he added after a moment.

"Is this the old 'Was it good for you, too?' question?"

"Was it?"

"You know it was."

"I *thought* it was. There's a difference."

"Not in this case," she said softly.

His cheek, abrasive with late-night whiskers, moved against hers in unspoken affirmation. "So what are we going to do about it?" he asked. "About this, I mean."

"This?"

"Us. Drew."

"What do you want to do?" She supposed she was still traditional enough that she needed to hear him say the words. She needed him to ask, just so she could say yes. A formality maybe, but that's the way she felt.

For too long, however, there was no answer to that question, which she had been foolish enough to think must surely be rhetorical. But the silence stretched so long that the slow burn of humiliation had started to grow in her chest before he spoke.

"I want to marry you. Claim Drew as my son, but..."

But... Again, she forced herself to wait, wondering if she could have been wrong. Wondering if the trust she had unthinkingly given Mark Peterson might truly have been misplaced. Not once, but twice.

"I don't have anything to offer you," he said.

Her first instinct was to ridicule, but the words had been too quietly spoken. Too...sincere. He believed that, she realized. And although she knew it for the nonsense it was, her eyes unexpectedly filled with tears at his earnest sincerity.

"I disagree," she said.

"I've got no money. No job. Not many prospects."

"You have a job."

He laughed. "Probably not after Shipley sees his chopper."

For the first time she realized the situation this crash had put Mark in. "They'll have insurance," she protested.

"I'm not sure it covers things like this. Things that aren't business."

She could have waited for Jake to send the plane, but she had jumped at the chance Mark offered. So...

"This is my fault," she said.

"Not everything in the world is your fault," Mark said.

Of course, that was her personality. Or her upbringing. If things went wrong, she was always ready to take the blame. Her father had trained her well.

"You didn't ask me to take you," he added. "I offered."

"But I let you. Did you tell anyone?"

"Get permission? I tried. Stumpy was supposed to keep on trying to get in touch with Shipley. I didn't figure it mattered all that much. Of course, I didn't figure on going down."

"It can be repaired," she said hopefully.

"Probably."

"So…how much does a helicopter cost?"

"You in the market?" he asked, his voice again amused. Or maybe that was just his form of whistling in the dark. "I know a pilot who'll be willing to work cheap."

"Maybe I could—"

"Minimally equipped, a couple of million," he broke in before she could make that offer. His voice was flat and hard, the amusement gone. "Do you have that kind of money?"

"Of course not. You know that."

"I wasn't sure. You had enough to buy the ranch."

"That bothered you?" She spoke the sudden realization aloud, her tone probably conveying her amazement that it might.

"Some."

"But…why?"

"I told you why. I've got nothing to offer you. Nothing that can compare."

"Nothing that can compare with *money?*" she asked. "Is that what you really believe? Because if it is…"

She hesitated, not willing to issue ultimatums. This was some kind of stupid masculine pride. Violet had left her some money, and Mark believed it put a barrier between them.

Maybe she thought what he was saying was silly, but she understood pride. Especially what it felt like to be on the receiving end of the handouts and the good deeds. As grateful as you might be for the helping hands, they could damage your fragile sense of self-worth.

She understood that on a gut level. And she was a woman

who had not even been raised to believe that standing on your own two feet was particularly desirable.

Mark had been raised by a man very much like her own father. A man who didn't believe in owing anybody for anything. A man who had always found it hard to accept favors.

"And if it is what I believe?" he prodded.

"Then...I guess I don't really know what to say to you to change your mind. I will tell you this, however. If money was what I was interested in, I'd already have married Jake."

"You still can. I'm sure he'll give you your ring back."

That stung. More than she wanted to admit.

"Yes, he would," she said, wanting to hurt him like he'd just hurt her. "All I'd have to do is ask."

"Then that would probably be the smartest thing to do."

The deliberately unemotional, controlled flatness of his tone angered her more than his pride. It was as if he didn't care whether she went to Jake or not. She knew in her heart that wasn't true, but damn it, he didn't have to act as if it were.

"And what about Drew?" she asked.

She was hitting below the belt, but if he thought this all came down to her going to the highest bidder, then she wondered what he felt about the fact that she would take his son with her.

The question silenced him, just as she had intended. He'd admitted his jealousy of Jake, of his possessive and presumptive behavior where she was concerned. Did he resent it enough to do and say the one thing she so desperately wanted him to?

"I guess it's no contest there, either," he said instead.

"What the hell does that mean?" she asked, shocked at his answer, despite how badly this exchange had been going.

"If you look at it objectively, Tyler can do a lot more for Drew than I ever could."

"For God's sake, Mark," she said, finally losing her temper. "Talk about sanctimonious. I didn't notice Drew asking you for anything. Did you?"

"Not yet. But…in all fairness, why should he? You're already giving him everything he could possibly want."

The arrogance of that took her breath. She had told him what her and Drew's life had been like. It was almost as if he resented the fact that they weren't struggling anymore.

"And you'd be happier if I couldn't give him things? Is that what you're saying? Because I have to tell you, that's what it sounds like."

Unconsciously, they had increased the space between their upper bodies, although they were still, embarrassingly now, intimately connected and almost yelling at each other.

"That's not what I meant. I just don't see what I'm supposed to do in this…arrangement. What my role is."

"Try being a father," she suggested. "I think Drew would welcome having one."

"For a change."

She hadn't said that, although to be honest, she had thought it. And the sarcasm she had tried to avoid was in his voice.

"Your words, not mine. But yes, he's never had a father. Jake's been the closest thing to one he's ever had. And I admit to being grateful for the effort he's made to fill that void."

"You didn't have any trouble finding me, Jillian," he said, "once you finally decided to come looking."

She laughed, the sound without amusement. "So it's my fault," she said. "The fact that Drew's never known his father."

"I just wondered why it took you so long to come looking."

"Maybe because I was busy raising your son. *Alone.*"

Now she was grateful for the darkness. Grateful she couldn't see his face. Grateful he couldn't see hers.

Awkwardly, she began to climb off his lap. There was something so brutally humiliating about having to disentangle yourself sexually from a man you were having this kind of argument with that she wanted to cry. Actually, she had wanted to cry for about the last twenty-four hours. She couldn't remember needing to weep this badly in years.

Slipping back into old patterns of behavior? Maybe they both were. Or maybe it was simply the bitter aftertaste of disillusionment. The death of a dream. The realization that some people changed, grew up, matured. And some didn't.

And talk about sanctimonious, she thought, pulling up her slacks and struggling with shaking fingers to fasten the hook and zipper. Reaction had set in with a vengeance, to the cold or embarrassment or disappointment over Mark's stupidity. She wasn't sure which. And she wasn't sure she cared, either.

To hell with it. To hell with him. To hell with all Violet's lectures about not settling for second best.

And talk about maturity.

Her throat constricted as she tried to keep the first revealing sob of self-pity inside. Violet was an old romantic. She had never made any bones about that. Except life wasn't a romance novel. If anyone was in a position to verify that, she was.

"Jillian."

"Don't," she said, hearing in her own voice how near to the surface tears were. She wondered if he could hear it, too. "Just...don't."

She fell back on the technique she'd always used with her father, willing herself to do anything other than give him the satisfaction of seeing her cry. Trying to think about anything other than how much she hurt. Or how humiliated she was.

She gathered her courage, rigidly holding herself together in the darkness. She had survived worse than this. This was nothing. *Nothing.* Old news.

Soon it would be morning. The searchers would spot the chopper, and then, if she could only hold on, she'd be on her way to Fort Worth. And to Drew. She wouldn't have to come back to the ranch. Not if she didn't want to.

Mark was right. Jake would give her the engagement ring back. Drew would adapt, just as he always did. He'd forget Mark. After all, she hadn't yet told him the truth.

Had she feared something like this? Had she known somewhere deep inside that no matter how things went between her and Mark, their relationship could never be what it once was?

Whatever the reason she had hesitated to tell Drew about his father, at least that was one regret she wouldn't have to live with. He'd forget Mark. And so would she. She would do exactly what she had always done. She would pick herself up....

The words echoed in her head. Reverberating with power. Without Mark around, she had had to pick herself up. Succor her own bruises. Bandage her own scrapes. And maybe that wasn't a role she wanted to give up.

She turned her head toward the window, using her knuckle to scrub away tears that she hadn't been aware were falling. They felt warm and almost pleasant against her cold cheeks. As she had when she was a child, she put the knuckle she had used to wipe them away between her lips and sucked the sweet, salty taste of them.

It was lighter outside. Almost dawn. The howl of the wind had died, and the snow lay gray against the black of the surrounding rocks.

The night was almost over. And when it was, she would, as always, pick up the pieces of her life and move on from here.

CHAPTER FOURTEEN

"LOOKS LIKE the oil line worked itself loose," the guy the co-op had sent out said. "Apparently it wasn't screwed in properly, or the safety wire slipped off. Eventually the engine vibration just worked it all the way out. Mr. Shipley will have something to say to maintenance, I'll bet."

And to me, Mark thought.

It was going to be necessary to send out a flying crane and sling load the downed helicopter back to the airport. Mark would fly into Amarillo with the crew of the rescue chopper, which the co-op had sent out first thing this morning to the crash site. He wasn't looking forward to whatever would be waiting for him when they arrived.

How the hell had everything gotten so bizarrely out of control? he wondered, looking at the damage to the chopper.

For a while last night it seemed that everything had finally fallen into place, like when the last pieces of a puzzle started to fit. And then suddenly...

He shook his head, knowing that going over the things he and Jillian had said to each other wouldn't help. Where it had all gone wrong wasn't suddenly going to become clear. If that was ever going to happen, it would have by now. He had been over the conversation a hundred times, and he was as baffled by how quickly it had fallen apart as he had been when it occurred.

"A mess, isn't it?" the mechanic said.

Mark glanced up, straight into his eyes. They were sympathetic. *If only you knew,* he thought.

"I'm glad it wasn't me trying to autorotate this thing down," the man went on. "Not around here."

Mark nodded. There were a few seconds of awkward silence.

"You ready?" the mechanic asked finally.

"Let me get my bag."

Mark walked around to the other side of the chopper, which was level now, thanks to the combined efforts of their rescuers. Jillian had flown out with the emergency crew from Amarillo, who'd arrived first. They would take her to the airport to meet the plane Tyler was sending for her. Mark, of course, had waited for the co-op's people to come and assess the damage from the crash.

As he opened the passenger side door to get his canvas carryall, the scent of Jillian's perfume filled the slightly stale air of the chopper's interior, assailing him with memories. Worse than that, underlying her fragrance was the subtle, yet distinctive scent of their lovemaking.

He jerked his bag out, jarring his back. Ignoring the pain, he slammed the door, as if he could shut off the memories as easily as he had the telltale smells.

Deliberately he dragged in a lungful of cold, fresh air. It cleared his head, which had begun to ache in sympathy with the cramping muscles in his lower back. Or maybe, he realized belatedly, the headache was from a lack of caffeine. He would miss the sure-fire rush Stumpy's coffee provided in the mornings.

Actually, he'd miss the old man's friendship even more, he thought, trudging through the three or four inches of snow that still blanketed the ground between the rocks. The snowfall had started to melt from the boulders as the morning sun heated them.

The rotor on the chopper the co-op had hired began turning, and Mark automatically ducked his head as he stepped under the blades. The mechanic had already scrambled into the back, and Mark steeled himself for the discomfort of climbing in. Only the first of the uncomfortable things he had yet to face, he thought as he used the strap to pull himself into the copilot's seat.

It was going to be a long day. The trip back to Amarillo. The confrontation with Shipley, if he was lucky, or with one of the other owners. Packing his stuff. Leaving the ranch where he'd grown up.

He didn't allow himself to think about what else he'd be leaving behind. He couldn't afford to do that right now. Instead, he turned his head as the chopper lifted off. The ship he had crashed faded away beneath them as they rose, nose slightly down, and turned north.

Had that been his last flight? he wondered. It wouldn't be easy to get another job flying. It didn't matter how many hours you had in the air, the specter of pilot error made people leery.

And he couldn't blame them. He could argue that neither crash had been his fault. He had been arguing that with himself for months now about the first. But still...

His throat thickened with an overwhelming sense of failure and loss. Only a few hours ago, it seemed he held everything that was important to him in the world in the palm of his hand. And then somehow it had all vanished so suddenly—

"I'm supposed to drop you in Amarillo," the pilot said, speaking loudly to be heard over the noise of the engine.

Apparently he'd been in radio contact with someone from the co-op. Mark was aware that the pilot had been speaking into his headset, but he hadn't paid much attention. Whatever they decided didn't make any difference to him now.

"They'll send the crane back out," the pilot went on, conveying the information he'd received. "Pick up the other chopper and bring it in."

Mark nodded, turning away from the safety of the side window and toward the front. Luckily, he didn't have to look anyone in the eye, he thought. Not yet, at least.

The mechanic had been nonjudgmental, even complimentary that he'd gotten the chopper down. And the other pilot would probably know exactly how he was feeling right now.

All he had to do was hold on through the interview with the owners at the airport. And after that…

He took a deep breath, thinking about his mother pulling the curtains over those windows every twilight. Shutting out the night. A deliberate act of will.

That's all this would amount to. Pack his bags, throw them into the back of the pickup and leave. There was nothing at the ranch for him, anyway. Coming back here had been a mistake. He had known that for a while.

So…nothing had changed. Just a matter of timing. Their decision instead of his, but the outcome was still the same.

"SO WHAT DO you think?" Jake asked, putting his arm possessively around her shoulder.

The same gesture Mark had found so offensive, Jillian thought. Just not offensive enough to suggest she not ask Jake for her ring back. Determinedly, she banished that memory and leaned tiredly against Jake's side. It wasn't where she wanted to be, but at least it was welcoming. And safe.

"I think he's going to be raring to go long before the doctor gives the okay," she said, relieved at how well Drew was doing. "He's already talking about more riding lessons."

"He did really well. Surprised me, I have to admit."

"Thanks for taking care of him. I felt guilty as sin that I wasn't here, but…all the time I knew he was in good hands."

Jake pulled her closer. "Rough day and night."

"You can't imagine," she said truthfully.

"Well, it's over now. I'm going to take you home and spoil you. And as soon as Drew is feeling up to it, the three of us can go somewhere warm and lazy. Soak up the sun. Forget—"

He stopped, but she knew what he had intended to say.

"Forget about the ranch," she finished for him.

She was too tired to be angry. Too discouraged. Maybe Jake was right. It would be the path of least resistance to give in and go along with his plans. Which, if she was completely honest, sounded tempting.

There had been way too much stress and hostility in her life lately. Drew's initial anger over the move out to the ranch. The subsequent harassment once they'd arrived. Mark...

And that was the bottom line, of course. After last night, whatever hopes she had had when she began this odyssey lay in ashes.

She couldn't believe she had let Violet talk her into that stupidly romantic quest to recapture the past. She couldn't possibly go back to being the girl she had been then. Even Mark had realized that. Why the hell hadn't she?

"Jillian? Are you okay?"

She came back to the present with a jolt. Jake was looking down at her with concern. And having gotten a glimpse at her face in the rest room mirror, she could hardly blame him.

"I'm fine. Just tired. Just...a little stressed."

"Come on. I'm taking you home and putting you to bed."

"Shouldn't we wait to talk to the doctor?"

"What for? Drew's fine. You saw that for yourself. The surgery was routine, no complications. All we're waiting for is the word that he can go home. You don't have to do that here."

She nodded, reluctantly.

"Hot shower, change of clothes," Jake began, guiding her down the corridor, away from Drew's door. "Something to eat. I think you've lost weight since you've been gone."

Less than two weeks, she thought. A period that had begun with such high hopes and ended this morning in a snow-shrouded dawn. *You can't go home again.* She had heard that all her life. Why hadn't she realized that, as with all old sayings, this one, too, contained more than a grain of truth?

HE HAD BEEN methodically throwing items into boxes and bags for almost half an hour now. Still working off the rage from the dressing down he'd taken. Stumpy hadn't been able to reach Shipley. No one connected with the co-op had known about yesterday's flight.

Shipley, in a typically Texan mindset, didn't seem upset that Mark had offered the co-op's chopper to take a neighbor to her child's sickbed. He was very upset that Mark hadn't let anyone know what he was doing. The good news was that the insurance would cover the damage.

All in all, Mark thought, he couldn't really complain about the way he'd been treated, but he'd resigned anyway. After all, it was what he'd planned to do a couple of days ago.

He had stopped by the bunkhouse on his way in, but Stumpy hadn't been there. He was hoping the old man would be back before he got ready to leave. He would like to say goodbye.

He started to close the lid of his old-fashioned, rigid-sided suitcase when something in the top slid forward, bumping softly against the edge. Hearing the noise, he stilled his hand in the act of turning the central latch. Instead, he opened the case again. Whatever he'd heard had disappeared back into the fabric pocket of the lid.

By now he remembered what the object was, and despite himself, he felt a small surge of excitement. He pulled the elastic edge of the pocket open and reached inside, removing the manila envelope he had put there himself. Almost eight years ago, he realized. Right after his father's death.

The envelope contained the papers that had been in Bo Peterson's desk the day he'd died. Mark had come home on compassionate leave, and after the funeral, he had cleaned out his father's dreary three-room apartment, boxing everything for the Salvation Army. Everything except these.

He had intended to go through them, but he had kept putting it off. He knew there was no insurance because Bo would not have been able to keep up the payments. There might have been a couple of bills, and even after all this time, Mark felt a twinge of guilt that he hadn't checked about those. Back then...

He shook his head, knowing that the issue right now

wasn't the failure of his relationship with his father. It was possible there could be something in here about his dad's financial dealings. Something that might shed light on where all the money he and Salvini borrowed had gone.

Pushing the suitcase aside, he sat down on the edge of the bed and lifted the metal prongs of the clasp. And then he hesitated, just holding the unopened envelope. There had been too many excursions into the past lately. And all of them of the emotionally painful variety.

Abruptly, without giving himself time to decide not to do this, he pulled the flap up and allowed the papers in the envelope to slide out into his hand. A couple of checks fluttered to the floor, but he ignored them.

He put the envelope on the bed beside him and began to sift through what it had contained. A couple of yellowed newspaper stories about his rodeo wins, clippings he couldn't believe his father had kept. Receipts for a variety of things, including a few visits to one of the walk-in clinics his dad had apparently visited in the days immediately preceding his death.

There was an old black-and-white snapshot of his mom, which Mark knew had been taken on the day his father had proposed. He held the photograph a moment, studying her face, surprised by how young she had looked at twenty-three.

There was also a small stack of canceled checks, held together by a rubber band. The top one was to the electric company. From the date it was obvious it was for the apartment's utilities rather than anything connected with the ranch.

He tossed the stack on the bed and ruthlessly plowed through the rest of the papers. Most were legal documents having to do with the lease on the apartment, rent for a safety-deposit box, his parents' marriage license, and birth certificates, including his own. He scanned each document as quickly and impersonally as he could.

Of course, he had no idea what he was looking for. And as he neared the bottom of the stack, he began to think this was a waste of time. Although he had plenty to waste now that he was unemployed, he gave only a cursory glance at the last few items.

When he finished, he stacked the papers together, tapping them against his knee to align the edges before he stuck them back into the envelope where they had rested, undisturbed, for the last eight years. As he stood up to put the envelope away, the checks that had floated to the floor caught his eye.

He bent, allowing the soft grunt of pain as his back protested. After all, there was no one around to hear it. He straightened, holding the checks, and put his other hand against his lower spine, pressing down against the sorest spot. He'd dig the aspirin out of his dopp kit and take a couple. It hadn't been quite four hours since the last dose, but what the hell.

He opened the envelope to stick the checks back inside, and as the top one slipped into it, the name of the recipient caught his eye. Suddenly, his tired brain kicked into overdrive. He fished around in the envelope, pulling them both back out. The recipient was the same on both of them. And the amounts...

"Son of a bitch." He said the words softly under his breath as his mind began to race.

"FOR YOU," Jake said, holding out the phone, his voice carefully neutral. "I tried to take a message, but he's insistent that he has to speak to you."

"He?" she asked.

She knew who Jake meant, of course. The question was simply a delaying tactic while she decided if she wanted to talk to Mark. If she was up to it. After the promised hot bath, food and a nap, she at least felt more human. And more rational, she admitted. Maybe Mark did, too.

Besides, it would be pretty childish to refuse to speak to the man she had just spent the night making love to. Her eyes lifted from the receiver to Jake's, wondering if he suspected what had happened between her and Mark.

There was nothing in them to confirm or deny that he

might. No emotion at all. Of course, Jake was pretty adept at hiding what he was thinking. In his business he had to be.

"Peterson," he said. "Says he needs to talk to you."

She hesitated a second longer, still trying to read what was in Jake's eyes. And trying to think what she and Mark could possibly have to say to one another that hadn't already been said.

Then suddenly, like a revelation, she realized Mark was calling to ask about Drew. She had never before had the luxury of sharing the responsibility for her son's welfare with someone else. Now that Mark knew that Drew was his, no matter the situation between Jillian and him, he would be concerned about Drew's health and safety.

She pushed herself upright, leaning back against the headboard of the bed, as she reached out to take the phone from Jake. She held the receiver, her fingers over the mouthpiece, rather obviously waiting for him to leave. Jake's lips flattened, but he didn't say anything else. Instead, he turned on his heel and walked across the room to the door. She didn't put the receiver to her ear until he had closed it behind him.

"Hello," she said, her voice a little breathless.

"How is he?" Mark asked.

"He's fine. More than ready to come home."

"Are they going to let him?"

Mark sounded surprised, but then he probably had had no experience with how quickly patients, especially young, healthy ones, were dismissed after surgery these days.

"Maybe later this afternoon. The doctors hadn't quite decided when we left the hospital."

She regretted the "we" as soon as she said it. Then she remembered that Mark had called her at Jake's. He knew she was with Jake. And why shouldn't she be? Mark had practically shoved her at him last night.

"So when are you coming back to the ranch?"

"I'm not sure," she hedged.

She was uncertain about where Mark's line of questioning

was headed. Was it triggered by a natural desire to see his son again, now that he knew? Or something else?

If she allowed herself to hope he might be asking for some other reason, it would put her right back where she had been before. Just as vulnerable and needy.

"I know what they were doing," he said, his voice softening as if he feared being overheard.

"They?"

Her mind had time to consider the rescuers this morning and the vandals at the ranch before he made the explanation.

"My dad. And yours. I know what they did with that money."

"What?" she asked, still a little confused by the abruptness with which he'd changed the subject.

"Drilling for oil." It took a second for the words to sink in, almost as if they had been spoken in a foreign language.

"They were drilling an *oil* well?" she said, incredulous.

And why wouldn't she be? After all, Mark was talking about two of the most pragmatic men she'd ever known. She couldn't imagine anyone less prone to the stars-in-the-eyes mentality necessary for wildcatting than her father and Bo Peterson.

"Hard to believe, isn't it?" Mark said.

"How do you know?"

"I found the cancelled checks."

"And you're positive that's what they were for?"

"The company's still in business. I called them this afternoon. Previous owner's dead, but the contract was still on file. The new owner thought he could put me in touch with someone who had worked on the job. If he can, I'll probably drive down there tomorrow to see what I can find out."

"There?"

"Odessa. It's a long way, but...I've got the time. So I figured why not. We might learn something interesting."

"You think maybe they were running some kind of scam?"

She was still trying to fathom that all that borrowed money

had gone to dig for oil. Of course, there *were* deposits of oil and gas in the Panhandle, but nothing had been found that would compare with what had been discovered farther south. And to believe that her father had really thought there would be—

"Company's as solid as they come," he said. "They've been in business a long time, especially for the business they're in."

Even after Violet's legacy, she had thought the amount Bo and her father had wasted was enormous. And for ranchers who had skimped and struggled all their lives just to get by…

"According to the contract, my dad went to them," Mark continued. "They didn't come up here and try to sell the two of them a bill of goods. Everything seems open and above-board."

"Then…someone else maybe. Scammed them, I mean. Someone must have made them think there was oil there."

"Then it must have been someone pretty damned convincing," Mark said. "Because whatever else they were, neither one was a fool. Or gullible." He was right, of course, which made this even harder to believe.

"So now we know," she said.

It didn't change anything, of course. Instead of wasting the money they had borrowed on some hybrid that had proven unsuitable for the country or on some other scheme involving cattle operations, their fathers had drilled for oil.

She couldn't imagine what had convinced them to begin, but she *could* understand the mentality that had kept them pouring good money after bad. They had probably gotten in so deep that if the well didn't come in, they knew everything was lost. Their land would be gone. Their families homeless. They couldn't afford to give up.

Maybe they had figured that once they reached the point of no return financially, they just had to keep borrowing to allow the company to drill deeper and deeper. Or maybe try in another, more promising location. Whatever they had thought about this idiotic venture, the outcome was preordained.

They had borrowed money they couldn't repay, and then the scheme had bottomed out. Her father had run out in the middle of the night, leaving his creditors without their money and Mark's father to face them alone. No wonder he had changed their name, she thought bitterly. He would never have been able to hold his head up again after that.

"I can pay some of them back," she said. After she sold the ranch, of course. "That's the least I can do."

After all, she acknowledged with a trace of bitterness, the inheritance she had gotten from Violet hadn't quite accomplished what she had hoped it would. It might as well be used to right some of the wrongs her father's uncharacteristic dream chasing had done to the people of this community.

"That's not your responsibility," Mark said. "Besides, most of them got a big chunk of their money back when the ranch was sold. And remember, they didn't have to make those loans. Maybe if they hadn't been so damn willing to do that—"

"They were the victims, Mark. Not my dad. Not yours."

After a moment he said, "I know. And you're right. I've still got the list of my dad's creditors and the amount each of them claimed he owed them. After the foreclosure, most of it was nickel-and-dime stuff. It might take me the next twenty years—"

"I didn't mean to imply that *you* should try to pay back what your father owed," she said.

There was a long heartbeat of silence.

"Just that you should. What's the difference, Jillian?"

The difference was that, thanks to Violet, she could afford to do that. And Mark couldn't. She wasn't about to say that to him, however.

"I'm going to sell the ranch," she said instead. "Pay off the people I can locate."

It was obvious that whatever she had been hoping for when she had come back wasn't going to happen. There had been time enough for Mark to make some comment about what had occurred between them after the crash. The fact that he hadn't spoke volumes. And of course there had also been no apology for the hurtful things he had said afterward.

"Tyler talk you into selling out?"

She laughed, shaking her head at the fact that he hadn't yet figured anything out.

"He won't be unhappy about it, but that's not the reason. I just came to the realization that...it wasn't working."

"If I'm what's 'not working' for you here, then I guess you should know I won't be around."

"Because of the crash?"

"Let's just say the co-op wasn't pleased. As soon as I figure this out, I'll be leaving."

"Figure what out?"

"Why two reasonable men would sink everything they owned, plus everything they could beg or borrow, into a wildcat well."

Because they had believed there was oil there, Jillian thought. And they had had to work together because they must have been told the deposit ran under their adjoining properties.

"Most people get wild-eyed when it comes to that much money," she said.

"There was nothing 'wild-eyed' about my dad. Believe me."

She did. She just didn't understand why taking this any further was so important. After all, Mark had solved the mystery of what they had done with the money. It was long gone, thrown away on the kind of dream that had lured plenty of others to destruction.

"Something or someone convinced him that there's oil here," he went on.

"Even if they did, what can it possibly matter now?"

"Maybe there is," he said.

Her mouth opened slightly in shock, and it was a couple of seconds before she realized it had. She closed it, shaking her head, although he couldn't see the gesture. She didn't even know where to begin with that remark. It was bad enough that their fathers had been bitten by the get-rich-quick bug, but Mark...

"And you're going to borrow money to try to find it?" she said, letting him hear the sarcasm.

"I'd have to, wouldn't I? Since I don't have any."

"I didn't mean that," she said evenly, hanging on to her temper because she understood now, better than she had last night, that the money really was an issue with him.

He let the silence stretch between them again, and when he spoke, thankfully it was on a very different subject.

"Will you give Drew a message for me?"

"Of course," she said, wondering belatedly if Mark understood that Drew didn't know about their relationship yet. And that she hadn't decided whether or not he should.

"Tell him...tell him I was really looking forward to the riding lessons." His voice was very soft, and from something in his tone, she knew that wasn't all he wanted to say. "Tell him I'm really sorry I'm not going to be around to give them to him."

"Okay," she said, her throat constricting.

"And tell him I said to take good care of his mom. Because she's very special. And because...as much as I'd like to, I won't be around to take care of her."

Afraid her own voice would reveal how moved she was by those simple words, she swallowed against the force of that emotion, trying to gather control before she answered. As she did, she heard the distinctive click of the connection being broken.

"Mark?" she said sharply.

Obviously not quickly enough. And despite the fact that she knew he was gone, she held the phone a long time, pressing the receiver against her chest, her eyes closed against her tears.

CHAPTER FIFTEEN

SHE STILL DIDN'T understand what she was doing here, Jillian admitted as she pulled the rental car into the yard of the Peterson ranch. Mark had told her he was leaving. Since he was no longer employed by the co-op, he didn't even have the legal right to be on these premises, which had once been his home.

She had come here, however, because she didn't know where else to start looking for him. He had mentioned going down to Odessa, which would be at least a two-day trip. If he had, he should be back by now. If he were coming back.

She turned her head, considering the child asleep in the seat beside her. His skin was pale, throwing the freckles across the bridge of his nose into stark relief. And the smudges that lay under the fan of dark lashes were pronounced enough to cause her heart to squeeze. She resisted the urge to push the fall of glossy hair off his forehead. The gesture might wake him, and she could almost hear his protest against her babying.

Although the doctor had okayed Drew making this trip, she felt a twinge of guilt that she had brought him so soon after his surgery. She couldn't leave him in Fort Worth, though. Not after she had finally told Jake the truth—that no matter what happened with Mark, she now knew she could never marry him.

She debated whether to wake Drew. But she would probably be back out in a minute. Mark wasn't here, she told herself with the same grim pessimism that had dogged every mile she had driven from the airport at Amarillo.

Before she left the ranch she could at least check with Stumpy Winters and see if he knew anything. Maybe Mark had left a forwarding address. If he hadn't, she supposed she could leave a message for him with the old man. Other than that…

Refusing to give in to the despair that had haunted her since that phone conversation, she put her fingers around the door handle, easing it open and then closing it as soundlessly as she could. Through the window, she took one last look at her son. Then she turned and ran across the yard to what had once been the Peterson home. She hadn't bothered to put on her jacket, which was lying on the back seat, and the winter wind cut like a knife.

She ran up the steps and crossed the narrow porch, the sound of her footsteps loud against its planks. She tapped on the door, listening for movement inside. There was none, so she knocked again, more loudly this time.

Then, for some reason, her hand closed over the doorknob. She turned it, fully expecting the door to be locked. The knob moved, however, and, almost by itself, the door swung inward. It was already twilight, and the shadows were deep inside the darkened front room it revealed.

She must have been in this house a thousand times, but nothing looked familiar. Or welcoming. Actually, it felt anything but welcoming. She shivered, reacting either to the cold around her or to the empty darkness that stretched in front.

"Hello?" she called.

There was no answer. No sound at all, except the moan of the wind blowing endlessly across the flat plains.

"Looking for Mark?"

Her heart leaped, reacting to the unexpectedness of the question before she had time to place the voice. She turned her head in the direction from which it had come and found Stumpy Winters standing at the far end of the porch.

"Didn't recognize the car," he went on, not waiting for her answer. "Thought I better check on who was up here. We don't get many visitors, especially not this time of year."

"It's a rental," she explained. "Is Mark back?"

"Back?" he repeated. The dusty black hat he wore shaded his face, making it difficult to see his eyes in the fading light.

"From Odessa?" she clarified.

Stumpy shook his head, the slow movement communicating his puzzlement. "Didn't know he'd gone. Been gone myself. 'Course the chopper ain't here, so I guess I should have figured Mark was off running an errand for the boss."

Apparently Stumpy didn't know about the crash. Or any of what had followed. "No, this was...something personal," she said. "He was going to drive down."

"All the way to Odessa? What in the world for?"

Mark hadn't told her not to tell anyone what he was doing, not even when he'd made that ridiculous comment about there possibly being something to what their fathers had believed. Her own inclination, however, was not to talk about what Mark had found out, if for no other reason than to protect any reputation her father had left as a rational man.

"He had some business. I'm not sure exactly what it involved," she said. Even to her own ears that seemed evasive.

"That a fact," Stumpy said, sounding interested. "Wonder why he didn't take the chopper."

That explanation seemed a little complicated to cover in a few minutes, especially standing out in the cold. And really it was Mark's place to give Stumpy the news that he was leaving.

"Do you think we could go inside?" She wrapped her arms around her body as if she had just noticed the chill. "I want to leave Mark a note. Or, if you see him first, I'd appreciate it if you'd tell him to call me. Tell him I'm back at my ranch."

She wasn't sure why she'd added the last. Stumpy didn't have any reason to think she would be anywhere else. He hadn't talked to Mark and knew nothing about what had happened since they'd flown out of here four days ago. Thinking that, she realized for the first time how strange it was he hadn't asked her about Drew.

"Sure we can," he said, starting across the porch. "Go on in. Switch is to the right of the door. Guess you know that as well as I do. You been in this house plenty a' times before."

By then he was beside her. He reached inside, flicking on a light that illuminated the front room, destroying the shadows. And that inexplicable sense of unease she had felt standing on the threshold, staring into its darkness, disappeared.

Feeling slightly ridiculous about her previous apprehension, she stepped inside. There had been changes, she realized. After ten years and who knew how many owners, that was to be expected. But there were also things that were exactly the same, producing a slight sense of déjà vu.

"There's a notepad by the phone in the kitchen," the old man said. He moved past her to lead the way.

That room, too, when they reached it, was subtly different, but she was able to walk over to the wall-mounted phone without having to think about its location. She tore a sheet off the pad that was hanging beside it and slipped the stub of a pencil out of the holder. When she turned, Stumpy was watching her.

"Been a long time," he said.

"Since I've been here? I guess it has," she agreed.

Her eyes found the wooden table where she had eaten dinner that last night with Mark and his father. She had been nervous because Mark had intended to tell his father they'd fallen in love. As tense as she was, the evening probably wouldn't have been pleasant, no matter how Bo Peterson had treated her. And his treatment hadn't been kind. Of course, given what she now knew about his worries that summer—

"What in the world you think Mark is doing down in Odessa?"

She lifted her gaze to focus on the old man. That was the second time he'd asked that question. Just natural curiosity? Or was he becoming a little forgetful with age?

She shook her head in response, at the same time lifting her shoulders in a small shrug. She crossed the room to the table. She laid the paper on it, and then, faced with its intimidating blankness, tried to think what she could possibly say to Mark.

"Why didn't he take the chopper?" the old man asked.

She looked up, surprised to find that he was now directly across the table from her, near enough that he would be able to see what she wrote. It wasn't that she minded him seeing her note. It just seemed strange. Most people would have kept their distance in order to provide some privacy.

"There was a problem with the helicopter during our flight to Fort Worth. Mark had to put it down in one of the canyons."

"Emergency landing? Bet that was scary."

"Especially since the turbine froze and then came apart. There was also some structural damage from the landing. You weren't able to get in touch with Shipley to tell him Mark was taking me to see Drew?" she asked, remembering that this was the reason the co-op owner had been so angry.

"Never did," Stumpy said. "Didn't figure it'd matter too much, your boy being sick and all."

"It probably wouldn't have—except for the crash," she admitted. "I don't think the co-op was too pleased with Mark because of that."

"Probably putting this one together with his other crash."

"He told you about that?"

She was surprised Mark would share an experience that had been so traumatic for him with the old man. Of course, he had known Stumpy almost his entire life. They both had.

"He tells me most everything. Not about Odessa, though. Didn't tell me about that. He probably would if he were here."

Again that sense of unease whispered along her spine. She didn't answer, lowering her eyes to the still-blank piece of paper before her. The message didn't have to be profound, she told herself. Just tell Mark that she needed to see him and that she was home. *Home.* The word echoed inside her head. It was strange how quickly the ranch had again become home to her.

"You know, don't you?"

She glanced up and realized that Stumpy had moved around the table to her side. He was so close she could smell him. The faintest miasma of age and dust clung to his body, along with a not unpleasant whiff of oiled leather and tobacco.

"Know what?" she asked, her heart beginning to beat a little irregularly. There was something strange in the dark eyes. Something…not quite right.

"That's why you come back here after all this time. Your daddy was afeared, but you ain't. Always knew you had backbone, Jilly. I didn't take you for a fool, though."

It took her seconds too long to figure it out. To put what he was saying together with what had been going on. And, more important, to put it together with what she saw in his eyes.

Before she had, he reached out, his fingers closing around her wrist. She jerked against his hold, trying to pull her arm free as her heart rate soared.

"What are you doing?" she demanded, twisting her wrist back and forth. "What's the matter with you, Stumpy? Let me go."

"You came here to take what's mine. Both of you. You're in on it together. And those two old bastards put you up to it. Didn't have guts enough to do it themselves, so they do it behind my back. Using you two."

To take what's mine… Again the realization came too slowly. He meant the land she had bought. Stumpy had once owned her ranch. A long time ago. Long before her father had.

"I don't know what you're talking about," she said.

She was beginning to, however, and it terrified her.

"Shut up your lying, girl."

"I don't know—"

His left hand, the one that wasn't wrapped tightly around

her wrist, exploded across her mouth with a speed that shocked her. She was almost too stunned by the unexpectedness of the blow to feel pain. At least not yet.

He might be old, but Stumpy Winters had done backbreaking physical labor all his life. His wiriness hid a strength that she was just now beginning to recognize. And to fear.

Instinctively, she put her free hand up to her cut lip, the salt-tinged taste of blood seeping into her throat. Wary now, and obediently silent, she held her fingers against the corner of her mouth, her eyes locked on his. The only sound in the room was the harshness of her breathing. Until...

"Mom?"

They turned at the same time, both of them considering the boy who stood in the doorway. His dark eyes were as questioning as his tone. Then, as they focused on her trembling fingers, still pressed against her mouth, they widened in disbelief.

"Run," she ordered, the single syllable holding every ounce of parental authority she could muster. It wasn't enough to overcome the shock of seeing her injured, captive. Terrified.

"Get over here, boy," Stumpy ordered the stunned child, raising his hand as if he intended to hit her again.

"No," she protested. "Get out, Drew. He—"

She never completed the sentence. Winters's hand struck once more. Her head rocked backward with the force of this blow, and involuntary tears started in her eyes. When she blinked them away, she saw that instead of running away, Drew had crossed the room, thin arms flailing at Stumpy's body. The old man turned his back to the child, shoulders hunched against the blows, but his clawlike fingers never loosened their grip on her wrist.

"Let her go!" Drew yelled. "You let my mom go!"

His hands pounded ineffectually against Stumpy's back. The old man attempted to ward off the boy with his free arm, while he controlled Jillian with the other. Afraid that he might injure Drew, Jillian frantically added her own blows to those of the boy's. At the same time she continued to twist and turn the arm he'd captured, desperately trying to wrest it from his hold.

She didn't know what Winters hoped to accomplish. Of course, if she was right about what she thought she had seen in his eyes, that mad malevolent gleam, he wasn't thinking. He was just reacting to what he perceived as a threat to his own grandly insane scheme. *As insane as my father's,* her mind suggested as she struggled. Because this, too, was all about that mythical oil Bo Peterson and her dad had bankrupted themselves to find.

Unexpectedly, with her last violent jerk, her forearm slipped free. At the same time Stumpy lost his grip on her wrist, he turned and viciously shoved the child away from him. Drew was propelled backward, the edge of the table slamming into his right side. With a scream of pain, he slipped onto the floor, sliding downward as if in slow motion.

Jillian was beside him almost before he fell. She knelt, putting her hand against his cheek to turn his face toward her. Drew opened his eyes, and she took a quick breath in relief. If he had lost consciousness, it had only been for a few seconds.

His gaze met hers, and in it she saw the same emotions she was feeling. The fear and uncertainty. And the questions.

"Get up."

Their gazes were drawn back to Stumpy by the command. He was holding an old-fashioned Colt revolver, its muzzle trained on the center of Drew's chest. He must have concealed the weapon in the pocket of the long, duster-type coat he was wearing.

"Both of you," he added, gesturing them up with the gun.

Jillian considered his eyes, reading in them only what she had seen before. This wasn't the man she had known all her life. This was someone who had gone over the edge of sanity. Someone who was now pointing a pistol at her son.

Afraid to take her attention off Winters, she put one arm around Drew's shoulders, and with her other hand supporting his elbow, she helped the child to stand. She heard his gasp of pain in response, but he made no verbal protest as he got to his feet.

"Whatever you want, Stumpy, you can have it," she said, forcing her voice to calmness. Coaxing. Reassuring. "No one is trying to take anything away from you, I promise you that."

"You already did. All I needed was for the price to go down a little bit more, and I'da had enough saved up to make the down payment. Then here you come with all your money and bought the place right out from under me. There's only one reason you'd a' done that, Jilly. Only one reason for anyone to a' bought that worthless piece of land. And I know what it is. Your daddy told you. That's why you come back here."

"My dad and I haven't spoken in almost ten years," she said. "He hasn't told me *anything*. You're wrong, Stumpy. So wrong."

"So why'd you buy that ranch?" he demanded. "Other than that oil, it's worthless. Ain't nobody made a go of it."

"I came back because Mark was here," she said.

Watching his face, she realized that he was at least thinking about that possibility. She had no idea how much Winters had known about their previous relationship, so whether or not he would believe her now...

"You telling me you spent all that money 'cause you wanted to see Mark again."

"Because...Drew's his son," she said. The secret she had kept so long was finally revealed. In a way that made her wonder if Drew would ever be able to forgive her for not telling him before. "I wanted Drew to know his father. I had hoped..."

"Mom?" Drew said softly, drawing her gaze to his face, despite the need to watch Stumpy's every move.

Drew's eyes were wide with something that looked almost like wonder. Or maybe hope. Joy. And in spite of what was going on, she nodded, smiling at him through a sudden veil of tears.

"You were hoping Mark'd still have the hots for you," the old man said crudely.

She turned back to him, and again she could see the thoughts moving behind the narrowed eyes. He was trying to decide whether to believe her. And at the same time she was trying to decide whether to keep talking, to keep trying to convince him she knew nothing about the oil, or to just shut up and let him think about what she'd said.

"I can't let you go, you know," he said, and hearing the tone of that, almost pitying, she felt her heart sink. "You tell somebody, and it's all over. They'll get it before I do."

"I won't tell anybody anything," she promised. "I don't know anything to tell," she amended.

"I wish I believed that. I really do, but if you didn't know, the two of you, then Mark wouldn't a' gone to Odessa. And you wouldn't a' lied to me about why he was down there."

"I don't know why he went. I told you the truth."

"You never could lie worth a damn, Jilly girl. You still can't. Your eyes give it all away. They are now."

"You're wrong, Stumpy," she said fervently. "Please don't do anything you'll regret."

"That's what I told your daddy. He knew I meant it, too. Only thing was, I didn't figure he'd just pull up stakes and run."

Run. That's exactly what her father had done, she realized. He had run away and hidden his family from this man. This threat. He had changed their names and left behind everything he had worked so hard for in order to protect his family.

And that's why he had been furious when he found out she had called Bo Peterson. He wasn't angry that she was trying to contact the father of her baby. He was terrified that they would be found by this madman.

In that final, terrible confrontation that had led her to leaving home, they had both been acting out of fear, but of very different kinds. Her fear was that Mark wouldn't be able to find her, and his that Stumpy Winters would.

"I came back to find Mark," she said again. It was the only argument she had. And it was the truth.

"Then tell me what Mark's doing in Odessa."

"Finding out all about a geologist who disappeared up here ten years ago," Mark said.

The old man's head swiveled in shock toward the sound of that quiet voice, the muzzle of the revolver following its movement. His eyes squinted, seeking to distinguish the features of the speaker standing in the shadows by the back door.

"You shouldn't be sticking your nose into this," Stumpy said, his voice almost plaintive. He sounded as if he really did regret that Mark had found out what he'd done.

"There was a newspaper clipping about his unexplained disappearance in the drilling company's file. Nobody ever found hide nor hair of the body, but they knew that when he left Odessa, one of the places he'd been planning to come was up here. You killed him to keep him from telling anyone else about the oil, didn't you, Stumpy?"

"That was *my* land. Been in my family for generations. And it broke their hearts. Then that bastard told Salvini about the oil, and I knew somebody else was gonna get the good out of *my* land. The only good there ever was about that place."

"And you couldn't stand that."

"It wasn't right. You can see that. It just wasn't right."

Mark nodded as if that made sense. He had taken a couple of steps into the room, moving away from the concealing shadows by the door through which he had entered.

As they talked, Jillian realized that the old man's attention was completely focused now on Mark's advance. It was as if Stumpy had forgotten about her and Drew. Forgotten they were even here. And it was up to her to take advantage of that.

Her arm was still around Drew's shoulders. As unobtrusively as she could, she began inching the two of them back and to the side, edging around the table that was between them and the door that led to the front of the house.

"But you thought it was right to kill that man?" Mark asked, his voice as soft as it had been before.

"Salvini wouldn't quit. I knew Bo wanted to, but Salvini said he'd gone too far to turn back. He'd a' kept digging up there if he'd a' had to shovel that dirt hisself."

"So you figured you had to scare him off."

Jillian wondered if Mark was guessing or if he really knew what had happened all those years ago. At least he was keeping the old man occupied, she thought gratefully, taking another step backward and silently drawing Drew with her.

"What'd you do to convince him, Stumpy? How'd you get Salvini to run off?"

Stumpy laughed, the sound harsh, but she could tell he was pleased with himself. Pleased with whatever he'd done.

"Sent him an anonymous note and a map. X marks the spot. Told him to go take a look at what was waiting for him and his."

"And what was that?" Mark asked, leading the old man on by the sincerity of his voice. Of course, he probably was just as interested in the story as he sounded. Vitally interested.

"That bastard's body."

"The geologist?"

"He didn't have no right to tell anybody about *my* oil. I killed him clean, but that ain't how that body looked when I got through with it." Stumpy's laugh was filled with delight.

"And Salvini ran, just like you thought he would."

"Took off in the middle of the night, tail between his legs, like a scalded dog."

"What'd you do with the body?"

"There's lots of places to get rid of a body around here. If you know what you're doing. If you know the land."

"And you do."

"Every inch of it," Stumpy said. "Lived here all my life."

Again Mark nodded. His eyes had never left Stumpy's face, but there was no doubt in Jillian's mind that he was aware of what she was doing. If he could keep the old man's attention for only a few more seconds…

"And then you tried to run Jillian away, too, didn't you?"

"You know all that now. You know it was me."

The old man sounded as if he were tiring of the questions. His eyes flicked toward her and Drew. Despite the fact that they had moved several feet away from where they had been before, he made no comment. And thankfully the muzzle of the pistol didn't shift in their direction.

"And the windmill? Was that you, too?"

When Mark asked the question, Jillian found she was holding her breath, expecting Stumpy to lose patience at any moment.

"I just wanted to scare her off. Figured she'd run like her daddy. I didn't know that the two of you already knew."

"And the chopper? Did you loosen that oil line, Stumpy?"

"It wasn't hard to figure out if you know something about engines. I know a little bit about most things on this ranch."

"But that wasn't supposed to be just a scare, was it? You tried to kill us. Just like you killed the geologist."

The old man didn't answer for a moment, the depth of the breath he took strong enough to lift his narrow shoulders.

"Always liked you, boy, but you started sticking your nose into stuff. Trying to find out who your daddy owed money to. And why. Made me wonder what you knew. What she knew."

"I think we've heard enough."

Startled, Jillian turned and found Ronnie Cameron standing in the doorway. He, too, was holding a gun. Compared with the long-barreled Colt Stumpy held, it appeared undersize.

And only now, seeing the sheriff, did Jillian realize that Mark's prolonged questioning had been deliberate. They needed Stumpy to make the confessions he had just uttered.

Ronnie had been waiting within earshot while Mark tried to draw him out.

Apparently Stumpy realized what was going on at the same time she did. His attention, too, had swung toward the door when the sheriff spoke. He had brought that long gray barrel around with him. And it was trained again on Drew.

"Don't nobody move," he said. "I ain't come this far to let this all go now. I been in Amarillo, getting some financing lined up...."

"It's over, Stumpy," Mark warned. "Don't make it worse."

"It can't be no worse, boy. You saw to that. The state can't kill me but once. I got nothing left to lose."

"I do," Mark said softly, his eyes for the first time meeting Jillian's and then falling to fasten a long, silent heartbeat on his son. "It's over, Stumpy. Let it go."

"Put the gun down *now,*" Ronnie Cameron said, his voice demanding, especially compared with Mark's reasoned tone.

"You move on out of that doorway, Ronnie," Stumpy ordered. "Get over there with him." He jerked his head toward Mark. "You do what I say, and nobody gets hurt. You don't...I've already told you, I got nothing to lose," he said again.

"You aren't going to shoot that boy," the sheriff said.

"Mark."

Jillian's voice was pleading. She wasn't sure how rational the old man was. Judging by the things he'd done, the sabotage of the windmill and the attempt to bring down the helicopter with both of them aboard, she wasn't nearly as sure as Ronnie that he wouldn't pull the trigger. It was a chance she couldn't take.

"Let him go, Cameron," Mark said to the sheriff. "Get out of the way and just let him go."

"I can't do that," Ronnie said. "You know I can't. He just confessed to one murder and to attempting to bring about a couple more. I got a duty to protect the citizens of this county."

"Then start with those two," Mark said, his eyes on Jillian and Drew. "Let him go, damn it."

"Put the gun down, Winters," Cameron blustered instead. "You aren't walking out of this house, so just get that out of your head. You fire that gun at anybody, and you'll be dead before the shot stops echoing."

Jillian could feel the tension escalating in the small room, her own included. The sheriff was laying down ultimatums, forcing the old man into a corner. Ronnie was stubborn enough, and self-important enough, not to back down if Stumpy refused.

Besides, Stumpy was right. He had nothing to lose by trying to shoot his way out. The old cowboy would probably prefer a bullet to that long incarceration while he waited for execution.

Her eyes were still locked on Mark's, but she didn't say his name again. He knew what was going on. He understood the personalities of the two men better than she did.

"Mom?" Drew whispered, edging backward, away from the gun, until he was pressed as close to her body as he could get.

Her hands tightened over his shoulders, trying to reassure him. She knew he was experiencing the same thing she was—the quiet-before-the-storm feeling that permeated the atmosphere. They were all waiting for the next move, wondering whose it would be.

"Get out of the way, Cameron," Mark said again.

The sheriff shook his head. Instead, he took a step toward the old man, his free hand outstretched. "Give me that gun."

"You want his blood on your hands, Ronnie?" Stumpy asked.

"It won't be on my hands. You pull that trigger, and you're the one who'll go down as a child killer. And then I'll shoot you like the mad dog you are. Now give me that gun, damn it."

Ronnie took a step forward. Automatically Jillian's eyes

followed him. At least they did until a sudden clang and clamor from the other side of the kitchen distracted them.

Mark had swept the pots and pans stacked on the shelf above the stove down on top of it. The ungodly noise was unexpected enough that they all turned automatically toward it. All of them—including Stumpy Winters.

And by the time the muzzle of the Colt he held in his gnarled fingers had swung away from Drew, Mark had taken a couple of running steps and launched himself toward the old man. He was still in midair when Stumpy fired, the gunshot reverberating in the enclosed space as loudly as the echoes of the falling cookware had only seconds before.

Mark hit Stumpy with enough force to throw him backward into the table. The front legs broke under their weight. Still entangled, they slid off the slanting surface and onto the floor.

Positioned on the far side of the table, Jillian couldn't see what was happening. She could hear the sounds of blows being struck. Once she saw the Colt lifted high enough to be visible above the edge of the broken table. Both Mark's hand and Stumpy's were on its stock as they struggled for control.

Finally, she regained enough presence of mind to turn Drew and push him through the doorway and into the front room. The sheriff, who had stepped forward, was in a position to see what was happening with the two men fighting on the floor, but he wasn't attempting to intervene.

By the time Jillian had gotten Drew out of the room and realized that she herself could intervene, it ended, as shockingly as it had begun. The sound of a gunshot echoed again, filling the room with the faint scent of cordite.

CHAPTER SIXTEEN

JILLIAN'S HEART crowded her throat, making it hard to breathe. Stumpy's shots had been fired at close range, close enough that she couldn't imagine how both of them could miss. If anything happened to Mark...

She tried to push past the sheriff to get to him. Ronnie put out his arm, barring her way. His weapon, which he hadn't used during the confrontation, was still held out in front of him. Terrified that he might be able to see more than she could—maybe more than she could bear to see—she hesitated, obeying, at least temporarily, his denial.

Finally Mark's hand reached upward, his fingers fastening over the top of the broken table. He used it to pull himself to his feet. He stood, head down, swaying almost drunkenly. During those few seconds, the echo of the gunshot had faded away, and the room had returned to that eerie, prestorm stillness.

Jillian pushed by Ronnie and put her arm around Mark's waist, offering support. He turned his head, looking down at her as if he had forgotten there was anyone else in the room. Then he gathered her close to his side and put his lips against her hair.

Unhurt, she realized, finally remembering to draw a breath. Apparently neither of the shots had struck him, although she still couldn't see how that was possible. She said a quick prayer of thanksgiving for that miracle before she allowed her gaze to fall to the body on the floor.

Stumpy Winters's hand was still wrapped around the stock

of his gun, his finger on the trigger. There was a dark, bluing hole in his temple.

She turned away from the sight, hiding her eyes against the soft chamois of Mark's shirt. After a moment, his other arm came around her, pulling her into his chest.

"It's over," he said, the words little more than a whisper.

"I didn't see how he could miss," she whispered.

Stumpy had fired at point-blank range as Mark made that reckless and heroic leap, deliberately drawing the old man's aim away from Drew. And in that split second, Jillian had truly believed she'd lost him. Mark's life in exchange for their son's.

"I don't think he wanted to hit me," Mark said. "I think he did exactly what he meant to do."

The old man had taken his own life instead of taking the life of the man he'd helped to raise. A man he'd put up on his first horse. A man he had welcomed back home, at a time when Mark had desperately needed a home and a friend.

Maybe it was one thing to cut a bolt on a ladder or to loosen an oil line when you wouldn't be around to see the results. In his madness Stumpy had apparently been willing to do those things, leaving the outcome of his actions to fate or to chance. Evidently he had found it was another thing entirely to shoot in cold blood a man who had been your friend.

"Come on," she said. Her arm still around his waist, she urged Mark away from the old man's body, turning him toward the door that led to the front.

"I better go call the office," Ronnie said, his eyes wide. "Let 'em know to get the coroner out here. And we'll need you both to come in and answer some questions."

Mark nodded. Jillian didn't bother to respond, remembering that Cameron hadn't done a thing while Mark was struggling with Stumpy for control of the gun.

The sheriff wheeled, putting his weapon away as he hurried out to his car and his radio. As soon as he disappeared, Mark laughed, the sound bitter.

"This will make Cameron's year. He's got himself something to talk about. Something he can let everyone in forty miles know about. In confidence, of course," he said caustically.

"It'll be interesting to see the version of the story he puts out," Jillian said as they moved into the front room, still arm in arm. All the silly things that had come between them seemed to have been destroyed by the danger that had just past.

"Is he dead?" Drew asked.

Apparently he had gone no farther than the other side of the doorway when she'd pushed him out of the kitchen. Jillian put her hand on his shoulder, trying to draw him into the embrace she and Mark shared. There was an unspoken resistance to that inclusion. The small shoulders stiffened, and Drew's eyes, too wide and dark, fastened on his father's face.

"I didn't kill him, Drew," Mark said, "if that's what you're thinking. Stumpy shot himself. That was the way he chose to end this, rather than be sent to prison for what he'd done."

The boy nodded, his throat working, and then he asked, "Is that true? What Mom said? About you being my dad?"

Obviously this question was far more important to him than what had happened to Stumpy. Mark's eyes found hers and held them briefly. Then he released her, stepping out of her embrace and stooping down so he was eye level with his son. Balancing on his toes, he put his hands on Drew's shoulders.

"What your mom said is the truth. I didn't know about it until a few days ago. Your mom thought I knew. She had her reasons, good reasons, for thinking that, but…I swear to you, Drew, I didn't know. I never knew you existed until the two of you moved out here. And even then…" The quiet words faltered. Mark would never be insensitive enough to use the boy's size as an excuse for not realizing Drew was his son.

After a few nerve-racking seconds spent studying his father's eyes, Drew nodded, apparently accepting that explanation. "So...now what?" he asked.

The pertinent question. Trust Drew to cut through all the rest of the unanswered ones to ask it, Jillian thought. Again, Mark looked up at her.

"That's up to your mom. Where we go from here."

Drew's eyes fastened on her face, and the too blatant hope in them almost broke her heart. "Mom?"

"Hey," she said, trying for a tone that was light enough not to reveal her reaction to that hope, "don't look at me. I'm the one who moved us out here in the first place. The whole reason for doing that was to reconnect with your dad. Besides," she said, turning to Mark, challenging him, "*you're* the one who has problems with the situation."

"Problems?" Drew repeated. "What kind of problems?"

Mark held Jillian's eyes a second or two longer before he turned to face Drew. "Not with you," he said. "I don't want you to ever think anything like that. But...there are a few things your mom and I have to work out."

"Like what?"

"Like money, for example. Jake Tyler, for another."

"Money?" Drew repeated. "What's that got to do with anything? Mom's got plenty. And as for Jake...I told you she gave him his ring back. What more do you need to know?"

"Maybe whether or not she regrets doing that."

"She doesn't," Jillian said truthfully. "The only thing I regret is that I didn't have the courage, or the good sense, to do this years ago. To come find you, I mean."

"Why didn't you?" Drew asked.

"Maybe because I was too busy looking after you," she said, reaching out to touch his hair. He moved his head enough to avoid the gesture.

"I told you, your mom thought I already knew," Mark said, obviously reading, as she had, the anger in that avoidance.

"And she thought you wouldn't care about your own son? That was kind of dumb, wasn't it?" Drew asked, looking up at her again. "I mean...you knew him and everything."

"Don't talk to your mother that way," Mark said. "She made her decisions based on what she knew at that time. And there were a lot of things going on that neither of us understood."

Drew nodded, again seeming to accept the explanation. At least for now. Jillian knew he'd have more questions about what had happened. It was natural that he'd want to know what had kept his family apart for so long.

Family. As the word *home* had earlier, this one triggered an emotional response she hadn't expected. They were a family, the three of them, even if they had never lived as one before. And it seemed way past time they did.

"Where will we live? Here? Or at our house?" Drew asked.

Without answering, Mark placed one hand on the boy's shoulder, using it to steady himself as he stood. Jillian had seen the carefully controlled grimace as he pushed upward.

"Are you okay?" she asked.

"Long drive."

And a chopper crash. Landing on a table hard enough to break it. Rolling around on the floor.

Rather than mentioning any of those things, Jillian put her arm around his waist again, leaning against his strength. A strength that would always be there for her and for Drew, just as it had been when Stumpy Winters had threatened them. Drew was right. Why hadn't she realized all those years ago that he would never have ignored her message?

"We can talk about that later, Drew. Work the logistics out," Mark said. "For right now...let's just go home."

Again the word reverberated in her heart. *Home.* That was exactly where she wanted to be. And it didn't matter where that was physically, as long as these two were also there.

There for one another. They would be. Drew was right.

about that, too. She knew this man, and she knew she could trust him to look after the two of them.

"Can we go riding this afternoon?" Drew asked, falling into step on the other side of his father as they slowly crossed the front room. "I want to show you what Jake taught me."

Mark put his hand on the center of the boy's back, and then slid it across to curl his fingers around his shoulder, pulling him close to his side just as he had Jillian.

"That might be pushing it," he said. "I've got a sore back and you've just had surgery. Maybe we better wait a few days."

The sound Drew made was both rude and expressive.

"That's enough, cowboy," Mark said. "There's no hurry about the riding. We'll have plenty of time for that. And time for everything else," he promised, his voice softening as he smiled down at the boy.

Then he turned his head, dropping a kiss on the top of Jillian's. "All the time in the world," he whispered, the promise loud enough for her ears alone. "And I swear this time we aren't going to waste a second of it."

"I THINK he's finally asleep," Jillian said, coming into the den. "Drew doesn't usually make such a fuss about bedtime. To be fair, there's been a lot of excitement today—not all of it conducive to sleep."

"You think he's upset about Stumpy's death?" Mark asked.

Her figure was silhouetted against the hall light before she flicked off the switch. Now there was only the light of the fire, low enough that the den was dim and shadowed.

As she moved across the room, he realized she had changed into a pair of well-worn jeans, which fitted her legs like a second skin, and a loose, faded sweatshirt. It was probably her normal at-home attire, at least here at the ranch.

Home. The word echoed in his brain. Although he'd only been here with Jillian and Drew for a few hours, this was already beginning to feel like home. Maybe too much so.

"I don't think he's as upset as he would've been if he'd known Stumpy better," she said, stopping at the fireplace to add a log to the fire. "And he didn't actually see what happened."

Regrettably Mark had, and if he wasn't careful, the image of the old man's body would flash in his brain, even when he wasn't thinking about the events of the afternoon. It had happened during supper and then again when Jillian had left to put Drew to bed.

He watched her replace the screen in front of the blaze, which crackled with renewed life. She stood, dusting her hands on her jeans and then looking down into the fire as if evaluating it.

"I think I've waited long enough for you," he said.

She turned her head to smile at him, and then she walked across to the couch where he had stretched out to give the aspirin he'd taken time to work. He reached up, offering her his hand. Despite the smile, her expression was pensive, maybe even a little sad, and it bothered him.

"What's wrong?"

"It just all seems such a waste," she said softly. "So many lives turned upside down over something that never existed."

"The oil, you mean?" He shifted carefully, moving over to make room for her on the edge of the couch. "Actually, there's a pretty good chance it does exist."

She had been in the act of sitting down beside him when he said that. She glanced up in surprise, and then, when she realized he was serious, her eyes widened.

"The reports the geologist did looked very promising," he went on. "That doesn't mean it will be cost effective to *get* to the deposit."

"We might just be throwing our money away if we tried?"

Our money. In reality there wasn't any money that was *ours*. There was only money that was *hers*.

"I guess that's something we need to talk about," he said.

"The oil?" she asked, watching his face. "Or the money?"

"Both."

He saw the depth of the breath she took, her breasts moving under the soft cotton of the shirt she wore. She was probably no more eager to delve into these issues tonight than he was. They could put off talking about the future. Or they could face up to the problems that still existed in their relationship and hopefully figure out a way to put them behind them.

"So talk," she said, obviously having decided the latter.

Her fingers freed themselves from his, but she laid her hand flat on his chest. He put his over hers, feeling the steady rhythm of his heart through them.

"Drew asked the right questions this afternoon," he said. "And if a nine-year-old can figure out that those are the right questions, then we ought to be able to figure out some answers."

"Whatever it takes for this to happen."

"This?"

"This family," she said, the word clear and distinct. "Me and you and Drew. I want us to be together."

"That doesn't have to be here."

"I know," she said. She lowered her eyes, watching her thumb move slowly up and down the side of the hand that covered hers. "In all honesty…this feels right. All of us being here, I mean. It feels like home. And there's enough left from Violet's money to keep us solvent for a while, even in the cattle business."

"Are you serious?" he asked, trying to tamp down the sudden surge of excitement at the thought that she might be. He hadn't dared to believe this could be what she wanted, too.

"Drew's happy here. Happier than I think I've ever seen him. And I've always wanted to try my hand at some of the less practical aspects of design. I could do that from here."

"What exactly does that mean?"

"I don't have to be coordinating fabric for the offices of someone like Jake. I could be designing it instead. I'd really like to try that. Besides…'' Again she looked down at their joined hands before her eyes rose to meet his again. This time they were filled with amusement.

"Besides what?" he asked, easily recognizing that look of mischief, even though it had been a long time since he'd seen anything like this in those dark eyes.

"Working from home would make a couple of other enterprises I'm interested in more possible," she said, the smile in her eyes beginning to touch the corners of her lips.

"Enterprises?"

"Given the speed with which I got pregnant with Drew…" Again she paused, but her gaze held his.

"Pregnant?" he repeated.

"Well, it *is* a possibility. We weren't exactly…prepared for what happened that night in the chopper."

"I'll be damned," he said softly, thinking about the possibility. Excited over it.

"I'm not saying I am. Just that I might be."

"I know."

"You wouldn't mind." Her inflection made it clear this wasn't a question, but a realization.

"I figure I've got some catching up to do."

She laughed. "Midnight feedings and dirty diapers. I have to admit I'm not looking forward to either of those."

"I'm so sorry, Jilly," he said, thinking how hard that must have been for her alone. He had always been there for her, kissing away the hurts, except when she had needed him the most.

"You can make it up to me," she teased, her smile widening.

He cocked his head a little, recognizing the tone as easily as he had the look in her eyes. "And you've got it all figured out how I can do that."

"Uh-huh," she said. "How's your back?"

"Am I right in thinking those two somehow go together?"

"Uh-huh," she said again, bending forward to touch her lips to his. Her tongue traced the outline of his mouth, while her hand slipped behind his head, her fingers threading through the thickness of his hair.

Her kisses were quick and insubstantial, a series of brief touches, mouth to mouth, and then a series of equally brief retreats. He could feel the sweet hard pressure of desire building in his groin, hot blood singing through his veins.

He reached up and grasped her shoulders, pulling her down against his chest. His mouth fastened over hers, which surrendered to his control without any further evasion. He slipped his hand under the loose waistband of the sweatshirt, bare skin like satin under his palm.

She wasn't wearing a bra. For some reason, that discovery excited the hell out of him. Adolescent, maybe, but her breast fit into his hand exactly as it had ten years ago. A little fuller, perhaps, the nipple hardened by their ever-deepening kiss.

Just as he realized that, she shifted position, stretching out beside him on the narrow couch. His arm, the one not already engaged, slipped behind her back to keep her from falling off. She put one leg over both of his, her thigh inadvertently coming to rest over his growing erection.

Her mouth lifted, moving only far enough from his to allow her lips to form the words. "That was quick."

"I told you. I've been waiting a long time."

She propped up on her elbow so she could look down into his face. "Floor," she whispered. "Or the bed if you're feeling mobile. I'm tired of never having room to do this properly."

He didn't remind her that "never" for them consisted of only two occasions. "Properly?" he questioned instead. "Are you implying we haven't been doing this properly?"

She smiled. "Let's just say that up until now it's been magnificent, but given the proper arena…" She leaned down, her mouth opening slightly, aligning to fit over his.

"And with the proper arena?" he asked just before her lips closed over his.

"Spectacular," she breathed. And then neither of them said anything else for a very long time.

"I'VE BEEN THINKING," Mark said.

Her head on his bare chest, she could hear the words rumbling beneath her ear. She was almost too exhausted to move. Or was that too sated to move? She felt like a cat curled by the fire, warm and content.

They hadn't made it to the bedroom, but the warmth and the subtle play of light from the fire had turned the rug in front of the fireplace into a more than satisfactory substitute. Far more than satisfactory, she thought, her lips curving in a smile.

"About what?" she managed to ask, but even forming the words was an effort. Her brain and body had been drugged by sensation after pleasurable sensation for the last couple of hours until both seemed lethargic. Sedated.

"About your folks. Your mom and dad."

The words were shocking enough to destroy both the lethargy and the sense of peace their lovemaking had engendered. She lifted away from his body, propping on her elbow so that she could look down into his eyes.

"What about them?" she asked, almost dreading the answer. Surely Mark wasn't going to suggest—

"Just that they're the only family we have left. It seems that we ought to let them know. Maybe your dad—"

"No," she said, the syllable harsh, almost explosive.

She sat up too abruptly, pushing away from him. Feeling the sleeve of his shirt beneath her fingers, she jerked it off the floor and across her breasts, covering her nudity.

"Jillian?"

She could tell by his face that he was surprised at the strength of her reaction. And she didn't care if he was.

"I suppose you want me to invite them for Thanksgiving or something," she said. "Have some kind of big family hour."

"Maybe," he agreed, his voice sounding calm and reasonable, especially in contrast to the bitterness she could hear in hers.

"Well, I won't. So just forget it, Mark. Let it go."

"I don't know what Stumpy did to that geologist's body, Jillian, but it was enough that your dad packed his family up in the middle of the night and left everything he owned behind him."

She didn't answer, because that wasn't what she had never been able to forgive him for. Mark didn't understand—

"Whatever he did or said, you have to remember that he was terrified. Scared for you, Jilly. Scared for your mom."

"I know," she admitted finally when the silence built to an unbearable tension. She did know, thanks to Stumpy's confession. It was just that she had lived with the bitterness so long...

"What'd he do?" Mark asked.

His fingers shaped her cheek, turning her face toward him as his thumb slid caressingly across her bottom lip. She took a breath, trying to be rational rather than emotional. Trying to put the anger she had carried in her heart all these years into some kind of perspective, now that she knew the whole truth about what had happened that summer.

"What did he do, sweetheart, that's so awful you still can't forgive him, even after all these years?"

"When my mother told him I was pregnant, he wanted to know if it was you. I told him the truth. I told him that I'd been trying to call you. It was like...I don't know. He just went...crazy. He called me a whore—his own daughter," she whispered, her voice breaking before she strengthened it to go on. "And then he slapped me. A couple of times. Harder than he ever had before. For the first time in my life I was really afraid of him. Later that night, I decided I had to leave. No matter what, I didn't want our baby growing up in that atmosphere."

"Jilly," he said gently, his voice rich with comfort.

She shook her head, thinking about the near panic of those days. "I was coming back here. I was determined to find you. I got as far as Pinto and I started bleeding. I was so scared. I went to the doctor there, and that's how I met Violet. He called her. She came right away and took me home with her. I told her everything. She's the one who found out that the ranch had been sold and you were gone. I didn't know about the bankruptcy. I didn't have any idea your family had lost everything.''

"And Drew?'' he asked.

"He came way too early, in spite of everything they could do. I blamed my dad for that. I kept thinking if only he'd given me some support. If I'd been able to stay at home, then none of that would have happened. And Drew had so many problems. Not just his foot, but…they told me at first he wouldn't make it. Couldn't make it. And they said that if he did—''

"It's okay,'' Mark whispered. "It didn't happen. He's fine. He's great. He's perfect. In every way that matters.''

"I know,'' she said, smiling through her tears at the quiet conviction in his voice. She hadn't cried back then. She had thought she had to be strong. For Drew. And for herself. Now, she didn't have to be strong for anyone. Mark was strong enough for all of them. "He *is* great,'' she said. "And perfect. Most of the time,'' she added, laughing a little soggily.

"I just think he needs a grandma,'' Mark said comfortingly. "Every boy does. Mine used to let me get away with stuff my mom would have killed me for. Now, maybe by rights your Violet should have the grandma honors, but since she's not around…''

"And a granddaddy, too?'' she said. "Isn't that what you're really getting at?''

"I guess I am. I didn't get a chance to make things right with my dad, Jillian. And no matter what he did, no matter how mad he could make me, I will always live with that regret.''

"I felt that way about the silly fuss I had with Violet. I know she understood. And I know she loved me, but…I would give anything if she could know how this turned out.''

"She knows,'' he said, his thumb caressing again. "So does my dad. If I didn't truly believe that…''

His voice faded, the thought unfinished. The only sounds in the room for a long time were the soft noises of the dying fire.

"Second chances," Jillian said into the stillness.

"We all need them. And we can only hope that the people who love us will be generous enough to offer them."

She nodded, and then slowly she leaned forward, studying his face, shadowed by the faint light from the low fire. Her eyes held his until her mouth was only an inch or so above his lips.

"I know someone who can find my mom and dad. Someone who specializes in finding people. In reuniting families."

"Then...I think we should do everything we can to make this one complete. We got our second chance. It seems the least we can do, sweetheart...."

Her decision. Her choice. She knew he wouldn't force this on her. But he was right. There were too many things in life that you couldn't ever make right. Maybe this one she could. And so, taking another deep breath, she nodded.

"I love you," she said. "I always have. I can't even remember a time in my life when I didn't."

He laughed. "Well, quit trying. You might come up with one."

"Not in a million years," she whispered. As she lowered her head the additional inch necessary to bring her mouth down to his, Jillian added a small, silent and highly improper prayer.

And there was no doubt in her mind it would be answered. Somewhere up in heaven a little gray-haired lady would be twisting some wings as she argued in her best Texas twang to guarantee as many of those million years as she could possibly arrange for them. And knowing Violet...

The smile that comforting thought engendered was hidden as her lips closed again over Mark's.

EPILOGUE

"I JUST WANTED to let you know how it all turned out. And to say my thanks to you, as Violet's emissary, since I can't say them to Violet herself."

"I couldn't be happier for you," Dylan said, turning his back to shield the phone from the sound of one of the Thanksgiving Day football games, which was blaring from the big screen television in the great room of the Garrett ranch. "Congratulations, Jillian. Or I guess I should say, 'Congratulations, Mrs. Peterson.'"

"I think Jillian will do. Since this is between friends and all," she said, laughing.

Just at that moment a cheer went up from the three men watching the game, almost drowning out her answer. Carrying the phone with him, Dylan headed down the hall to escape the noise.

"I appreciate your letting me know," he said as he walked. "I'm glad I could find your folks. And glad the call went well."

When he reached the kitchen, he stopped, leaning against the center island. Gracie Fipps, the Garrett housekeeper, was finishing the final preparations for Thanksgiving dinner. The mingled smells of it surrounded Dylan, reminding him of a hundred holidays spent in this house.

Through the opened service door that led to the dining room he could see Lily setting the table. Watching his sister's deft placement of each piece of silverware, each stem of crystal, he recognized again that subtle glow of contentment about her. And unless she hurried, Dylan thought in amusement, that "glow" would give away her secret before she got a chance to tell the family.

Another successful love story. Like his holiday memories, he seemed to be surrounded by those, too.

"Well, I don't want to keep you from your family," Jillian said, probably noticing his distraction. "I just wanted you to know that, as usual, Violet was right about everything. This really is where I need to be. I don't know how she knew that, but…maybe she just had a sixth sense about people, somehow. A special radar. Part of her wisdom."

A special radar. As she had had about Sebastian? The thought seemed disloyal, but what Violet had said about his friend having an impure heart had always bothered Dylan. Of course, everyone was entitled to one mistake. Maybe that faulty evaluation of Sebastian could be considered Violet's.

"I'm truly glad it all worked out for you, Jillian."

He was, of course, but being around Lily and her husband Cole's obvious happiness and then hearing the undisguised joy in Jillian's voice had made him envious. He wanted that kind of relationship for himself. And the only woman he'd ever loved had married his best friend instead.

"Happy Thanksgiving, Dylan," Jillian said softly. "And again, thank you for making all this possible."

"Not me. But we both have a lot to thank Violet for."

"Okay, I know I'm embarrassing you. I just needed to share our happy ending with someone, and thanking you was as close to thanking Violet as I could come. Enjoy your day."

"Stay in touch," he suggested.

Even over the noise coming from the den, he heard the deep, distinctively melodic chime of the front doorbell.

"I'll give you a report about our Christmas visit with my family when I see you at Violet's memorial service. Until then…have a wonderful Thanksgiving."

Jillian broke the connection just as Gracie made a shooing motion at him with her kitchen mitt. Obligingly, Dylan moved away from the island, giving her room to put the pecan pie she had just taken out of the oven down beside a pumpkin one, already cooling on the butcher block counter.

Dylan handed her the phone and then headed toward the front of the house to answer the door, a flutter of apprehension moving through his stomach. Max Santana, the ranch foreman, had already arrived and was ensconced in front of the TV with Cole and William. Although the senior member of the Garrett clan was noted for inviting anyone in the community to the family celebrations, Dylan wasn't aware that they were expecting guests. Other than Sebastian Cooper, of course.

Lily glanced up as he passed the double doors that led into the dining room from the wide entry hall. He waved her back to the task at hand, indicating that he'd see to whoever was at the door. It was a relief to have something to do. Although he had always enjoyed watching football with his father, today he was almost too excited about his news to sit still. And if this was Sebastian—

He opened the door and felt an overwhelming sense of disappointment. Schooling his face not to reveal that emotion, he extended his hand to Reverend Donald Blair, who was standing on the threshold with his left arm around his daughter, Rachel.

"Happy Thanksgiving," the minister boomed.

His long fingers fastened around Dylan's with a strength that was belied by his slimness. Dylan endured the handshake, then stepped back to allow them to enter the foyer.

After the appropriate exchange of greetings, he took their coats, pressing a quick kiss against Rachel's cheek as he stood behind her. Her eyes followed her father as he walked in the direction of the noise of the television, guided unerringly to where the other menfolk were gathered.

When Dylan had hung the coats in the closet, Rachel slipped her arm into his, lowering her voice. "Have you told Sebastian?"

"Not yet. I decided I should do it in person."

Rachel nodded as if that made perfect sense. Which was

reassuring, since Dylan had been wondering if it had been a cruelty not to call his friend immediately.

Of course, since Sebastian had been invited to dinner today, it had seemed an ideal time to break the news that there had been some progress in the disappearance of his wife. *Seemed* to have been progress, Dylan amended the thought, fighting his own elation that after all this time—

"Do you think this could really be Julie?" Rachel asked.

She was referring to the answer Dylan had just gotten to the personal ads he'd been tracking through the newspapers at the library where Rachel worked. He had always considered the personals a source of information about possible cases, and in helping him with them, Rachel had, during the last month, almost become his unofficial researcher.

And Dylan must have asked himself the question Rachel had just voiced a thousand times since he'd noticed those first lines of poetry in the *San Antonio Express-News*. Even when he had finally posted a reply, he had wondered if he could possibly be corresponding with Julie. He supposed he wouldn't have a definitive answer until he got some response to the photo he had been instructed to send to a box at the paper, but still…

"It has to be," he said, maybe as much to convince himself as to answer Rachel. "Julie always loved Dylan Thomas's poetry."

They both had, quoting it to one another as they studied for their lit classes in college. Besides, Dylan had been named for the Welsh poet, which made the series of ads he'd found seem to be clearly directed at him. And it was just the kind of thing Julie might use to send him a message, especially since she knew about his habit of checking the personal columns.

"You still don't have any idea why she would be doing this?"

This. Disappearing, Rachel meant. Hiding from everyone, including her husband.

All along, despite what the police had told them, Dylan

had been sure that Julie was alive. He would have known in the depths of his soul if she wasn't. As for why she had left Sebastian and was now attempting to make contact with Dylan through a series of rather cryptic lines of poetry...

"Not a clue," he said truthfully.

Maybe when he confronted Sebastian with his discovery he'd get some answers, and until then, this break in Julie's case was enough to give him reason to celebrate this Thanksgiving. More than enough reason.

"A TOAST," William Garrett said, holding up his wineglass and waiting for those who gathered around his table to lift theirs.

Unconsciously, Dylan considered each of the people who had come to the Double G tonight to celebrate with the Garretts. The Reverend Blair, whom William would surely ask to say grace. Rachel, sitting beside Max Santana, the Garretts' ranch foreman, with whom she'd been in love for years and whom she had finally been dating now for almost three months. His sister Ashley. Cole and Lily, surrounded by that aura of happiness he'd noticed earlier, seeming oblivious to anything but each other.

His gaze then considered Gracie Fipps, who at William's repeated urging had finally agreed to join the family at the dinner table. Sharing a smile with her employer, who, Dylan knew, was also becoming a friend, the housekeeper had slipped into the empty place that had originally been set for Sebastian.

Cooper had never shown up. And he hadn't called to explain why he wasn't here. As he thought about the implications of that uncharacteristic behavior, Dylan's lips tightened in frustration.

There had been too many instances lately of Sebastian doing things Dylan would never before have thought him capable of. Of course, when everyone was telling you that your missing wife was dead, maybe you were entitled to a few aberrations of behavior.

"And how about you, missy?" William demanded.

At that familiar chiding tone, Dylan glanced up to find his father's eyes focused on his oldest daughter. The rest of the guests were waiting, wineglasses raised.

Lily glanced toward her husband, her lips curving into a small, almost secret smile. Again the surge of envy Dylan felt was so strong he was afraid it would be obvious to anyone who might be looking at him.

Of course, no one was. Everyone was focused on Lily, seated at the opposite end of the table from the Garrett patriarch.

"My toast will have to be made with water, I'm afraid," Lily said, "at least for the next few months. But if that's all right with you..." She lifted her water goblet, moving it toward her father in a gesture that was almost a salute.

Dylan smiled, understanding that this was Lily's way of letting their friends and family in on a secret that, as far as he was concerned, hadn't been a secret for a couple of months.

"Oh, my goodness," Rachel said. "You don't mean..." Her mouth opened in delight, green eyes widening as they moved first from Lily's face to Cole's. And then to William's.

"Congratulations, Lily," Gracie said.

The quiet sincerity in her voice was obvious. Of course, Gracie had children of her own, Dylan remembered. Two beloved sons, now married, whose letters and exploits she shared daily with William over their morning coffee.

"Congratulations for what?" William asked, instinctively turning to Gracie for an explanation.

And even her eyes were smiling as she answered him. "I think you're going to be a grandfather, William," she said.

There was a second of stunned silence. The shock on his father's face was almost enough to make up for the disappointment of Sebastian's desertion. At least, it was when combined with the joy on Lily's...

"Well, I'll be damned," William Garrett said. "Begging

your pardon, Reverend. Now, that's news that calls for a re.
Thanksgiving celebration. And, Lily honey, you can toast
with anything you want, just as long as you take care of th
grandson of mine.''

"What makes you think this is going to be a grandson?
she asked, her eyes leaving her father's to laugh into Cole
again.

"I'm trusting that man of yours to have taken care of tha
My best, heartfelt congratulations to both of you. And Dyla
I guess you know what this means, don't you, son?''

Although he managed a smile, Dylan was hoping that h
father wasn't going to suggest that it was time he get marrie
and follow Lily's example. After all, she was the Garre
firstborn, something she never let him forget. And until…

Until what? he asked himself bitterly. Until Julie decide
that she'd married the wrong man? Was that what he w
waiting for? Was that what he'd been waiting for all the
years?

"It's your job to see to it that our girl doesn't over
things," his father continued. "No more tearing all over t
country on those cases of yours. No more late hours or n
eating right. No more… Hell, you know all the things the
better be no more of as well as I do. We got us a Garre
grandbaby on the way.''

"Here, here," Gracie said, raising her wine in Lily's
rection. "Here's to a safe delivery and a healthy baby.''

"Here's to my first niece or nephew," Ashley said, sm
ing at her sister, "whom I can't wait to spoil.''

"Here's to a dozen more," Dylan said, lifting his glass
Cole's direction, a silent acknowledgment of his brother-i
law's role in all this.

"And here's to happiness," Lily said softly, her eyes
her brother's. "Here's to happiness for all of us stubbor
ornery Garretts. And to our friends," she said, her eyes mo
ing around the table.

"God bless us every one," the Reverend Blair boome

n unintended parody of that famous line that somehow
eemed ridiculously appropriate for the occasion.

And God keep you safe, my love, Dylan added silently, his
wn Thanksgiving prayer for Julie.

And then, with the rest, he raised his glass, joining in his
ather's toast to the next generation of Garretts.

Isabella Trueblood made history reuniting people torn apart by war and an epidemic. Now, generations later, Lily and Dylan Garrett carry on her work with their agency, Finders Keepers. Circumstances may have changed, but the goal remains the same. The legend continues with the fifth book in our exciting new continuity series

TRUEBLOOD, TEXAS

Watch for
THE BEST MAN IN TEXAS
by
Kelsey Roberts
Coming next month
Here's a preview!

CHAPTER ONE

"YOU'VE GOT A BROKEN ankle that I need to set," Justin explained. "Lie still so I can do an assessment. You've been in and out of consciousness for quite a while since you were found at the accident scene."

The woman looked up at him. Her brown eyes were thickly lashed and golden starbursts radiated from her pupils. He chastised himself for noticing that at all. He was supposed to note that her pupils were equal and reactive, not incredibly beautiful.

"Forget my ankle!" she insisted.

"I'm a doctor, Miss Parker. I'm not allowed to forget fractures."

"Who is Miss Parker?" she demanded urgently.

Justin, who had been taking her pulse, went still. "Excuse me?"

He saw a flash of emotion—anger or frustration or both— in her expression.

"Am I Molly Parker?"

Justin whipped out his penlight and again checked her pupils. "Are you telling me you don't remember your name?"

She swatted the penlight away from her face. "I'm telling you I don't remember *anything*."

"Then I think the hospital in Fort Worth will be better equipped to deal with your injuries, and—"

She cut him off by gripping the sleeve of his jacket. "Please don't send me anywhere. I don't know why, but I just have this feeling that I'm safe here. That doesn't make sense, does it?'' She lowered her eyes and nervously drew her lower lip between her teeth.

''It makes perfect sense,'' he assured her. ''X rays showed you have a cracked rib and, if I may be so bold, you look like you went a few rounds in a boxing match and I bet you weren't the winner.''

She closed her eyes, apparently taking in his assessment. ''You said I was in an accident?''

He nodded. ''That isn't what cracked your rib or caused most of the cuts and bruises on your face. Most likely, you were the victim of a crime or—''

''Or what?''

''Domestic violence. Which, by the way, is a crime.''

''Am I married?'' she asked, horror in her tone.

He shrugged. ''No wedding ring. No pictures in your wallet. You don't have to be married to someone to get beaten, Molly.''

She rubbed her face with her hands. ''I think I would have preferred it if you'd said I was in a barroom brawl.''

He put a gentle hand on her shoulder and told her, ''Technically, you weren't in an accident.''

''It gets worse?'' she asked in a defeated voice.

''Pretty much. There were no witnesses but Sheriff Younger told me you were a pedestrian and there were no skid marks at the scene.''

''Meaning?''

''The driver who hit you was either seriously distracted or...''

''Or?''

''Or aiming for you.''

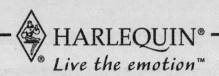

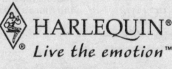

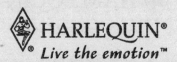

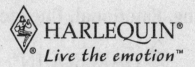

HARLEQUIN®
INTRIGUE®

BREATHTAKING ROMANTIC SUSPENSE

Shared dangers and passions lead to electrifying romance and heart-stopping suspense!

Every month, you'll meet six new heroes who are guaranteed to make your spine tingle and your pulse pound. With them you'll enter into the exciting world of Harlequin Intrigue— where your life is on the line and so is your heart!

THAT'S INTRIGUE—
ROMANTIC SUSPENSE
AT ITS BEST!

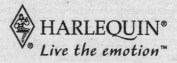

REQUEST YOUR FREE BOOKS!

2 FREE NOVELS PLUS 2 FREE GIFTS!

 HARLEQUIN®

E V E R L A S T I N G   L O V E™

Every great love has a story to tell™

YES! Please send me 2 FREE Harlequin® Everlasting Love™ novels and my 2 FREE gifts. After receiving them, if I don't wish to receive any more books, I can return the shipping statement marked "cancel." If I don't cancel, I will receive 4 brand-new novels every other month and be billed just $4.47 per book in the U.S. or $4.99 per book in Canada, plus 25¢ shipping and handling per book and applicable taxes, if any*. That's a savings of about 15% off the cover price! I understand that accepting the 2 free books and gifts places me under no obligation to buy anything. I can always return a shipment and cancel at any time. Even if I never buy another book from Harlequin, the two free books and gifts are mine to keep forever.

153 HDN ELX4   353 HDN ELYG

Name	(PLEASE PRINT)	
Address		Apt.
City	State/Prov.	Zip/Postal Code

Signature (if under 18, a parent or guardian must sign)

Mail to the **Harlequin Reader Service®:**
IN U.S.A.: P.O. Box 1867, Buffalo, NY 14240-1867
IN CANADA: P.O. Box 609, Fort Erie, Ontario L2A 5X3

Not valid to current Harlequin Everlasting Love subscribers.

Want to try two free books from another line?
Call 1-800-873-8635 or visit www.morefreebooks.com.

* Terms and prices subject to change without notice. NY residents add applicable sales tax. Canadian residents will be charged applicable provincial taxes and GST. This offer is limited to one order per household. All orders subject to approval. Credit or debit balances in a customer's account(s) may be offset by any other outstanding balance owed by or to the customer. Please allow 4 to 6 weeks for delivery.

Your Privacy: Harlequin is committed to protecting your privacy. Our Privacy Policy is available online at www.eHarlequin.com or upon request from the Reader Service. From time to time we make our lists of customers available to reputable firms who may have a product or service of interest to you. If you would prefer we not share your name and address, please check here. ☐

HEL07